"An Unsustained Charge"

By Janys Thornton

*To Richard
Best Wishes
Janys Thornton*

Contents

No Job for a Lady

The Beautiful Game

Unwanted Attention

Did She Encourage Him?

Showing Her Legs

A Plan is Hatched

The Tournament Begins

Watching the Opposition

Cissie and Ernie

The Day of the Kings Visit

The Cup Final

The Women's Day

Armistice Day

Afterword

November 1913

Sheerness Naval Dockyard

No Job for a Lady

The girl waits on the corner by the dockyard railway station, early in the morning. She shifts from foot to foot, whether because of the weather, or her nerves, cannot be said. She feels sick, but her Mum made her eat a breakfast of porridge to keep the cold out, and the weight of it sticks it to her stomach.

She has arrived first, and wishes one of the others were here already. She is conscious of the men going by and feels small and vulnerable on her own, but no one looks her way. They are all intent on not being late. Other women hurry by swaddled against the November day; one catches Alice's eye and gives her a reassuring smile.

Just then, Tilly Jackson and Kitty Pritchard come into sight, and Alice McDonald immediately feels happier not to be on her own. "What kept you? I've been here ages," she calls, as soon as they are in range.

"I had to take our Percy to Mrs Flynn's, so she can take him to school with her own kids," Kitty explains. "Mum has to be at the bus depot by six o'clock. She's the clippie on the first bus out, so I have to get his breakfast before school."

"It's already half past seven, and we've got to report to the naval stores supervisor at eight o'clock sharp," says Alice, "We can't be late on our first morning."

Working in the dockyard is no job for a lady, but when the Labour Exchange advertises roles for women in the yard, the three girls apply straight away. It is more money, and they will be doing their bit for the war. Women have never done so many different jobs before the Great War began.

It's a long walk down the dock road, passing sailors and soldiers, who are either going about their duties or walking into town for a few hours leave. So, the girls are glad of each other's company.

"What do you think our duties will be?" muses Alice, as she pulls her collar up against the autumn wind, which cuts straight across them, whipping their long skirts round their legs, and the sea salt stings their eyes, making them weep.

"The Labour Exchange says it's working in the stores, so perhaps we will be issuing uniforms out to handsome sailors!" responds Tilly, with a cheeky smile.

"More like giving out bags of nails to old shipwrights, whose faces look like bags of nails!" jokes Alice.

"As long as he's earning a good wage and can keep me in sweets, I might not mind," Kitty says, practical as ever.

"I'm just glad to be able to give more money to Mum," Alice says, screwing her eyes up against the weather. "She works so hard taking in washing, I'd really like to be able to contribute more."

"Yes, but we should be able to afford some nice things for ourselves too," Tilly says, dancing around her friends with excitement.

"We can save up for after the war," Kitty says, "We can get some money behind us for when we have to go back into domestic service."

"Not bleeding likely!" laughs Tilly.

"Me neither!" Alice agrees.

Their boots slap against the granite flagged path laid by the Admiralty a century before, as they hurry to their new jobs. Stray tendrils of hair escape their pins and get caught in their mouths as they chat, keeping their first day nerves at bay. The wind also brings the smell of engine oil and hemp ropes to them, together with the odour of working men.

"We've been told to report to Mr Phillips," Tilly says, to the soldier guarding the dockyard gate.

"Through there to the Quadrangle building," the soldier replies, pointing into the dockyard, "you can't miss it."

The girls giggle as they pass the uniformed men. Tilly tries to catch the eye of one of them, and the three of them dissolve into further giggles, when he winks back.

Once inside the yard, they can't miss the "Quad", as it dominates the centre of the dockyard. It was built in 1824, as a fireproof structure to store all the necessary equipment and paraphernalia needed for the Royal Navy. The yellow stock brick walls are four feet thick, and four storeys high, with a weather-boarded clock tower in the centre of the roof, chiming the hours to the workers below.

"Blimey, that must be it!" Alice says, as the large, imposing building comes into view.

"It looks more like a prison than a storehouse!" Kitty responds.

Fortunately, Mr Phillips, the stores' manager, is there to greet them on their arrival, and stop them getting lost. He is waiting under the central granite archway that accesses the courtyard to the Quad, together with their supervisor, Mrs Blueitt. He is almost forty; of medium build, with thinning hair, which is kept in order with brilliantine. At the front of his mouth, one of his teeth crosses over slightly, giving him a cheeky grin, when he finds something funny enough to bestow his smile upon. He wears a bowler hat rather than a cap, to mark him out as part of the management, but he worked his way up through the ranks from being a messenger boy, to get where he is today. Always sensible, he keeps a spare pair of socks in his work drawer. just in case his feet get wet and bring on a chill. He likes to joke with the men, but, at the same time, he is protective of his own staff. The men are already making lewd jokes about the women, so he will need to ensure that no impropriety takes place.

"Are you three girls Katherine Pritchard, Alice McDonald, and Matilda Jackson?" he asks, checking their names against a clipboard.

The three girls whisper, "Yes, sir," and stand demurely, as they would have stood in the past when they were employed in domestic service. Only Tilly risks meeting Mr Phillips' eye.

"I'm Mr Phillips, the stores' manager. I'm going to hand you over to Mrs Blueitt, who will be your supervisor. She will tell you your duties and tell you the rules. If you have any problems, go to her, and she will tell me." And with that, he turns and walks back to his office, leaving the new recruits with Mrs Blueitt.

"This way girls," she calls over her shoulder, as she leads them inside the Quad, through the iron columns and York slab paving, past endless offices, and storerooms, where anything and everything is kept behind locked iron doors.

Ruby Blueitt has worked in the dockyard before the war in the colour loft, where the flags and sails are manufactured. She is a robust woman of middle age, with knotty forearms from years of wrestling heavy fabrics. She wears small glasses for reading, but takes them off if anyone comes into her office when she is wearing them, as she had once been remarkably pretty and is still vain. She is going grey, but dyes her hair with henna, which gives her pink strands where the silver once was. Her ample bosom (which she happily allows Mr Dennis to fondle once a week, in exchange for a trip to the pictures and a fish supper) strains against the buttons of her dockyard issue overall as she inspects the girls. She has taken the opportunity that the new *Military Service Act* of 1916 presents to move over into a supervisor role. The Act imposes conscription on all single men aged between eighteen and forty-one, but exempts the medically unfit, clergymen, teachers, and certain classes of industrial worker. Most of the skilled dockyard workers fall into this last category, but not all. This led to a labour shortage that creates opportunities, and other women are now supervising the munitions, foundry, and other workshops across the dockyard.

"This is the locker room. I'll need you to sign for your uniforms," she says, as she leads then into a large room containing lockers and coat stands. She pushes a ledger towards them, where their names are recorded. She hands them each a heavy brown smock to wear over their clothes, and a snood to cover their hair. These serviceable uniforms are made in the colour loft, along with the flags. "Put these on and I'll introduce you to the others and show you around." She has a West Country accent, and emphasises the "r" sound in "around". She had moved with her late husband from Plymouth to Sheerness, when he was promoted to shipwright. But his untimely death, twelve years ago, when he missed his footing on an icy gangplank and fell into the unforgiving sea one cold January morning, has left her to raise their three sons alone, sons who had all joined the navy, and one of whom will not be coming back.

"You three will be in the Loan Tools Stores. It's in a separate building, so you will work without me in there all the time. You will need to be trustworthy and grown up enough to be left unsupervised. Any trouble, tell me."

"Yes, ma'am," they respond dutifully. Tilly pinches Alice's arm discreetly, indicating that the prospect of working without Mrs Blueitt watching them is a bonus, on top of the better wages they will receive. Alice knows Tilly will be flirting with the men if there is no one watching over her.

Mrs Blueitt busies herself, completing her record book as the girls don the smocks. "Look how ugly this makes me look," Tilly whispers to Alice. "I'll never marry a handsome naval officer dressed like this!"

"This snood is so itchy," Alice says, rubbing her forehead where the heavy fabric sits.

"At least they will save our own clothes," Kitty adds.

"Yes, these uniforms are almost as practical as you are!" Tilly jokes, and giggles louder than she means to, causing Mrs Blueitt to turn around. But just then, Mrs Pamplin, the foundry supervisor, comes in slightly out of breath, as she has been rushing, and says to Mrs Blueitt, "I'm a girl short. A new girl was due to start this morning, but she hasn't turned up, and I need at least one more to start production today. Can I take one of yours?"

Mrs Blueitt immediately agrees. "Which one do you want?"

Mrs Pamplin casts her eye over the girls. Alice is small and, if she were a man, you would call her wiry. Tilly is bigger, but has a delicate bloom to her pretty cheeks, which belies her feistiness. Kitty is more vigorous looking, with a bigger frame and sturdy legs. She chooses Kitty, saying, "She looks the strongest."

"Right, Kitty, you are off to join the Munitionesses. You will be helping make the torpedoes to sink them German U-boats. Its an extra five shillings a week. Get your things and go with Mrs Pamplin," Mrs Blueitt directs her.

Kitty doesn't get a say in this transaction, and casts a quick glance at the other girls as she meekly follows the big woman out into the cold autumn morning, whilst clutching her bag and coat to her chest.

Alice and Tilly watch her go, then obediently follow Mrs Blueitt, as she takes them around the stores, keen to convince their new boss that they are the sort of girls who can be left to work alone. The male store workers follow them with their eyes. The men's own supervisor, Mr Dennis, (Mrs Bluiett's paramour) warns them to leave the girls alone saying, "Canoodling is not permitted." He does not suggest that such attention might be unwelcome by the girls.

*****

At lunch time, when there are any new girls joining the dockyard, Victor Banks likes to sit where he can see them in the canteen. He tries to ignore Teddie Taylor, but Teddie isn't so easily dismissed. He is part of a younger set of lads, who tease Victor mercilessly about his love life, or rather his lack of one. Taylor is the ringleader, tall and good looking, the sort of popular, confident lad who has an answer for everything.

"Have you dipped your wick yet?" he shouts out at Victor, whenever he sees him. His cronies laugh with him. He calls him "Victor the Virgin," or just "Verge," for short.

"Victor the Virgin, tell us which one you fancy, and I'll put a word in for you," Teddie jokes, as Mr Phillips, the stores' manager, leads a half dozen girls into the canteen, together with their supervisor, Mrs Blueitt. "Even you should be able to charm the knickers off one of them," he laughs, to the entertainment of his mates. Mr Phillips directs the new women to a table that has been reserved for them to eat their packed lunches. Looking towards Taylor and his gang, Mr Phillips calls out, "No harassing my girls. Mrs Blueitt or Mr Dennis will let me know if you do!" and he gives the signal that he has his eye on them, before he turns and leaves the canteen.

Arthur Dennis feels it is incumbent on him to stand up, and also give the signal that he acknowledges what Mr Phillips has said. He points at Taylor, then sits back down to eat his solitary meal. Teddie ignores the small man with his thick glasses and twitchy nose that give the impression of a small rodent, and sits down with his pals on Victor's table, uninvited, and starts telling lewd jokes as they gaze towards the women, most of whom look back at the lads defiantly, making it clear their attention is not welcome. Victor risks a direct look over at the girls. One of them catches his attention; she is small, with a scattering of freckles across her nose. She is smiling shyly at her new colleagues, as she joins in their conversation. She seems just the kind of girl he would like to meet.

After that, Victor makes it his business to find out as much as he can about her. In a small town like Sheerness, that isn't hard to do. Her name is Alice McDonald; she is almost sixteen years old, and lives in West Minster with her large family. He walks past her house a few times, in the hope of seeing her. He begins finding excuses to go to the stores on errands that don't need doing, or he pretends he's forgotten to get all the equipment he needs, in order to go a second or third time.

Then, one day, Teddie Taylor comes into the workshop, bursting with some news. "Oi, Verge," Teddie calls across the benches, "I know something that will interest you."

Victor tries to ignore him, but his other workmates enjoy his discomfiture, so urge Taylor in his baiting with questions like, "What is it, Ted?", and "It must be important, Victor." Teddie needs little encouragement to continue. "That little girl in the stores you fancy has joined the women's football team that Phillips has set up! You should see her in her kit. You can see her legs! But it might be too much for a virgin like you!"

The other men laugh, as Victor's face turns bright red.

As soon as the dockyard siren sounds at the end of the shift, Victor goes to find the sports and social notice board in the canteen, where all the recreational activities are advertised. There it is in black and white: a women's football league, with fixtures and squad names. Alice is down as an outside forward, playing on the wing in the stores team - *Naval Stores Ladies*. The next practice is Tuesday. Victor makes up his mind to go over to the sports field to see what is going on.

*****

Tuesday comes around, and Victor ambles nonchalantly across to the recreation ground. A number of other men are heading in that direction. They are laughing and joking, saying things like, "How funny, women playing football," and "They will trip over their skirts," but when the women run out for their training session, it is clear they are taking it seriously, and the men are forced to concede that they are good players. "Some of the girls are quite skilful," one man observes, "Many of them play in the streets with their brothers and neighbours," says another.

But Victor doesn't join in the conversation about the merits of the players. He only has eyes for Alice in her long black socks, which show the shape of her calf muscles. Her shorts finish just above her knees, but, as she runs, they ride up, exposing her naked thighs. Even her red and white striped football jersey flattens itself against her chest in the breeze, revealing the curve of her breasts. Most of the girls are wearing mop caps to protect their hair from the mud, but brunette curls escape prettily from Alice's around her neck, and the exertion brings on a rosy glow to her cheeks.

After that, Victor can't get the picture of Alice in her kit out of his head.

*****

The Beautiful Game

"I've tried weeing into my new football boots, but they are still stiff and unyielding," Alice tells Tilly, as she examines them once again. "It is really difficult to do in the privy at home. My long skirts are in danger of getting wet. I have to balance over the lavvie to hold one boot, then the other between my legs. There isn't room to swing a cat in there, and first our little Rab comes out, then Joe saying they need to go."

"Have you tried to do it here at work?" Tilly asks her, as she joins Alice in inspecting the boots. The new girl, Enid, stops unpacking a box of nails into the cabinet to listen. Alice has popped out several times over the last week, between customers, to urinate into the boots. But there is always a queue for the lavvies, so it is difficult to do uninterrupted, especially as she then had to carry the urine filled boots back to the stores, and place them out of the way to cure.

"That's why I decided to bring the boots into work and try to soften them here. It reminds me of how Miss Dobbs, who I used to work for, sometimes used the "bourdaloue" to go in when there were no lavatories nearby."

The "bourdaloue" is a boat-shaped jug with a raised lip at one end and handle at the other. It looks a bit like a gravy boat. Miss Dobbs expected Alice to carry the thing in her basket, if she accompanied her on an outing, and to empty it discreetly after use.

"Once, there was a new kitchen maid who was a bit drippy, and she poured the gravy for dinner into it as I had left it on the side to wash out. Fortunately, the cook spotted the silly girl's mistake and stopped her. The cook then filled the gravy boat straight from the bourdaloue without hesitation, and sent it up to accompany Miss Dobbs' dinner. Nobody said anything!" she laughingly recounts to Tilly and Enid.

Alice worked for Miss Dobbs as soon as she left school, at just under twelve years old. She hadn't been a bad employer, but she was very demanding. She barely moved off her day bed and expected her staff to be always at her beck and call, and at that of Phoebe, her little pug dog.

"I couldn't wait to get away from domestic service. When the dockyard advertised jobs for women to help with the war effort, I went straight down the Labour Exchange. The pay is so much better here. I'm getting twenty-four shillings a week," Alice tells Enid, continuing to inspect her boots, as there are no customers to serve. The girls have worked in the loan tool stores for almost a year and feel quite the old hands, now that someone new has joined them. Their job is to issue tools on production of a signed voucher from a manager of one of the workshops. These loans are recorded in a book and signed for, and the voucher filed away. On return of the tools, the book is noted, and they put the items back in their place.

Once the store is swept and clean, Alice and Tilly take it easy between customers, and chat. Alice perches on a high stool behind the counter, reading a book, whilst Tilly does some sewing when it is quiet, but mostly they just chin wag with the other girls until a customer comes in. They take advantage of this slack moment to tell Enid about themselves.

"The hours are better than domestic service too, Monday to Friday, eight o'clock till six o'clock, and Saturday till twelve," Tilly continues. "Plus two weeks paid holiday. Not that I've ever had a holiday!"

"But the downside is that we have to work overtime when requested, except for the extra money we get paid! That's an upside!" Alice laughs, "When I worked for Miss Dobbs, I had to work from daybreak till she went to bed, with only Sunday and Wednesday afternoons off. There was no such thing as paid overtime, working for Miss Dobbs. And she made me wear a horrible green dress that I had to buy. At least the dockyard supplies the ugly uniforms we wear." Alice feels she has certainly landed on her feet when she got a job in the dockyard, even if her feet are still hurting in her new football boots.

The men's union objected when the women are first employed, calling it "dilution", as the jobs are picked apart for the women to do. Any unskilled men are wanted for the Western Front, and their jobs are filled by women. The Admiralty has not said what will happen to the female workforce at the end of the war, whether some might remain, or if some jobs can be done by women permanently.

"I hope that when the war is over we can still work here," Tilly says.

Alice puts her football boots down in the corner, out of the way. She returns to perch on her stool and picks up her knitting. "I'm making a little cardie for Cathy's baby," Alice says, holding up a tiny yellow garment for her friend to see. Her sister

Cathy is married to a soldier who is away at the front, and they already have a little boy calls Stanley, who is just three years old. Cathy fell for him when she was scarcely fifteen. Alice's Dad, Rab, visited the barracks, to ensure that Wilf would marry Cathy as soon as she is sixteen. "My Dad took me out of school and found me the position with Miss Dobbs as a "maid of all work" to help out at home, until Cathy was married. Once she received her allowance from her new husband, it was too late for me to go back to school. Mum and Dad wanted to ensure that the town busy bodies didn't say we couldn't afford to keep baby Stanley. So, it's all Cathy's fault that I went into domestic service," she explains.

"I had to go into service because my Mum was remarrying, and my stepdad has five children and, with my two younger brothers, there are just too many indoors. I'm lodging with a neighbour, now that I'm not living in with my employer."

Alice once again picks up her boots; she can't leave them alone for five minutes. "I saved up for weeks to buy these new boots. I've been wearing my brother's old ones and they are too big. I really wanted to break them in for Saturday afternoon's game."

Mr Phillips, the stores' manager, started a ladies team to play against the women in the electrical department under Mr Apps, at the beginning of the 1917 football season. Now, all the dockyard departments have women's teams, and they also play against the girls working in the industries at Queenborough, in the glue factory and the tile works.

"Do you like football, Enid? I play on the wing, and I love it, simply love it," Alice enthuses to her new colleague.

"I play in defence. You should come along," Tilly tells Enid, as she takes a turn perching on the only stool in the store, "It will help you make new friends."

*****

At the end of the day, Alice sets off for home; the McDonalds live in Khartoum Road in West Minster. It is not in the town of Sheerness, nor is it really a suburb. It is more like an appendix, two streets of terraced houses running parallel to the railway line on one side, and the road to the dockyard on the other. Each street only has houses on one side, with an alley running through the middle. At both ends of Gordon Road stands a pub, the *Duke of Clarence* at one end, at the other end is

The Pride of Kent. On the corner of Khartoum Road stands a grocers shop and at the other a Post Office. In the middle of one road there is a Methodist chapel and Sunday school. Over the railway is the Co-op's dairy and pastureland. It is a sandwich of a village, squashed into a piece of land the military doesn't want.

As it is next to the sea, there is a jetty, where colliers regularly arrive to unload their cargoes of coal for the gas works, whose blue grey gasometers rise and fall almost imperceptibly as the gas levels change. Her father is employed as a stoker there, as had been her late grandfather. The sewerage station is also on the same piece of seafront. These salubrious industries stand between the hamlet and the sea, so any possibility of looking like a picturesque fishing village is scuppered. Alice's street looks towards the railway line.

"I'm home," Alice calls out as she goes through the back way. Since leaving Miss Dobbs, where she had lived in, she has returned to the family home to live with her parents and her siblings.

Alice's mother, Maggie, would have liked to have had a couple of service men billeted with them, as the money is good, but there is not a spare bedroom that can be allocated. The house only has two rooms upstairs, and Alice's parents sleep in the parlour, since the children got bigger. It seemed more modest to divide the boys from the girls into the two bedrooms, rather than have them separated by just a curtain. So, her mother takes in washing from soldiers billeted about the town in other people's houses, filling the air every day with the smell of carbolic and "dolly blue" as the copper boils away in the corner of the scullery.

Alice's eleven-year-old sister, Dolly, is pressed into service helping with the ironing, when she comes home from school each evening. What little space there is in the house is taken up with clothes drying or piled high, waiting to be ironed. Dolly's face is set in a permanent sulk, as she feels none of the others work as hard as she does, which leads her brother, Walter, to jokingly threaten to, *"iron that sulk off her face unless she cheers up."*

Dolly looks up from the ironing and greets her sister with, "It was your turn to empty the piss pot from our room. I had to do it."

"I did it yesterday, it must have been Mary's turn," Alice retorts.

Their sister Mary is quick to dodge this chore and whines, "Mum says it's too heavy for me. You two must do it till I'm bigger."

"I was doing it when I was your age. Seven is plenty old enough to carry a piss pot!" Dolly snaps at her.

"Cissie slept again last night, she should take a turn," Alice replies, "She's the same age as you Dolly, Anyway, I pay Mum fifteen shillings for my keep. I shouldn't do it at all, now I'm contributing so much."

"You take up fifteen shillings worth of the bed and just leave Mary and I five shillings worth!" Dolly counters.

"I don't! Mary kicks like a mule. When Cissie and little Ernie are in the bed too there is hardly any room."

"When the war's over and you go back into domestic service, I'm going to spread out in that bed!"

"Whatever happens after the war ends, I'm not going back to work for Miss Dobbs!" Alice says, and stomps back out again.

*****

"March smartly girls," Harriet West, better known as Hattie, calls over her shoulder, as she leads her crocodile of students towards the south gate, after she has been teaching the girls to swim in the dockyard pool. She hopes that a couple of the stronger swimmers will enter the annual swimming gala in the summer, where she also likes to compete.

As she is about to pass the guard, she hears her name being called behind her.

"Miss Roberts, Miss!"

She stops her line of girls for a moment, as a young woman in a heavy brown dockyard smock runs up to her.

"Hello, Alice, I'm Mrs West now. Aren't you working for Miss Dobbs anymore?" Hattie asks, not really surprised to see her former student here in the yard, as many girls in domestic service are finding other employment whilst the war rages on. All the teachers know Miss Dobbs, as she was also a teacher before an inheritance enabled her to join the leisured class, although her former colleague is more a professional invalid than anything else. Hattie can see why Alice prefers a job in the dockyard, rather than be at her previous employer's constant disposal for her every whim.

Alice is a little out of breath as she catches up with her and says, "Sorry, I hadn't heard you'd got married, Miss. I work in the stores here. I've been here nearly a year now. I love it. We have a great social life, and the pay is better too. You won't believe it as I hated doing drill, but I play football now."

"You may not have heard either that, sadly, I'm already a widow because of the war," says Hattie, with an acceptance that her marriage was so brief. She brightens up to exclaim, "But football! You are out of breath just running up the road! I don't know anything about the game. I've always played cricket myself, but I can help with general fitness," Hattie suggests; she has always been a keen sportswoman. She would have liked nothing better than to be a professional, but such opportunities are not afforded to middle class women, so being a physical education teacher is the next best thing. She had first become interested in sport by playing cricket with her eight brothers and some cousins. Now, four of her brothers will not be returning from the front, and her brother Aubrey has lost a leg. It was he who had taught her to ride a bicycle, and he used to sing *Daisy Bell* to her if he gave her a ride on his crossbar. She can

28

no longer listen to the words *"A bicycle made for two,"* without a tear in her eye,

"When and where shall I meet you?" she asks.

"We can meet at the dockyard recreation ground, the Wellmarsh, next Tuesday after work. We are allowed to use the facilities there, now that we are employees of the yard. I will bring my friend Tilly and some of the other players with me, if that is okay?"

"Yes, of course. See you next week, then. I must get these girls back to school. They will be getting cold as their hair is wet. Straighten up girls!" commands Hattie, giving a little dismissive wave to Alice, as she regiments her pupils into an orderly line, and parades them through the high dock gates.

*****

Like Alice, Gladys Finch and Gertie Brongar don't mind the war; they had escaped domestic service and receive twenty-four shillings a week working in the dockyard stores. It is monotonous, but they have such a laugh with the other women.

The girls are not from Sheerness, like most of the others. The Employment Exchange in Sittingbourne advertised the dockyard vacancies as "war work," and they jumped at the chance to apply. They are thankful not to end up at the glue works, where the smell of carrion clings to your hair, as the factory is designated as "munitions work" because the glue is needed in the manufacture of so many things, but it is hardly most people's idea of "doing your bit"!

Their only complaint is that their ten-hour shift ends at six in the evening, but the railway company maintains a pre-war timetable. This means there is a train at quarter past six, which is almost impossible for the girls to catch, as they have to change out of their smocks, wash their hands and faces, before legging it up the road over half a mile to get to the station on time. If they miss it, which is more often than not, they have to wait for the one at quarter to seven, kicking their heels in the cold November air.

On payday, the two girls are once again facing the long wait, when Gertie says, "Let's have a bit of a warm by the pub fire whilst we wait."

"But we'll have to buy a drink," responds Gladys. "If we have a pint of beer, I'll need the lavvie before we get home."

"Have a whisky then," replies Gertie. "It's cheaper than beer at the moment anyway, and it'll warm you up even more."

"I can't argue with that," says Gladys, so they stop at the first pub outside the dock gates that looks welcoming. The public bar is crowded with men from the yard, spending their wages before going home to their families, but the snug bar is empty and inviting. It is cosy in front of the fire; the smell of beer welcomes them in. The lights are bright enough to see properly, and the velvet upholstered chairs are pleasant to sit on – the first time they have a proper sit down all day, as the main store house has been busy with deliveries. The glasses behind the bar sparkle and the brass beer pumps shine. It is delightful after a hard day at the dockyard.

The landlord sees them come through the glass of the door; it's etched pane bearing the word "Snug" in icy letters. Business is not as good as it should be, as the Government are talking about curbing licencing laws, to cut alcohol consumption interfering with the manufacture of munitions.

The landlord served in the army across the Empire in his younger years and is not one to miss an opportunity to make a shilling or two, so he strokes his luxurious moustache, throws his polishing cloth over his burly shoulder, and goes to serve the two girls. It is obvious they have never been in a pub by themselves before, by the way they are looking around.

"What can I get you, ladies?" he enquires.

"Whisky, please," responds Gertie decisively.

"Which one? I've got Irish or Scotch, single malt or blended? James Eadie's malt or John Crabbie's blended? A quarter gill or half?"

They don't know how to order, or what measure spirits come in, or that there are several different types of whisky to choose from, but it isn't illegal to serve alcohol to under eighteens, so the landlord gives them half a gill each of Crabbie's, and charges them for a malt.

"Drink up, ladies," he encourages them, as they finish their spirits, "Have another? Its only fourpence a glass."

The beer is as weak as gnat's pee, now that the Government has limited its strength, he thinks, but he doesn't say that to the customers.

Gertie and Gladys treat themselves to another glass each. Both girls have their wages to spend, and it is already burning a hole in their pockets.

"We're doing the men's jobs and getting paid their wage, well most of it, anyway," says Gertie, toasting Gladys. "We can go in the pub and buy our own drinks."

"Tomorrow afternoon, after work, we're going shopping!"

"I want a red lipstick, like the suffragettes wear, and some new stockings and a fish supper."

Two more glasses of whisky later, Gertie and Gladys realise that it is almost quarter to seven. They run up the road in their heavy boots with sparks flying off the flag stones, but are too late to get the train. The two girls giggle like crazy things, and hang onto one another on the empty platform amidst the disappearing smoke from the 6:45 to Sittingbourne.

"Goodness, I haven't laughed so much in ages! You'd think that Charlie Chaplin himself had appeared on the platform and done a little dance just for us!" laughs Gladys, as she bends over to get her breath.

Meanwhile, the landlord returns to the snug, having heard the door bang shut, only to find they'd already left, taking their drinks with them.

Gladys and Gertie calm down and finish the whiskies that they are still cradling, hoping to get another half hour's warmth out of the dregs. Just then, the landlord comes onto the station platform with the local constable and accuses them of stealing the glasses.

"We didn't steal them, just forgot we'd got them," Gertie protests.

"There's a war on and glasses are hard to come by," retorts the landlord. The constable takes their particulars in his little notebook, as the girls stand there chastised.

Gertie and Gladys are summoned to court on Saturday morning for theft. Mr Ranger-Jones, the magistrate, isn't interested in their answer that they forgot they still had hold of their glasses in their rush to get the train. He remains righteous that theft is theft. Once he satisfies himself that the girls don't know any better, he gives out a hefty fine, together with a sermon on abstinence and the war, and the dangers to young girls from behaving like men.

"What can we do with our Saturday afternoons now we are paying off our fine?" Gladys wonders, when she recounts their story to the other women in the stores on Monday morning.

"Simple," responds Alice, "Play football with us!"

*****

December 1917 doesn't start well. There is an air raid in the small hours of Thursday the sixth. Seven bombs land in Invicta Road, killing four people, and injuring a further twelve. Several houses are wrecked in the process. Cavour Road takes a pasting, as does Granville Road, and St. George's Avenue. Some bombs fall on the recreation ground at the Wellmarsh, and three fall on the yard, with another four at the dockyard railway station, damaging three buildings and a railway carriage.

Hattie gathers her things together at the end of the school day; the raid has resulted in a difficult day, as most of the children are unsettled because they were kept awake and out of bed from almost half past two in the small hours until seven o'clock.

"My class were really out of sorts, because of the constant gunfire during the night," she says to her colleague, Betty Dale, as she gets her kit together ready for her first fitness session with the footballers. "It must have gone on for at least two hours repelling the air raid."

"A lot of parents kept their children at home to catch up with their sleep," Betty says, in response. "Those children who lived in the bombed streets are either too upset to come to class or are helping clear up. I know some had to care for the smaller children, whilst the grown-ups dealt with the aftermath of the raids."

The air raids are far too commonplace in Sheerness, but not all result in bombs being dropped on the town. Often the Zeppelins and the new heavy Gotha planes, built specifically for bombing, fly overhead with other targets in mind, as Sheppey marks the entrance to both the River Thames and the River Medway.

It doesn't help that the Broadway School has been requisitioned, and is currently functioning as a military hospital. The school is now located in the

Congregational Church Sunday school building and the Methodist Hall, which are at opposite ends of Napier Road. Neither hall has a playground for the girls to get fresh air and some exercise.

"I hate this place. I will be glad when we can go back to the Broadway School. I can't teach physical drill properly here. There is nowhere in either Sunday School big enough. And Miss Garrett has cut the length of the lessons to just ten minutes every day. She's introduced a class that she calls *"indecipherable words,"* or as I call it, *"difficult spelling tests,"* which she thinks the girls will find fun! The girls look decidedly peaky from being indoors so much! It's not just the air raids that are taking a toll on their health," Hattie laments, as she packs her plimsolls in her bag.

"Yes ,but every time the siren goes it has to be treated like it will be a full raid, as we don't know what the enemy is planning. It's no wonder the girls are tired."

"There were no raids last month, and only five in October."

"Yes, but there were ten raids in September, and sometimes there have been two in one day," Betty responds. "We have to be alert. Anyway, where are you off to?"

"I've arranged to meet some of my old girls for football training at the Wellmarsh. I'm not sure what state that will be in after last night's raid. Wish me luck!" she says, as she heads out the door.

*****

Fortunately, there is no damage to the gymnasium at the Wellmarsh, where she has got permission to use the equipment there for the girls. There are lots of men about clearing up, and the smell of sweat hangs heavy in the air. She feels in the way, but she waits outside in the vestibule, as arranged. She is wearing her gymslip, to give her freedom of movement, when the door opens, and Alice and her friends troop out from the changing rooms. There are seven of them, all dressed in their football kit, including their boots. Hattie is shocked for a moment, as the girls are all wearing black shorts and red striped jerseys. Even though Hattie always wears very practical clothing, like a divided skirt, so it is easier for her to ride her bicycle, she is not prepared to find other women resisting convention when it comes to how they dress.

"Goodness, I wasn't expecting you to be wearing shorts. How silly of me not to realise that!" She introduces herself to Alice's colleagues. "I'm Mrs West. One or two of you will remember me as

Miss Roberts, but I think you should call me by my first name, Hattie, for ease."

This makes her former pupils Alice and Tilly feel very grown up, as they have been telling the other girls what a good fitness coach Hattie will be, but they still find themselves calling her Miss Roberts, out of habit.

"I feel quite overdressed in my gymslip," she continues, looking down at her navy-blue skirts. She doesn't favour gym bloomers, as she finds them cumbersome, but she can see that shorts are more suited to the fast pace of football.

"Do any of you have plimsolls or canvas sand shoes to wear, as your boots will be too heavy for gym work? If not, you can do it in bare feet."

The girls strip off their boots and their long thick woollen socks to expose their bare legs. Hattie regularly wears a one-piece costume to teach her swimming lessons, and is used to revealing her legs, but some of the girls are initially uncomfortable. As Hattie puts them through their paces, they become less self-conscious and more relaxed with the exercise regime.

At the end of the session, the girls troop back to the dressing room to change into their normal clothes. Hattie follows them and notices that they use the room marked "Away." Inside, along with the benches with the coat hooks above, there is a washroom area with clean white tiles, which houses communal showers and some toilet cubicles, but these are outnumbered by the urinals, which give off a pungent aroma that pervades the whole place.

"Goodness, it's a bit whiffy in here," she says, fanning her nose.

"We're used to it," responds Gertie Brongar. "We have to share all the men's facilities in the dockyard, although, because of complaints about Peeping Toms, a couple of the lavatory blocks are sign posted as "Women's" now, but you still get the odd bloke wandering in after you, pretending he's forgot it has changed."

It seems one man in particular goes into the toilets with his manhood out and heads for the redundant urinals, but only if there are two or three girls in there already; he is never there by himself, it is noted. He obviously waits somewhere out of sight to use the toilets, if a woman has already entered. The girls all agree, saying things like "dirty old man," and "creepy pervert."

Hattie is momentarily shocked. It has never occurred to her that the dockyard girls will have to share facilities with the men. Some of the girls are school leavers, and just twelve years old. She hopes they are watched over by a responsible matron.

"Do you complain?" she asks the group. "Do they take any action?"

"It depends," says Gladys Finch. "The ladies of the colour loft are treated differently, as there have been women there for years, but the rest of us can get a bit of a rum do. I know a couple of girls who complained to Mrs Eames, the colour loft supervisor, and then the senior officers of the dockyard took notice. But the other male managers sometimes think we bring it on ourselves."

Hattie feels sorry for the girls. "Well, I'll see you all again next week," she says, as the changing room begins to empty out.

*****

Beryl Eames has set the women to scrub the colour loft ahead of the Superintendent of the dockyard, Rear Admiral Bennington's regular weekly visit. She doesn't do any of the cleaning herself, so she doesn't wear the smocks which the others do to protect their clothes; she wears a navy-blue skirt and jacket, with just a clean white apron over her slightly spreading hips, to mark her out as their superior. The loft is the one place in the dockyard where women have always been employed, and so she tries to keep it spotless. Traditionally, the staff are the widows of the dockyard workers who have been killed in accidents at work, leaving the family without a breadwinner. The dockyard had offered work, in a time before pensions, to stop the dependents falling into poverty, but the custom remained. Since the war began, some of the women have moved onto other dockyard work and been replaced by those whose husbands are at the front.

Back in May 1915, the ship the *Princess Irene* had exploded, taking seventy-seven dock workers with her. All those widows in one small town. Hundreds of pounds were raised to help the families, but not enough to keep them going on a daily basis forever; they needed to earn a living. Some women remarried, others moved away. Some women had just lived with a man, supposedly as housekeepers, and are not their lawful wives. But, after some campaigning, the fund has recognised them as *"unmarried mothers acting as housekeepers"* and ensured they don't go without.

One of the widows works in the loft, but there are a couple of others elsewhere in the dockyard, who may transfer over once the war ends.

"Do you want me to sweep down the stairs?" Katie Willis asks Mrs Eames, as the women scuttle around to ensure the loft meets the Superintendent's standards. It isn't under Beryl's remit to clean outside of their allotted space but, as there is a shortage of labour, until the war is over and the men return to their old jobs, there is no one else to do it.

"Yes please, Katie" she responds. She will be glad when the onetime workers will come back to the loft. The jobs in the foundry and stores will revert to the men, but the loft ladies are established Civil Servants, and will be able to reclaim their old jobs too. Not like the dilution women doing the men's jobs now, who will find themselves out on their ears, she thinks.

"Are Mrs Blueitt's girls sweeping the bottom corridor?" Katie enquires, wondering how far to go down the stairs.

"I doubt it," Beryl replies. Mrs Blueitt is one of the ones whom she thinks will revert to her old job as a machinist in the loft. Secretly, Mrs Eames doesn't think that Mrs Blueitt is up to the role of supervisor, as she has "sloping shoulders" and manages never to take responsibility or the initiative, but she keeps her own counsel on the matter.

Everyone knows that Mrs Blueitt is "carrying on" with Mr Dennis. But she only does so because he has helped her secure the position as supervisor, and she relies on him to help her with the daily paperwork. She will drop him if someone better comes along. It is said she has her eye on Mr Phillips, but he seems impervious to her charms. Mr Dennis doesn't realise that Mrs Blueitt is the type of woman who looks for opportunities to put herself forward, however she can, so he happily continues to spend his wages on her.

"Just do down the top stairs, we can't do them all," Beryl instructs Katie. The colour loft is part of the Quadrangle. and is on the top floor, where it is flooded with light from the cast iron sash windows. Along the dividing wall there are dozens of pigeonholes, where the flags are stored. It is the only part of the dockyard built for women to work in, and has its own female lavatories and a separate kitchen, where the women can prepare and eat their own food, away from the men.

"Peggy and Mabel, can you ensure all the colours are properly folded in their pigeonholes, please?" she asks, indicating where some of the flags are looking a little forlorn. It is heavy work making the colours, and will take two women to refold them. The Battle Ensign is twenty foot by forty foot, and made from heavy drill fabric, and the Union flags are even larger. They are made on the bigger than normal industrial sewing machines that hum and rattle all day long. The women will spread the finished items out on the floor and inspect them for any faults. Any missed stitches will leave a tiny hole that the wind will poke its finger through, and worry at day by day, until one day when the wind is angry, it will rip the thing in half. You need to be strong as well as a good machinist to work in the colour loft; there is no place for delicate ladies doing fancy needlework in the yard.

Just then, Mrs Johnstone, the supervisor from the Electrical Department, pops her head around the door. "Can I ask your advice on a staffing matter later today?" she asks.

Mrs Eames is finding that many of the women throughout the dockyard are looking to her to intercede with the management, even though they aren't in her department. Some of the men don't treat the new women with the same respect they did her ladies, causing friction and complaints, all of which are ending up with her to deal with. The Admiralty doesn't pay her any more than they pay the rest of the supervisors, but the others all look to her for advice.

"Yes, of course, come back at two," she responds.

She looks around; it will be difficult to keep the loft this clean until the Rear Admiral's visit. She doesn't even think he notices. But she has her standards, and is not regarded as the most senior women's supervisor for nothing.

*****

The war is dragging on, and far from being over by Christmas, three Christmases have now passed, and a fourth will soon be upon them. 1918 will see another year of conflict.

The late headmistress, Miss Morrison, had been unwell for some months, and Miss Garrett had been covering her work, as well as taking her own classes, whilst her colleague only undertook light duties. Then, Miss Morrison died unexpectedly, and Miss Garrett found herself promoted to headmistress, which was only to be expected. It had been very distressing, as Miss Morrison had collapsed in the Methodist Hall vestry, which she had been using as her temporary office. The room was shared with the school secretary, for want of more space, and poor Miss Windley didn't know what to do. Miss Garrett had taken charge as usual, but they had had to keep the children away, whilst first the doctor, then the undertaker had attended to Miss Morrison. Now, all the responsibility for the school sat firmly on her narrow shoulders.

Miss Garrett, (no one ever used her first name, Elsie) is dry and severe looking. Her hair is dragged away from her face so tightly, that it lifts her eyebrows into an expression of slight surprise, as though she has discovered that an acquaintance is having an affair, but that she suspected as much all along. She dresses soberly, but in skirts that allow her to walk at the brisk pace that she favours. She is quick, like a bird looking for something interesting, although most people see her curiosity as nosiness. But the glint in her eye at those who displease her is more like a beady eyed magpie than some songbird. She is well respected and independent, and known for her dislike of mankind as the bringers of all sorrows on women.

Miss Garrett completes the daily log for the school in the same temporary office in the Methodist Hall that Miss Morrison had used, with its mismatched furniture and smell of dusty hymn books. Miss Windley refuses to work in there again, and now has a desk, in what had been the walk-in store cupboard, where the robes had been kept. Fortunately, it has a tiny window to give the secretary some light and air, but the only heating comes from what might drift in lazily from the main hall. The vestry has a tiny fireplace, but there is not enough coal to heat the room when the main hall takes so much to heat with its ancient central stove.

The headmistress purses her thin lips in disapproval, and thinks of the lovely wood panelled office in the Broadway School with its modern boiler and radiators, now being used by the army. "No doubt, when we're able to reclaim our building back from the military, all the fixtures and fittings will be ruined," she complains to Miss Windley.

"I heard that when the troops moved out of Queenborough School, they had broken most of the locks, not just on the stock-cupboards, but also on the class-room doors," Miss Windley says timidly, as you never know if Miss Garrett wants a response or not, but on this occasion she does.

"Yes, I heard that the piano was broken open, no doubt whilst the men caroused after going to the pub when they are off duty." She gives a disapproving sniff. "And that's not to mention the whole inconvenience caused by all the coat pegs being removed by the troops."

"Whatever did they want them for?" Miss Windley asks, but Miss Garrett is now on her favourite hobby horse, and there is no stopping her.

"The Education Board say their aim is to turn out girls fit to be wives and mothers! Why don't they give then an education, so they can pursue an independent career? That is why they are so willing to sacrifice the girl's school for the war effort. They will never do that to the boys!"

Cooking, knitting, and needlework are key features of the curriculum, but so is swimming and nature. Miss Garrett wants her girls to appreciate where they live, and to fully enjoy God's gifts – the sea and the countryside.

"We've had to give up teaching the girls gardening, as there are no grounds here for them to practice what they learn. I've had to instruct the staff to take the girls on a ramble in the surrounding countryside, when the weather is fine. The girls look decidedly peaky. I don't know what Mrs West thinks she is doing about their PE classes, I really don't."

Miss Windley doesn't dare interrupt, even though she knows that most of the teachers only walk the girls along the promenade and back, as it takes too long to get beyond the town and back again.

"And Miss Briggs can't teach cookery properly, as there is only limited kitchen space here. All she can do is demonstrate how to bake, and prepare a few rudimentary meals with a small group of pupils. It really isn't good enough. They will never treat the boys like this."

Ena Briggs is Miss Garrett's closest friend and colleague. She also teaches science and mathematics, but the School Board make little demand on those subjects for the girls at the Broadway School. Miss Garrett would rather coach those girls who might get to the County Grammar School; the few talented girls might be able to get office jobs, or even be teachers. So, between her and Miss Briggs, they do their best to teach those girls the wider subjects they will need.

Miss Garrett hasn't finished, and Miss Windley resigns herself to the fact that until the headmistress has done complaining about the makeshift school, she has little chance of getting on with her own work.

"Do you know why the Board chose these church halls over the premises on offer by the Masons and the Conservative Party in their big headquarters? Both have more spacious halls on offer," she asserts, not waiting for an answer. "It isn't because it will inconvenience their fellow masons and party members. They would have paid them well, and that's usually enough for a contract to head their way. No, it's because the church halls are full of moral messages and imagery for the girls to learn from. But that's not to say that the war isn't making unmarried mothers of the local girls, but once they leave school, they are no longer the concern of the Board," Miss Garrett muses primly.

In a town where there is a naval dockyard and a large army barracks, underage pregnancy is not uncommon. One of her former pupils was married two weeks after her sixteenth birthday, and is expecting again. She already had a babe in arms, conceived before her fifteenth birthday, and she isn't the only one. Miss Garrett gives a little tut to herself at the thought. People are less judgemental about war babies. But that is only if the father stands by the girl. Those not so lucky, often sought help with putting the child up for adoption, or into the workhouse.

She starts moving back towards her own desk and leaves Miss Windley to her own work, but she is not yet done with putting the world to rights, and starts a new line of attack on the girls' education.

"I was heartened when the dockyard recruited women clerks for the first time – not just writers and typists, but clerks, who are established Civil Servants," she says, settling in the doorway so Miss Windley can't escape, even if she tries. "But the Admiralty played a bit of a trick on those female applicants, saying they needed to pass the dockyard entry exam to be able to be clerks. It is so unfair, as the local boys are schooled to take the test from the time they are seven. The whole school year begins and ends to coincide with the exams. Elsewhere in Kent, it follows the agricultural seasons. The boys learn the necessary maths, grammar, and composition to get through the exam," she tells Miss Windley, even though the secretary is already aware of it, as Miss Garrett has told her several times before.

The boys of school leaving age are ranked annually by the Admiralty, and the best boys get the best apprenticeships, whilst lesser boys get jobs like labourers. But it is still a job for life with a pension. Boys that fail the exam have to find other work.

"The girls' knitting classes don't equip them for the exam, so it is a big surprise that as many as six women managed to pass and become clerks. But at least now they will work in the offices, and also have a job for life like the men – a proper career. If they continue to employ girls after the war, I will change the curriculum, so more will pass the exam now I'm headmistress. Miss Briggs can teach most of the skills they need to pass," she says, planning ahead. "Can you make a note to remind me to look at the timetable to see how we can do it, please." She gestures to Miss Windley to make a note in her diary for further consideration.

But most of the dockyard girls are doing heavy work. Recently, the women have been unionised by Mary Macarthur of the *National Federation of Women Workers* (NFWW). The NFWW had made fair pay representations to the Admiralty, together with the *Workers' Union*. They attempted to ensure that women dockyard workers are not left out of pay advances awarded to munitions workers under the Ministry of Munitions.

They are successful, and wages are raised considerably from pre-war rates, although hours remain long, and conditions are poor, or downright dangerous. The local paper reported that a woman doing munitions work in the yard, had broken her arm in three places – although the upside is she will benefit from being treated at the naval hospital to nurse her back to health. The unions worked very hard to ensure the employers didn't find loopholes in the equal pay agreement. Otherwise, the Admiralty would claim that women were not doing EXACTLY the same work as men, even when it is clearly highly skilled. Miss Garrett applauds the dockyard women for this achievement, as the teachers have been trying for some years to gain equal pay, without success.

She turns her mind back to the job in hand of completing the school log, and asks Miss Windley, "Have you finished sorting the money out from the children's war effort moneybox?"

"Yes, Miss Garrett. We received a very nice letter today in acknowledgement of the children's contribution to the *Fund for Christmas Presents for the East Kent Buffs.* The men are currently stationed in Aden, in Arabia. It won't feel like Christmas there. We sent them ten shillings," Miss Windley says, passing Miss Garrett the letter.

"We must remember that Aden is not far on the map from where Our Lord was born," Miss Garrett responds piously, then she adds wryly, "At least they won't get trench foot there!"

"The remaining nine shillings was spent on various comforts for Mr Johnson's parcel," Miss Windley reports. Mr Johnson is one of the teachers from the boys' school, who is now serving at the front. Miss Garrett summons up her dry smile in appreciation of the news.

Just then, Hattie knocks on the Vestry door, and interrupts their conversation. "Come in," invites Miss Garrett, leaving Miss Windley to finally get on with her work and return to her own desk. She puts down the letter and removes the reading glasses that she increasingly finds she needs.

"Sorry to disturb you," Hattie says. "I've been asked to help give fitness training to some of the dockyard girls for their football. I was wondering if there are any bigger sized plimsolls in lost property, as the girls only seem to have their boots, and they need something less heavy for the gym."

"Help yourself, but I expect there are only odd ones rather than pairs." Miss Garrett gesticulates to the box of oddments balanced on the filing cabinet above Miss Windley's head. Hattie rummages through the contents, and manages to make one pair, with two shoes that almost match.

"Alice McDonald (do you remember her, Miss Dobbs' maid?) and the other girls tell me that they have to share the men's facilities, and that the men sometimes walk in!" Hattie recounts to her colleague, in disgust.

"How unpleasant," says Miss Garrett, wrinkling up her narrow nose, as she gives a sniff of disapproval. She looks like she has just tasted a very bitter lemon.

"They say there are few avenues of complaint open to them," Hattie continues, as she tries further matches of odd shoes.

Miss Garrett pulls a face. "If that was me, the man in question would be leaving there with more than just a flea in his ear!"

Hattie doesn't doubt that, as Miss Garrett can be very formidable; she once chased some thieves who attempted to steal her bag through the streets of Paris.

"It must be difficult for the girls having to work in such a male dominated workplace," Hattie ponders, before saying, "Perhaps I will ask Marie Beesdale and Suki Wendle if there are any lost property plimsolls to spare in their schools. Maybe I can make a couple more pairs that way." She throws the unmatched items back into the lost property box, and returns it to its home on the filing cabinet.

*****

Saturday afternoons are when the women's football matches take place. Kick-off is as close to noon as possible, allowing for the away players to arrive following their morning at work, and to ensure that ninety minutes can be played before the light fails in the winter. This means that Alice, Tilly, and the rest of the *Naval Stores Ladies* team, go straight to the dockyard playing fields as soon as the siren sounds the end of the shift.

The Wellmarsh is a huge recreation ground, which serves both the army and the navy, as well as the dockyard. There are separate pavilions for different sports, and enough facilities to accommodate dozens of service men at one time. But the women are allocated the furthest pitches from the changing facilities, and are given the poorest equipment: nets with holes, and ragged specimens of corner flags. Mr Phillips stands guard outside their changing rooms, on these occasions, leaning against the green and cream painted walls to bar the way, and ensure no stray men wander in with poor excuses for why they are there.

The *Stores Ladies* are playing against the electrical department women, so there is a lot of rivalry between the teams, as they run out onto the pitch. It had been raining the day before, so the water splashes up through the grass. It will soon be a quagmire. Hattie has helped with their fitness training for about four weeks, and it is really beginning to tell, increasing the *Stores Ladies* stamina and strength. John Phillips now calls her "Coach", instead of Mrs West, although she still only has a rudimentary understanding of the off-side rule.

"Well, Coach," he addresses her, as she stands beside him on the touch line, "what do you reckon to our chances in the cup this season?"

"The girls haven't mentioned a cup to me," she responds, looking at him in surprise.

"Ah, that's because it's new, Mrs West! There's a competition running in the North-East calls the *Alfred Wood Munitions Girls Challenge Trophy*, but local people are calling it the *Munitionettes Cup*. I've been talking with the other managers, and we've decided to run our own tournament, and we've approached the Dockyard Superintendent for a cup for the girls to play for. There are already a number of tournaments for the men, for almost any sport you can think of, so they won't miss out," says John Phillips, warming to his subject now.

"It may surprise you to learn that there are a number of cups in the trophy cabinet that no one ever plays for anymore. And there are trophies for almost every sport imaginable! The *Plunge for Distance* looked like it was going to become a regular event at the annual swimming gala, but it was dropped, after just one appearance in the 1904 Olympics. It hasn't been a competition event since. No one is interested in it anymore! The cup has never even been engraved! It's like new! The Rear Admiral says we can have it, and what's more, his wife, Mrs Bennington, is going to champion it. After Christmas, we will do a blind draw for the eight teams that will eventually lead to the cup final on the weekend of the *King's Birthday* holiday, on the first of June. Are you up for helping our girls to win it, Coach?"

Hattie gives him a broad grin. "Too right I am!"

*****

Unwanted Attention

Victor Banks is once again hanging about near the stores, trying to catch a glimpse of one of the women who have been brought in to fill the ever-increasing vacancies caused by the conscription of all the able-bodied men under forty-one. Victor had been called up, but as the breadwinner for his widowed mother, and a semi-skilled labourer needed to repair the navy's ships, he has an exemption from the Board, as a man needed for urgent war work.

As more women come to work in the yard, he often finds himself hanging about near where they are located. He has developed a knack of conspicuously carrying a large brown envelope containing messages, or pieces of vital equipment that are needed elsewhere, and disappearing for at least half an hour on these missions, so that he can spy on the girls.

Victor is a bit of a loner, and tries to steer clear of the other lads, like Teddie Taylor and his cronies, with their ribald banter. They are always discussing which girls they have kissed in the shelters on the sea front promenade. He has few friends, as his own peer group, now in their mid-twenties, are nearly all married, or have steady girlfriends, leaving him with the company of the younger lads like Taylor. There are a few bachelors who like to play the field, and it is speculated that one or two of them may be queer, but no one knows the truth of that rumour. They certainly don't seek out Victor's company, and he, in turn, doesn't seek theirs.

Victor's mother teases him and says, "You've just not found the right girl yet," whenever any friends or family enquire about his love life. She smoothes his lank hair down, and brushes the dandruff off his bony shoulders with her hands, smiling indulgently into his water-coloured eyes. He is her baby, an only child in a time of big families, and it has been just the two of them since he is ten.

But Victor knows that no girl will be good enough for his mother. He sees the way she looks down her nose at the munitionettes, who work in the dockyard. "They are brazen hussies, who give the glad eye to all the officers. Their skirts are a good six inches above their ankles," she says. He also hears her talking to her friends about the local girls, all of whom are, "No better than they ought to be," according to his mother. Then again, few girls are as good as his mother, in his opinion. Who could love him as much as she did? Who else will put his wants first?

But he still has needs, like any other man, and often considers visiting one of the many brothels in the Bluetown area of Sheerness, outside the dockyard walls. One day, after work, he goes down the High Street, looking for somewhere to take his custom. He notices the soldiers and sailors are coming and going from a couple of "respectable" looking houses set amongst the many pubs. These houses have lace curtains, like any other, but the front doors stand open, and each has a ferocious looking doorkeeper barring the way to the inner door. These doormen are all of the same sort, stocky with the evidence of their pugilism written on their faces, with flattened noses and bent ears. He watches from across the street, trying to blend into the bleak dockyard wall. He has to tell a mangy dog who comes sniffing to "shoo"; the poor thing is hungry, but it is against the law to adopt a stray dog, as there are no rations for them. Victor notices how some of the brightly dressed women are entering and leaving, their days finished, or evenings beginning. They look across to where he stands, and dismiss him with their eyes. If I can chat to one of them first, it might calm my nerves, he thinks. After much dithering, he finally gets up the courage to approach one of the strumpets in the street, as she is about to go into *The Jolly Jack Tar* with her friend.

"Excuse me, miss, can I take you for a drink and a chat?" he asks, noticing how she is less pretty and older close up, with cold eyes and a hard mouth, her blouse not as clean as it might be. She smells of gin and something more masculine that he can't quite name, but is familiar. And she is missing the bottom of her ear lobe. It is said locally that an amorous client had bitten it off in the throes of passion.

"Sure," Ivy Dummott replies, ready to take his skinny arm. "It's five shillings for a chat, and half of light ale. I've got to get back to my kids, but I can spare half an hour. You can have a fumble in the alley after."

Her friend Pearl gives a gap-toothed smile, knowing that Ivy won't go home till the pubs chuck out.

"No," he replies, pulling away, "I don't mean like that."

She laughs in his face, "My time's precious. I don't drink with the likes of you for free." She turns and walks into the pub with Pearl, leaving him humiliated on the threshold.

He makes do with buying some obscene picture postcards from Mrs Bennet's newsagents and tobacconist, a few doors down. You can easily see the cards on display through the shop window, and the activity of the matelots alerts him that he will be able to buy some without anyone taking any notice. He goes in and selects a few, which he takes to the counter.

Mrs Bennet takes them from him. "Sixpence each, and you'll need this," she says, as she produces a newspaper for him to buy to conceal the cards in. "And don't you want some sweets for your mother?" She passes him over a quarter of pear drops, already bagged up, concealing the broken lumps from the bottom of the jar. She smirks, as she charges him an arm and a leg for the lot. It would have been better value to pay the doxy five shillings for her time.

"Do you need anything else?" she asks, in a suggestive way glancing up to a top shelf, where there is a tray of contraceptive sheaths tucked behind some sweet jars.

Victor makes a hasty retreat out of the shop, his face burning.

When he gets home, he gives his mother the pear drops, and tells her that the newsagent is selling dirty postcards and respectable people can clearly see them through the window. "I'm glad you didn't see them, Mum," he says.

He knows how his mother will react and, sure enough, she wastes no time investigating the shop herself, and stops at the Police Station, on her way back into the respectable part of town, the other side of the dock gates, to make a complaint about the obscene matter on display. He later reads in the local newspaper that the cards are seized and destroyed, and Mrs Bennet is sentenced to a hefty fine of twenty-five pounds – about six months' pay, or three months in jail for her trouble.

*****

"Your admirer is outside again," May Ballard calls across to Alice, as she comes into the stores one January morning, having spotted Victor lurking near the bins.

May had joined the footballers at the beginning of the season. She has five brothers, and regularly plays with them in the back streets of Sheerness. She has footballer's legs and a no-nonsense attitude. As the boys got older, they joined local teams, and teased May by calling her "May-Not," as she always asked, "May I join in?" to which they reply, "No, you May-Not." So, when the

Naval Stores Ladies team are looking for players, she signs up immediately.

"Doesn't he have any work to do?"

"He's always hanging about," Alice responds, eyeing him through the window, from a safe distance. "I suppose he's missed me, as we weren't here over Christmas."

Gladys Finch joins them, taking advantage of the opportunity for a gossip and a break. "He looks a bit creepy to me," she says, and the others nod in agreement.

"When he comes in here, his hands are clammy as he passes over his voucher from his manager. He always tries to touch my hand as he does so." Alice grimaces.

"He's too old for you anyway, and everyone says he's a mummy's boy."

"Yes, a good ten years older," Gladys observes. "His eyes are a really funny washed-out colour, like a cold, dead cod."

"When he takes off his cap, his hair is lank and greasy."

"And he's got dandruff!"

"He's so skinny, and he has a long neck like a goose!" May contributes to the assassination of Victor.

"Yuk," says Alice, with a little shudder. "He watches me at football, and afterwards tells me how much he enjoyed looking at my legs as I ran." The girls join her in her shudder. "Sometimes, when I'm getting the things he wants from the stores, he sidles up to me, so I have to squeeze past him. He is so repulsive."

"Have you complained to Mrs Blueitt?" May asks. "Can't she get Victor's boss to send someone else on his errands?"

"I don't know what I would say to her," Alice responds.

So, the girls decide to discuss it with Hattie at their next training session.

*****

Miss Garrett assembles her Girl Guides on Tuesday night, as usual, in the Napier Road Hall, that just a couple of hours earlier was functioning as the Broadway Girls School. That is one of her pet hates about being in temporary accommodation; at the end of each school day, they have to pack up everything and store it in cupboards, as the hall reverts to being the Sunday school building used by different community groups each evening, or used for concerts to entertain the service men and women, as well as being a Sunday school on the Sabbath. As Miss Garrett is engaged in many of these activities, it feels like she is living there instead of in her semi- detached house in Crimea Road.

She feels sorry for Mr Moss the caretaker, as he is having to do no end of cleaning and getting the hall ready for its next use. The Broadway School caretaker remained at the school when it became a hospital, so the Education Board provides no extra help to keep the Sunday school hall clean.

Tonight, Miss Garrett is teaching the guides the basics of first aid. They are also using the hall's small kitchen to learn some "war cookery", where they substitute margarine for butter, and learn how to cook macaroni instead of potatoes, and what to eat the "foreign" pasta with. Just as she is explaining how the Italians make a "ragu" sauce from tomatoes, and how she has eaten such sauces on her various holidays to Italy before the war, Mr Pope, the scout master, bursts in through the main doors.

"Miss Garrett, I need you to change your Girl Guide night to another day, so I can lead my scouts on Tuesdays. I've volunteered to be the chief air raid warden, and need a regular day to brief the VAD men. They meet on Thursdays at the Masonic Hall, which they use as their HQ, so I will need to be there. You will have to move to Thursdays, so I can fit it in," he says, with his whiney voice that resembles the air raid siren turned to low volume.

"Why don't you volunteer to lead the wardens on Tuesday evenings when you are free?" she asks him, with a look that if it doesn't kill could certainly leave someone maimed.

"Because Mr Barrowman already has Tuesdays for first aid practice for the VADS, and won't swap, so I had to take Thursday," he says, bobbing his bald head about so the gaslight shone dully off it, his attempts to cover his pate with a comb-over stuck down with brilliantine failing miserably.

"Can't you have your VAD meeting after your scouts meeting?"

"The Hun don't run their air raids to a published timetable, you know!" he responds sarcastically.

Colonel Bate, the secretary for the London branch of the Red Cross has offered the services of the Voluntary Aid Detachments (VADs) to the police, for air raid duty. They believe that the emblem of the Red Cross inspires a feeling of confidence in the crowds which assemble in the underground railway stations and other refuges in the poorer districts of London. Soon VADs across the country are helping bring order to chaos inflicted during the raids. Mr Pope evidently feels that his contribution is needed as Mr Butler, the previous commander, has been unwell recently.

But Miss Garrett thinks that nothing will drive people out into the streets screaming more than this horrible little jobsworth. She is convinced that he is abroad at night reporting houses to the police, if so much as a chink of light is showing. Winston Churchill, First Lord of the Admiralty, had plans drawn up to black out British coastal towns in the event of a war, back in 1913, even before most people believed that war might be declared; Sheerness is amongst those towns named. These plans are implemented on the twelfth of August 1914, just eight days after Great Britain and her Empire enters the war. Since then, there are reports in the local paper every week of people summoned to court for showing a light; from the nurses' hostel to ordinary citizens, no one is exempt.

Only the other day, a landlady of a boarding house was summoned. Miss Garrett followed the case in the local paper, which said the woman had failed to attend court when she was first called, but appeared at the next session and pleaded guilty. It seems a pity the woman is summoned at all, as she is not really to blame. She said that the light was left burning for the army officers who are lodging with her and had not returned. On a previous occasion, a light was left burning in the officers' bedrooms and was shining out to sea.

The paper reports that the magistrate says, "I can't understand three officers in His Majesty's service disobeying the law in these days of Zeppelin raids. Everybody else is expected to obey the law. How can we expect a woman like the defendant to do so, when the law is defied by those who should be the first to obey it? It seems to me that the officers are really to blame. It is a very grave thing indeed. However, the defendant is in the house, and has made herself responsible, and therefore I must call on her to pay a fine of two pounds." Although the poor woman expressed her regret, it is she that has to pay the hefty fine.

Miss Garrett thinks that checking the blackout is just the kind of small -minded thing Pope enjoys doing. But she knows she will have to concede and swap days. Mr Pope will have all the great and the good behind him.

"Very well, Mr Pope, we will swap from next week," she says, giving him her most vinegary of smiles, whilst seething inside.

*****

Hattie is not shocked when Alice tells her about Victor's unwelcome attention; she is only surprised that more of the girls don't have similar complaints. She volunteers to speak to Mr Phillips on the girls' behalf, and suggests that Alice keeps a diary of the events. Indeed, later that day, she sees Victor for herself lurking outside the gym as the girls begin their training, and he is still there when they come out. He starts to speak to Alice, but stops when he sees Hattie giving him a hard stare, and calls out to him, "Can I help you, sir. You seem to have been standing outside the gym for some while in this cold weather?" He looks shifty and disappears around the corner. Hattie West is not seen as being quite as formidable as Miss Garrett, but she still had a fierce reputation, as she is known to play sports like cricket and tennis against male opponents. Victor is nowhere near man enough to face her.

Hattie decides to stop at Mr Phillips' home, on her way to the house she still shares with her colleague, Ena Briggs. When she married Bill West in April 1915, the couple decided she should remain in lodgings until he is demobbed, after the war, whenever that might be. But Bill was killed just over a year later, during the Battle of Jutland, when his ship *HMS Black Prince* was sunk with all hands, on the night of the thirty-first of May 1916. With nowhere else to go, Hattie stayed living with Ena. Tibby the cat still lives with her too, and Hattie knows that even if she was to move on, Ena had become so used to the animal, that she will keep it. After Bill died, she often held the cat tight and sobbed into its soft fur. Tibby deigned to put up with this treatment, as Hattie is one of those people who can charm any four-legged creature.

Hattie left her employment at the Broadway School, as married women are not permitted to be teachers. However, she reapplied when she became widowed, as she did not qualify for a pension and needed to support herself. The Ministry of Pensions, set up in 1916, doesn't view her as "deserving", because some town gossips report her as having "relations" with other men. The wagging tongues saw Hattie playing cricket and tennis, and the Ministry judges her to be of low moral fibre as a result, and rules that she is not entitled to a pension. It is lucky that she has a profession which she can call upon, or she may have been desperate.

Mr Phillips lives in Trafalgar Parade, near the seafront. His house is one of the bigger terrace kind, with a large bay window and a small garden at the back. Hattie knocks at the door and waits. Mr Phillips's unmarried sister, Biddy, who keeps house for him, answers the door and views Hattie with suspicion through her half-moon spectacles that she wears for needlework. She knows who Hattie is, as two of her nieces go to the Broadway School, but it isn't usual for men and women to be friends, so she can't imagine what brings the teacher to their home.

When Mr Phillips opens the door, it is the first time Hattie has seen him in just his shirt sleeves, with a *Fair Isle* pullover over the top. Usually, he wears a waistcoat, with his silver pocket watch chain strung across his chest. He looks quite different, warmer, and less formal. Hattie launches straight in with, "Some of the girls are expressing concerns about the unwanted attention of some of the men in the dockyard. I saw one of them myself hanging about through our training session, and he accosted one of the girls afterwards. He left when he saw me, but she tells me it's a common occurrence, and happens during the working day as well. Can you tell the men to keep away?"

"I can ask them to, but if they are not under my management, then I have no authority."

"Can you take it higher, to your superiors?"

"Look, I'm sorry if the girls are put out, but no one is doing any real harm. Some of the girls give the men the glad eye. Everyone knows the single girls all hope to marry a naval officer and, failing that, a shipwright, someone to give them status and security. So, it's not fair to expect all the men to keep away, when the girls are just as much to blame."

"Well, surely the Admiralty can see that the men are not getting on with their work. Can't you tackle it from that side?"

"I will have a word, but I can't make any promises," he concludes. He notices her disappointment and tries to make amends. "We need to start planning our campaign to win the cup, now that the draw has taken place and the fixtures are known." He produces his notebook from his back pocket to show Hattie the dates of the matches. "I will see you Saturday," he finishes, trying to be conciliatory.

Hattie smiles and nods.

*****

Maggie McDonald, Alice's mother, is again looking for her "cousin by marriage", Ivy Dummott, in the pubs in Bluetown, where the smell of beer is supplemented by the smell of men and cigarette smoke, and sometimes a scented tobacco that the Caribbean sailors smoke, sending them into a dreamy state.

She has tried *The Jolly Jack Tar* to no avail, and pokes her head around the door of the *Shipwright's Arms*.

"Have you seen Ivy?" she calls out to the landlady, who is propping up the bar and talking to some sailors, whilst her barmaids run around doing all the work. The landlady just shakes her head.

"She's needed at home to look after her children, tell her," Maggie says.

"What's happened?" one of the sailors is moved to ask. "Can we help you look for her?"

"Her son Ernie has hurt himself again," Maggie replies, pulling herself up to her full four foot eleven as she stands in the doorway, her wide child bearing hips blocking the way. She swings around and sets off for the next pub.

Maggie's family, the Keppels, have been osiers in Faversham, for as long as anyone can remember. They weave the big wicker baskets for the hop pickers and the bushel baskets the tally man will measure the picked hops into. The family moved to West Minster when she was ten, and her father got a job at the gas works, as the family's osier business can't support the whole of the extended Keppel tribe. Maggie has left the hop gardens behind, but she doesn't really mind, as the smell is really overpowering, and makes her feel sick and faint at the beginning of the season, until she becomes immune to it again. She didn't realise that she was replacing it with the ripe stench of the sewage works. Now, after more than twenty-five years, she has forgotten the scent of the hops, except sometimes when she pokes her head round a pub door looking for Ivy, and the memories come flooding back.

Seeing the sailors around Bluetown reminds her of her first love. At just fifteen, Maggie fell pregnant with her eldest, Billie, to a sailor off one of

Her Majesty's ships, who promised to marry her as soon as she is sixteen. He was handsome and strong, and called her a "right canny lass" in his Geordie accent, but he sailed away without giving her his real name. Her father tried to track his ship down, but the Royal Navy heard so many similar stories, that he got nowhere. Fortunately, her mother agreed to raise Billie as her own, but Maggie is dubious of any help that the sailors in the pub may be offering from her previous experience.

"How's Rab," Mrs Jinks, the town gossip, calls across the road to her as she hurries along, "Is he over his cold?"

"You know men, always iller than we are. But he still goes to work, can't afford to lose a day's pay with so many mouths to feed."

Maggie tries to save a few shillings every week in the Co-op for a rainy day. A family can easily become destitute if sickness strikes the bread winner, especially as diseases like consumption are still commonplace. Rab can't afford to be sick.

"Are Ivy's two with you again?"

"Yes, Ernie's cut his head open, and Ivy's nowhere to be found."

"Your Rab's a good'en taking on her kids, as well as your own brood."

Maggie nods. "That he is," she says, as she heads to the next pub.

When Maggie was nineteen, her Dad brought Rab McDonald and his brother Ginger home from work for Christmas Day, as the two Scots lads had nowhere to go to celebrate the festival. Her Dad couldn't resist a hard luck story and takes pity on them, sharing what little they had with the two lads.

It wasn't long before Maggie and Rab were walking out together. When she fell pregnant with Cathy, he kept his promise to marry her, unlike the sailor who was Billie's father. Rab also took on the four-year-old Billie to raise as his own, and the child's birth certificate was amended, at some expense, to bear the McDonald name. Many a man would not have done that.

"Is Ivy in here?" she calls out from the doorway of the *Maid of Kent*.

"Not seen her today," the potman calls back, as he collects the dirty glasses from the windowsill.

Ivy is usually to be found in the pubs in Bluetown, where she will proposition sailors for drinks, in return for sexual favours in the back alleys. She had been pretty once, but has lost her looks to her lifestyle. However, she still manages to attract enough customers to keep her going. Most of the time, every penny she makes is spent in the pub, but, occasionally, she will find a generous benefactor with whom she might spend both days and nights, until his shore leave is over. Then, she may return home triumphantly, bringing fish and chips for her children, Cissie and Ernie. If she isn't too intoxicated already, she will enjoy the sight on their little faces, accepting without question the treat she has brought them.

Maggie often takes the two of them in until Ivy appears, contrite, and promising to mend her ways. When Ivy's mother, Agatha, had been widowed, she had married Maggie's Uncle Frank, and the two girls become cousins by marriage. It is this tenuous relationship which led Ivy to rely on Maggie.

"If she comes in, tell her I'm looking for her, will you?"

There had been no room for the teenage Ivy in her mother's new home, so she had gone to work in a ladies outfitters store in London, whilst living with her mother's sister in Pimlico. The family had great hopes for her, as Ivy showed promise at bookkeeping and managing the stock. She was good with people and knew how to make a sale. She had worked her way up on the shop floor to become a senior sales assistant. Then, her aunt died, and Ivy needed to find new lodgings quickly. One of the other women in the shop said she knew somewhere that took in boarders, and Ivy moved into an attic room near Euston. But without the company of her aunt, she soon found herself at a loose end in the evenings and started joining a friend visiting some of the pubs near the station. There are many well to do gentlemen in such establishments, killing time before their trains are due to depart, and they are happy to buy drinks for a pretty girl.

Soon, Ivy found it hard to get up in the mornings and increasingly she was late or missed work. When her employer sacked her, she thought of returning home to Sheppey, but the gentlemen still kept buying her drinks. To make enough to pay her rent, she found that if she agreed to be nice to the gentlemen, she could earn her keep and quite a bit extra. This became Ivy's way of life away from her family. If it hadn't been for her brother, she would probably still have been there.

Next, Maggie tries the *Green Dragon*, where her brother Eddie was the landlord before the war. Her sister-in-law, Dierdre, is currently the licensee as her husband is in France.

"Are you looking for Ivy again?" Dierdre asks, almost before Maggie has entered the bar. "You're too good to her, she's not even real family."

"Tell me about it. Her own family tried to turn her life around, and for a while she was back on the straight and narrow, you know."

Her sister-in-law gives her a look, which suggests she is sceptical about Ivy's own family's concern for her.

"Her brother really cared for her. He went looking for her in London and found her drunk one afternoon, and brought her home with him to Sheerness. He made her promise to give up the drink, and helped her to get a job in a dress shop," Maggie tells Dierdre. "She was doing fine there; her London manners made the navy wives and gentry feel they were getting an up-market service. It was when she was working in the shop in the High Street that she met Eli Dummott. They fell in love and got married. Then, she had Cissie, after which everything fell apart."

Dierdre remains unconvinced. "Yes, but playing the good wife and mother was tiresome for Ivy after living it up in London. Everyone knows she is bored at home with only housework to do. That's when she started drinking again. She used to come in here looking for Eddie. She is all smiles at him trying to get free drinks, till I sent her away with a flea in her ear. She's not changed any over the years."

Maggie knows she can't change Dierdre's mind about Ivy, so she says her goodbyes and sets off again. On the off chance, she tries the Congregational Church, where Eli is a lay preacher. He is a riveter in the dockyard, and older than Ivy by some years.

"I don't suppose Ivy's been in to see you today Eli?" she asks.

"Not today. Has she gone missing again?" he asks as he sweeps the steps. "I've tried to get her to change. I've tried to beat the drink out of her, but it is no use; she won't learn from the beatings I administered for her own good. I'd take her back in a heartbeat, and Cissie too, if Ivy will only take the Lord into her heart and repent her ways."

Eli announces this from the top step, to anyone willing to listen. He is looking for both public sympathy and admiration. Maggie bites her tongue on his hypocritical ways. He didn't claim Cissie when Ivy left, because it is a commonly held belief that a daughter of an alcoholic mother will become an alcoholic herself. Eli thinks there is no hope for the little girl, and more or less washes his hands of her, but not quite.

"I'm a God-fearing man and know my duty. I still pay maintenance for them both, despite the behaviour of my wife," he continues, in his pulpit voice, for the benefit of any passers-by.

Maggie grudgingly concedes this point, as Ivy had fallen pregnant with little Ernie, with no knowledge of who the father is, but Eli Dummott still pays maintenance for Cissie, despite this indisputable evidence of his wife's infidelity. Ernie's birth certificate says *"father unknown"*, where the name of his parent should be, but Ivy gave him the surname Dummott anyway. However, it is Maggie and their extended family, that rallies around Ivy and helps her when the boy is small, but many tire of Ivy's inability to take control, and soon only Maggie is left helping out.

Ernie was damaged at birth by his mother's heavy drinking during pregnancy. People say he will grow up to be an "imbecile", and have to live in the workhouse with the other inmates classed as imbeciles, as he will be unable to earn a living - if he lives that long. But Cissie loves her little brother, and does all she can to care for him, and shield him from society. She soothes his outbursts and interprets his utterings. But he is clumsy, as both his eyesight and hearing are impaired; his current injury is evidence of this.

Maggie decides to cut across Eli and stop his preaching. "Ernie has fallen and cut his head open. Mrs Embleton has stitched the wound, but Ivy needs to come home and care for her children until the boy is better again. I've got my own children to look after. I can't take on nursing a sick child not my own, not when Ernie's mother should be taking responsibility. If you see her, tell her I'm looking for her, will you?" Maggie finishes and, without giving Eli the opportunity to start preaching about Ivy's sins being visited upon little Ernie, she walks away.

She eventually finds Ivy in the *Dockyard Arms* with her friend Pearl. They are keeping company with a couple of sailors, who are standing them both drinks, despite the "*no treating*" order introduced to help curb drinking affecting the war effort.

"Ivy, you must come home, Ernie has hurt himself again," entreats Maggie.

"Can't you look after him?" her cousin asks. Ivy and Maggie are around the same age, but have little in common. Ivy had been very pretty once and the envy of her peers. She had golden blond hair with natural curls that framed her face and clear blue eyes. Her eyes are often bloodshot now, and her hair is no longer her crowning glory.

"I can, but it's your duty, not mine!"

"He'll be okay with Cissie. I'll see them later."

"No! Now Ivy, or I'll get my Rab to drag you home!"

Ivy reluctantly leaves the pub, and promises to return as soon as she can. "I'm a devoted mother," she tells her companions, waving farewell drunkenly, as Maggie shoos her out. Once outside, Maggie locks arms with her, so she can't escape.

"If you're not careful, they will take those children away!"

"I can look after them," Ivy slurs, and draws herself up as she attempts to walk in a straight line next to Maggie. They pass Phyllis Banks, Victor's mother, who is gossiping to a friend outside the drapers shop. Mrs Banks is a notorious town busybody, who knows how to use the information she gathers to her best advantage. She wears horn rimmed spectacles to ensure she misses nothing. She is a stringy woman, and when she is wearing her disapproving face, which is often, the cords in her neck stand out. She always smiles at people as she stabs them in the back, and she carries a shopping basket both day and night, so that she can always look purposeful when she has gone out to glean snippets of news for later use.

"No better than she ought to be," says Mrs Banks to her companion, nodding towards Ivy and cording her neck. "It breaks my heart to see a woman brought so low." But really she can't wait to tell everyone how she has seen Maggie McDonald weaving down the road, arm in arm with that infamous woman, Ivy Dummott.

Did She Encourage Him?

There is another heavy air raid on the twenty-eighth of January. The dockyard comes under attack at five past nine that evening, when five bombs damage the destroyer, *HMS Violet,* as well as the lighter, *Winkle.* The steam vessel, *Swale,* and the steam launch *No. 121* are also wrecked. The bombs are indiscriminate, and also sink a custom's boat and a revenue cutter. Another falls near the Rear Admiral's office and smashes many of the windows. Mrs Bennington has to do her best to calm the servants, who are panicking, much to her annoyance. At Gun Wharf, a bomb destroys the explosives stores, lighting up the night sky, but fortunately not setting off a chain reaction. The same bomb also partly demolishes some workshops, and a wall between the Gun Wharf and the dockyard. Other offices and storerooms also suffer damage, and the blast breaks dozens of windows in the town. Five men are injured, and one, a stoker, later dies.

There is a lot of clearing up to do, and the dockyard is very busy as a consequence. Every available man is set to making repairs or clearing rubble. The women in the stores are run off their feet, fulfilling orders to help with the clear up operation.

Victor is only temporarily put off by Hattie West making it clear his presence is not welcome around the *Naval Stores Ladies* football team. He uses the pandemonium to run his petty errands, so that he can find an excuse to speak to Alice. However, whenever he arrives in the stores, one of the other women come to serve him.

"Isn't Alice here today?" he asks, knowing that she is out the back, as he sees her disappear through the door.

"She's busy, and so should you be, not finding excuses to come here and bother her. Can't you see she's not interested?" Tilly Jackson tells him, in no uncertain terms. She takes his voucher and sets about fulfilling the order.

But Victor remains undeterred. He understands little about women and most of what he thinks he knows; he has learnt from the likes of Teddie Taylor. He firmly believes that all women want to be chased, and that they are driven by their sexual desires. His mother is always telling him how handsome he is and what a catch he will be for some girl, whilst at the same time ensuring that he knows that no woman will ever love him like his mother does. He has placed his mother on a pedestal, and doesn't realise that the kind of respect he gives to her should also be given to other women.

When he returns to the stores, later on, another girl is there to intercept him and prevent him speaking to Alice, and the same thing happens every time he goes there for the next week or so. But Victor is not so easily thwarted, and he makes a plan to catch Alice on her own. He will watch the stores until whoever is Alice's working partner for the day, be it Tilly, May, Enid, Gladys, or Gertie has gone to the lavatory, before he goes in. The tools loan store is not part of the rest of the stores complex in the Quadrangle, where the nearest lavatory designated for the women is situated. It is located in some huts several blocks away, and it is almost an expedition for the girls to pop out when nature calls. As there are only two women's toilet blocks in the whole of the dockyard, there is often a queue and plenty of other women around for a gossip. This will give him about fifteen minutes, when Alice will be alone and unprotected.

The manager of the loco shed, where he is currently working, is less tolerant of Victor going missing all the time than the fitting shop manager was. But there is a spot near the end doors where he can see the loan store, so he can nip over when he sees the coast is clear.

Later that day, Victor's stars align, and he spots an opportunity to catch Alice on her own. But, as soon as he goes into the loan store, a second man follows him in with a voucher for tools. Alice serves Victor quickly and reaches her hand out for the other man's order, indicating that she is done with Victor.

"I'm not sure if we've got any of these left, I'll have to hunt for them out the back," she lies to the second customer, ducking away to escape Victor, and leaving the two men together.

Victor hangs about for a bit, trying to engage his colleague in conversation, but he knows nothing about sport, or any other subject that men pass the time of day with, and his conversation soon falters, so he decides to return to the loco shed.

After this scene is repeated a couple of times, over the next few days, he finally gets Alice on her own. She is sitting on the stool behind the counter, making a bonnet for the new baby girl that her sister has given birth to, just a few days ago. Her body language indicates her defensiveness against him, with her legs crossed, and as soon as she sees him, she puts her crochet down and folds her arms.

Victor tries to make idle chit chat with her, "What are you making today?"

"An elephant," she answers trying to cut the conversation off.

"A toy one for the baby?" he asks, revealing that he knows all about the goings on in Khartoum Road.

"No, a real live one that I will ride through the town!" She holds the item up so he can see it is a baby's bonnet, but he doesn't take the hint. "What do you want, Victor?"

"I need a wench!" he jokes, laughing at his own near pun.

"A wrench," she corrects him, rolling the "R", as she snatches the voucher and turns her back on him to go into the store.

Victor lifts the counter flap quietly, and follows silently behind her into the back of the stores. As Alice raises her arms to reach into the cabinet, where the locomotive tools are kept, he comes up behind her and grabs her arm to swing her around. She is taken by surprise, as he tries to put his hand up her skirt and kiss her.

"Stop it! Get off me!" she says, trying to push him away, as he roughly gropes her.

Just then, the bell on the door goes, signalling that someone else had come into the stores. Victor beats a hasty retreat, knocking into the other man as he leaves.

Alice is shaking, and she is on the verge of tears, when Tilly returns. She can immediately see that Alice is upset and goes to her, saying, "Are you okay?"

Alice nods, as Tilly steers her to sit down. "What happened?" she asks, addressing this question to Reggie Symonds, the other customer who has just come into the stores.

"I just saw Victor Banks leaving in a hurry," he responds, looking slightly bewildered.

Tilly takes his voucher and quickly returns with the tool he needs. She closes and locks the door after him, and puts a little star next to the man's name in the record book, so she will remember who it is.

"Now, tell me what happened," she says, fussing over Alice, passing her a handkerchief, and putting the kettle on the stove to make some tea.

After Alice recounts what Victor has done, she says, "We must tell Mrs Blueitt. You can't let this go. It's too serious."

"No one will believe me," says Alice.

"Well, I do for a start," Tilly replies. "We will shut up shop temporarily and go and find her."

*****

They find Mrs Blueitt in her small office in the Quadrangle; all the women supervisors seem to have rooms that had probably started out as walk-in cupboards. She is not surprised to hear Alice's complaint, as she has expected one of the girls to come to her like this since the women were first employed.

"The men have no respect," she says, as she wonders what she should do. It doesn't occur to her that she sets a bad example by carrying on with Arthur Dennis. She knows that some of the senior officials will just brush it under the carpet and, for all her faults, she doesn't want that to happen. She will have to get someone with authority on her side. They need to make an example of Victor, to deter the other men from harassing the girls.

She decides to take the girls to Mrs Eames. The colour loft supervisor is held in high regard, and the senior officers will defer to her opinion. But she will need to make it seem that it is Mrs Eames' idea on what action to take. That way if it all goes wrong, no one will blame her, Mrs Blueitt thinks.

"We will go and see Mrs Eames," she announces to Alice and Tilly. "She will know the correct action to take. She's been a supervisor the longest."

******

Beryl Eames is in her cramped glass office at the end of the loft doing her paperwork. All the windows had been shattered in the air raid, and are now repaired, but small fragments of glass keep turning up in odd places, such as in the folds of the fabrics stored on the racks or in the ink well. Several of her ladies have received tiny cuts, as a result, and there is a busy trade in first aid plasters dispensed by Lottie Payne, the first aider trained by the St John Ambulance Brigade. When Mrs Blueitt knocks on the door, the more experienced woman can see straightaway that something has happened, as Alice is very pale and has been crying. At first, she thinks the young woman might have been injured, but her face is too drawn to be something as simple as that.

"Whatever is the matter?" Mrs Eames asks, indicating that Alice should sit down, as Mrs Blueitt closes the door. Through the internal window, she can see the women of the loft craning their necks to see what is going on, so she reaches up and drops the blind; a few fragments of glass showers down, having hidden there after the bomb blast.

Mrs Blueitt says, "Tell Mrs Eames everything, Alice." And it all comes spilling out: how Victor Banks follows her, how he goes to watch her play football, and how he had cornered her today.

"How old are you, Alice?" the supervisor asks.

"I was sixteen last week."

Mrs Eames looks thoughtful for a moment, "And he knows you had a birthday?"

"Yes, we celebrated after football, by going to the pub. He was hanging about as usual. He offered to buy me a drink, but I refused, I used the no treating rule as an excuse. Is it important that it was my birthday?"

"Yes, the law is slightly stricter concerning assaults on underage girls, but as you are now sixteen, all the work is on proving that you are not to blame. Have you ever given him any encouragement?"

"No, Miss. Never. I told Mrs West, our football team coach, about it, and she spoke to Mr Phillips, but she didn't give Victor's name. She just said it is one of the men. She suggested I kept a record, which I've been doing."

"That is good, but it only proves that Victor is a pest. Are there any witnesses?"

"Tilly made a note of the man's name, the one who came into the stores when Victor assaulted me."

"But the other man said he didn't see or hear anything," Tilly says. "But he did say he could see that something had happened."

"Okay, girls, leave it with me. I will speak to Mr Phillips and see what must be done."

Mrs Blueitt interrupts her, saying, "Alice, show Mrs Eames your bruises."

Alice shyly lifts her skirt to show Mrs Eames a fresh purple bloom at the top of her thigh, which clearly resembles finger marks. She rolls her sleeve up as far as she can to show more bruises on her arm, where Victor grabbed her.

"You can see that he physically assaulted her. We need to treat this seriously," Mrs Blueitt says, ensuring the other woman takes responsibility for what will happen next.

"Ah, this throws it in a different light; it is more than just harassment," the supervisor says. "Wait here a moment."

She opens the door and calls out to two of the women making colours. "Mrs Pegg, kindly fetch Mr Phillips for me and tell him to come immediately. Mrs Dawson, please fetch Sergeant Oliver from the dockyard police station and tell him the same."

This causes a fresh twitter of speculation in the loft, as the ladies there try to guess what may have happened requiring the attention of the two men, especially the police sergeant. Within a few minutes, both arrive, and Mrs Eames outlines what has taken place in the loan tools store.

"A lot of these girls encourage the men to behave like this," Mr Phillips says, annoyed that the supervisor has called the sergeant, instantly escalating the issue. "I'm sure we can sort it out with a reprimand."

"I have seen the girl's bruises," Beryl Eames replies. "Can you ask the police matron in the town police station to examine Alice, please?"

Mrs Blueitt nods in agreement with her colleague. "Mrs Eames is right, we can't let the girls be treated like this by the men," she says. "Where will it end if we don't nip it in the bud?" She ignores the fact that everyone knows that she sometimes allows Mr Dennis to pat her bottom as she goes by, sending out the wrong signal on acceptable behaviour.

The town police employ Mrs Strike as the female police matron. Her role is to attend and counsel female prisoners, who are vulnerable to the harsh conditions of a male-dominated prosecution regime within police stations. She also performs any searches on women or children who are suspects, or to check any woman who has been a victim, for signs of sexual assault.

Sergeant Oliver summons Mrs Strike to the dockyard. The matron wears a dark blue serge tunic that is based heavily on the men's uniform. However, it buttons on the opposite side. She also wears a full-length skirt with lace-up boots. She removes her broad brimmed hat when she arrives, and puts on a clean white apron to protect her uniform. She then takes Alice to the loft ladies changing room to examine her. She asks Alice to strip naked and, as well as inspecting the bruises, she effects an intimate examination, to determine if Alice is a virgin or not, despite being told that Victor has not attempted to have intercourse.

"It will help your case if you are a virgin," explains Mrs Strike. "If you are not, then the magistrate will question your morals, and that would throw in doubt if you encouraged Mr Banks or not."

Once she is satisfied, Mrs Strike goes back into Mrs Eames's office to give her report to the sergeant, who notes her evidence down. Alice is left in the changing room to get dressed. Tilly goes in to help her.

By this time, not only is the colour loft a twitter with the incident, but word has gone round the whole dockyard; over two thousand employees are speculating on what has happened. In no time at all, the sergeant calls for Victor Banks to report to the dockyard police station, where he promptly denies all the charges.

*****

Reggie Symonds feels awful after Tilly served him in the loan tools store earlier that day, before she sent him on his way. He knows that something has happened, but he came into the stores too late to prevent it. He usually goes a few times a week to pick up supplies, and he has become friendly with the women there, including Tilly and Alice. When he learned that Tilly and Alice played football, he started regularly chatting with them for a few minutes most days about the game, but he is conscientious and doesn't like to waste time, so always returns to his work before his boss notices he has gone.

He is an apprentice carpenter, with only one year left on his indenture, after which he will be able to work unsupervised. He is proud to be working on repairing some of the ships that are seeing service in the war; he feels he is doing his bit. He is mad keen on football, and had played for Sheppey United briefly, as many of the regular players were called up for military service. However, an accident in the yard broke his foot, and he now walks with a slight limp, leaving him unfit for both military service and football, as he can no longer run or march properly.

Reggie has heard rumours about Victor; it is hard to avoid hearing Teddie Taylor's taunts. There was a rumour concerning Banks and one of the colour loft ladies. However, there was no evidence to support the claim as far as Reggie could see. Recently, Teddie has been saying Victor is obsessed with one of the girls, but Reggie hadn't put two and two together to realise it is Alice whom he meant, until today. Reggie was surprised to see Victor coming from behind the counter in the stores, where he shouldn't have been. He knew that something had happened, but he hadn't really seen or heard anything.

When Reggie goes home to his family in Kipling Road, at the end of the day, he is quiet and withdrawn as he eats his dinner. His mother has cooked a bacon dumpling and mash, and Reggie has barely tasted the sweet salty meat, which is one of his favourite meals, as he is preoccupied with the afternoon's events.

"That's not like you, son, to not enjoy your food," she says, as she clears the plates away.

"I know, I'm in a dilemma," he responds, lighting up a "*Cup Tie*" cigarette and offering the packet to his father. He explains what took place in the stores to his parents, then says, "I know something happened. Alice was so upset. But I didn't see or hear anything. If there are no other witnesses, it will be Alice's word against Victor's. And they will believe Victor."

Reggie's Dad grunts. "That's the way of the world, son," he says, and returns to his newspaper.

His mother ruffles his prematurely thinning hair; he will be as bald as his father soon. "Hopefully, with women working doing men's jobs, things will start to change, and a girl won't be held responsible when a man makes a pass at her."

"You can only say what you saw, you can't perjure yourself. And if this Victor just came on a bit fresh, there's no serious harm done," says Mr Symonds, once again returning to the reports on what is happening on the Western Front, where Reggie's two older brothers are serving.

Reggie knows this is so, but he still can't get it straight in his head. "I think I'll take Patch out for a walk," he says, reaching for the Manchester Terrier's lead, "He helps me think."

Patch just looks forward to the chance of catching some rats and wags his tail nineteen to the dozen.

*****

When Alice gets home, her mother is feeding the rabbits in their hutches. The animals don't have individual names, as they are kept for the table, but Maggie calls them all "Bunny", as she attends to their needs. When she first took a pair from her Uncle Frank, they had been from the same litter. He told her to separate them, but she couldn't see the need for two hutches. She was shocked one day when she found them mating.

"Not brother and sister!" she kept repeating, disgusted at the low morals of the animals. After that, she had segregated them and kept a stud book to avoid interbreeding.

Maggie can see that Alice has been crying, and asks, "What's happened?" cutting straight to the heart of the matter.

Alice tells her mother everything, whilst Maggie continues to feed the rabbits.

"Come inside and let me look at your bruises," Maggie says, when Alice finishes.

Maggie looks in the old biscuit tin on the top shelf of the pantry, where she keeps the family's medicines and other first aid items, like sticking plasters and an eye bath, and brings out a tub of Ellman's embrocation, which smells strongly of eucalyptus that has pervaded all the lint bandages in the tin. She gently rubs some on her daughter's bruises to bring them out. She then makes her some tea and sends her to bed to rest. When her husband, Rab McDonald, comes home from the gas works, where he is a stoker, Maggie tells him what has happened to Alice.

"Not that pasty weed that hangs about on the corner?" he asks, when Maggie says it is Victor, his Scot's accent giving his words the edge of menace. "I would nay thought he had it in him. Looks too much of a mammy's boy to me!" Rab goes back out the door, and looks up and down the street, before returning to say, "He's nay there now. Lucky for him, or I'd wring his wee scrawny neck for him."

"Let the police deal with it," Maggie responds. "They are taking it seriously. Alice has made a statement and everything. Her boss in the yard is backing her up."

Rab is only partially mollified. He is not a big man himself, but he is wiry, and was raised in Glasgow, so knows how to look after himself. He and his brother Ginger have won many battles, and they will not let their daughters be treated badly by any man.

"Aye, we'll see how that works out," he says, stripping down to his waist and reaching for the carbolic soap to wash the coal dust from his skin, before his evening meal.

Alice lays in the bed she shares with her sisters, listening to her mother and father talking about the incident, and knows they love her.

*****

At the next football training session, there is no sign of Victor, and the team wastes no time in bringing Hattie up to date on what has happened. The girls believe that the court decision is a foregone conclusion, and that Victor will be sent to prison. However, Hattie is not convinced. She doesn't want to disillusion Alice, but she is aware that there will be an uphill struggle facing her.

The next time Hattie takes a class of girls to the dockyard swimming pool, she sees John Phillips walking across the yard towards the Quadrangle and corners him. "Have you had a chance to raise the question of men like Banks showing an unhealthy interest in the girls with the senior dockyard officials yet?" she asks.

John squirms under her scrutiny, before confessing, "No, I haven't. Many of the girls like the attention, and with the war on, the men are working long hours. A bit of harmless flirting helps the day along. This is the first time it's got out of hand. A reprimand would have been better than a police investigation. If I had been able to deal with it myself, I would have got Victor Banks' exemption from military service removed, and he would have been sent to the front. I got rid of someone who was pilfering like that."

"But justice won't have been done," Hattie replies.

"And you think it will be like this?" he retorts.

Hattie knows he is right. Few sexual assault and rape cases came to court, and those that do often don't go the victim's way.

Later that evening, Hattie decides to tell her colleague and landlady Ena Briggs about the impending court case. Ena's full name is Serena, but she doesn't like the name. She thinks she is too busy a person to have a name like that. She is the shape of a pippin apple, but, like Hattie, she keeps fit by riding her bicycle everywhere. Although famed for her ostentatious jewellery, which she wears around the house, Ena is never seen to wear it outdoors. She is too practical a person to encumber herself with such trappings, although her spectacles have a couple of rubies set on the top edge of the frames.

Ena immediately says, "We are going to have to give Alice some coaching in how to respond to the lawyer's questions in court. The defence will try to prove she encouraged Banks, that she has low morals, and that he is the victim in all this."

"That is a tall order. How can we do that?" responds Hattie.

"Miss Garrett has been coaching girls taking the dockyard exam for office jobs. They are interviewed as part of the process, and it is very tough because they are permanent jobs, not just war time work. If she can teach Alice some of the tricks to improve her confidence, we may be able to get her through the court case. Only problem is, if she appears too confident, they will still blame her."

"So, dammed if you do, and dammed if you don't!"

"Precisely!"

"Well, that's decided. We will enlist Miss Garrett's help in getting Alice through the coming ordeal."

*****

Miss Garrett tries not to be judgemental about the behaviour of the young girls working in the dockyard, but she can see that a magistrate might not look kindly on Alice's complaint. The onus is on the victim to not only prove that an assault took place, but that she is of good character, tried to fight her assailant off, and didn't encourage the attack in any way. Here is a girl who regularly shows her legs in public, when she plays football, her sister had a child out of wedlock at only fifteen, and she is chatting to men at work, unchaperoned. Meanwhile, Victor Banks goes regularly to church with his widowed mother, is a semi-skilled labourer in the dockyard, and is of unblemished character. She knows the defence will try to make mincemeat of Alice.

Alice's brush with justice will not be straightforward. First, there will be a Committal Hearing at the magistrates' court, at which evidence of a crime will be presented. A date of Tuesday 12 February 1918 is set for this, to determine if there is a *prima facie* case to answer. This is to establish whether there is probable cause to believe the defendant committed the crime with which he or she is charged. Only if the hearing decides there is evidence of possible guilt will the case go forward to the next level. It means that Alice will first need to convince the magistrate that Victor has assaulted her. If the magistrate does not believe a crime has been committed, then Alice's case will not go forward to the Assizes to be heard before a judge and jury; and that will be the end of that.

The Committal Hearing is just two weeks away, so Hattie, Ena, and Miss Garrett have to work hard with Alice to get her ready for the ordeal. Every evening, after their various activities of football, Girl Guides, and sewing and reading groups, the company meet up at Ena's house, to drill Alice in how to answer in court.

"What do you intend wearing for the hearing?" Miss Garrett asks Alice, looking her up and down critically.

"I'm going to wear my Sunday best," the girl responds.

"Do you mean that pink blouse you were wearing last week in church? That isn't suitable, it draws too much attention to you," the headmistress responds. Alice looks worried; she doesn't have an extensive wardrobe to call upon.

"Don't worry, I thought that it might be an issue, so I've made you a new blouse, so you will look smart in the witness box," Ena says, producing a beautiful pin tucked blouse, of light blue cotton, which she gives to Alice. "If you give me your best jacket, I will press and sponge it for you." Alice tries the blouse on, and she looks quite the lady in it. "I've got a plain black hat I can lend you too. I keep it for funerals, but it will make you look more grown up and serious." Ena produces a small felt hat, with a minimal amount of netting around the brim, and no flowers or feathers, which she fixes to Alice's hair with an enormous, jewelled hat pin. "I don't have any plain hat pins I can spare," says Ena apologetically; she is known to have some very flamboyant jewellery, and the hat pin proves the point.

Miss Garrett's role is to prepare Alice mentally. "You need to stand up straight in the witness box, no slouching or leaning against the bar," the headmistress schools her, trying to correct sixteen years of bad posture in a few evenings. She sniffs and tuts in disapproval whenever Alice forgets herself and lets her shoulders droop. "Now, you need to keep your eyes downcast and speak out clearly when addressing the bench. They will try to catch you out, but you must be firm about what you say."

"I promise you I will be there in court with you. If you are nervous, just look up at me in the public gallery. You will gain strength from a friendly face," Hattie says, doing her best to allay Alice's fears. Her cat Tibby gets up on her lap and gives Alice a hard stare, as if to say, "You can't trust men, look how many kittens I have been left with over the years."

Miss Garrett's latest lodger, Lucy Hardcastle, comes along each evening and makes the tea, whilst Tilly tries to give her friend reassurance that everything will be all right. Lucy joined the school back in September, straight from one of the new teacher training colleges. Since the war began, Miss Garrett has taken in half a dozen different women, who only seem to stay a few months before moving on. One left to be a nurse, a couple were too scared of the air raids and had quickly sought posts elsewhere, one had sadly died of scarlet fever, and one married a naval officer. Lucy is the longest serving new member of staff since the outbreak of hostilities.

They arrange a final coaching session on the Sunday before the court case, and Ena invites Alice and Tilly to tea at four o'clock, after the group of teachers have taken their Sunday school classes at the Congregational Church. By now, Alice is getting very nervous, and Hattie is concerned that she will forget everything they have told her, so she decides to concentrate on the forthcoming cup game against the women from the foundry. As an outside forward, playing on the wing, Alice's job is to help make goals for the striker. Tilly is a full-back, whose role is to sweep-up the ball if an opponent manages to breach the defensive line. Neither girl is afraid to get into a tussle, if needed, and there is concern that their football aggression will also come out in court. Hattie has long since learned the necessary strategies to win games, so tries talking tactics to the girls.

"We need to go to court as though we are playing a cup game. Your role, Tilly, is to defend Alice. You need to stop any doubt about her character by emphasising that she doesn't have any boyfriends, that she is a hard worker, and that she doesn't encourage men. Don't answer back and don't call names.

"You, Alice, need to give the prosecution everything they need to score. You need to be clear about what happened, and need to leave no doubt about what kind of girl you are, and you must be deferential to the magistrate."

After the girls leave, Hattie turns to the other teachers, and says, "I wish we'd let Mr Phillips deal with this in his usual way."

*****

Showing Her Legs

Phyllis Banks smoothes the embroidered tablecloth on her dining table as she perches on the high back chair. She straightens the cutlery and ensures the tea plates all have the transfers of sprays of roses facing the same way. It is only then that she once more holds forth on her current favourite topic, which she returns to again and again, over the next few days, until the day of the court case.

She is appalled that some girl from a family of ne're-do-wells is accusing her son of interfering with her. "That family have always been no good. When their Cathy got pregnant, I felt it was my duty to report her to the *Society for Befriending Women and Girls.* She is a bad influence on her younger sisters and others."

The 1913 Mental Deficiency Act enables unmarried mothers to be categorised as "moral imbeciles", for having a child out of wedlock, so Mrs Banks is always the first to point the finger. It makes her unpopular with many in the town, as unplanned pregnancies are commonplace, but she is too self-righteous to care what others think of her.

"I told Mrs Flint, when she stopped me in the street, my Victor isn't interested in that kind of thing.

That's why he doesn't have a girlfriend. Why would he look at that skinny plain thing anyway, I asked her?" she says, as she brushes his Sunday best suit.

"Well, we will have to get your Uncle Albert and his friends from the Masonic Lodge to speak about your good character. Albert is friends with Mr Ranger-Jones, the magistrate. He's in the same lodge. It's about time Albert nominated you for membership," she says, as she launders his whitest shirt.

"And I will speak with Reverend McNeil. He can tell the court how you help put out the chairs for Sunday school, and how you cut the grass in the church yard. He owes me a favour from that time I didn't report him when the communion wine went missing, and I found Mrs McNeil drunk in the vestry," she confides, as she polishes Victor's boots.

"And we need to tell Mr Ranger-Jones that you are the breadwinner, since your father died in the service of His Majesty's dockyard, when that thoughtless crane driver knocked over that pile of timber killing him instantly," she muses, as she irons a clean hanky, with corners so sharp you can cut yourself, another weapon of morality to go in Victor's breast pocket.

"Did I tell you it was driven by Mrs Ranger-Jones' cousin, once removed?" she asks Victor; she always knows the genealogy of everybody in town. "No? I must remind her too." She makes a mental note in the debts owing column of her brain.

"I know some people say it was his own fault. The other workers said he was asleep in a sort of little den he had built behind the wood, and shouldn't have been there. But the dockyard couldn't prove it, and paid us compensation just the same," she gloats, as she starches Victor's shirt.

"And what sort of girl works in a dockyard surrounded by workmen and lewd servicemen? Or plays football showing her legs, like some common music hall act? We must remind your lawyer, Mr Herbert. I'll remind him too how I saw him hanging around the alleyways in Bluetown, where the sailors go," she sniggers, as she sends him to the barbers at half past eight on the Tuesday morning of the trial, for a shave and haircut.

When she is done, the magistrate will see that her son is a fine up-standing boy. When they enter the court, Victor's mother gives him a last-minute spit wash, and tells him to remove his hat, so that she can comb his lank hair as he takes his place in the dock.

*****

As Miss Garrett sits in her office, she hopes all will go well in court, but she also thinks that it is unlikely to be the result they all hope for. Over the years, many of her former pupils have confided in her how their bosses try to take advantage of them. It is all very well striving for independence, but men are still just sex pests! She purses her narrow lips, as she fights down her impotent indignation.

Miss Windley asks if Miss Garrett would like some tea. She instantly regrets it, as the headmistress follows her back to the kitchen area. I won't get back to my desk to finish those receipts, the secretary thinks, as Miss Garrett starts chatting.

"Yesterday was a funny day," she recalls to Miss Windley, as though her colleague wasn't part of it. "We abandoned the timetable in the afternoon, as Miss Pettett's brother came in to talk to the girls, as he's on leave from the front." Miss Windley knows this, as the children sang some patriotic songs and she could hear them even with the door shut to her tiny office. "He told them some interesting stories about the war. They all particularly liked the one about a little French girl named Pauline, whom his platoon rescued from a barn and then adopted, until her family was traced. I think some of them imagined they were Pauline!"

Miss Windley knew that Miss Garrett had enjoyed the story as much as the children, as she had suggested that the pupils pool their treats so they could send Pauline some chocolate and sweets.

"This morning, the students gave Miss Pettett a big parcel of eatables for her brother to take back for the soldiers in France. It is amazing that so many delicacies can be found, as many everyday items are in short supply," Miss Garrett muses.

"People can be so generous," replies Miss Windley, hoping that the headmistress will let her return to her work.

"Has the nit nurse arrived yet to inspect the children for head lice and other vermin?" Miss Garrett enquires, the thought of which still makes her skin crawl, even after all these years of being a teacher. She gives a sniff of disgust, in anticipation.

"Not yet," responds Miss Windley, whose job it is to note down the results and write any letters to the parents of verminous children.

These thoughts about dirty children remind Miss Garrett of Alice's cousin Cissie. Cissie has been sent home in the past with a note for her mother saying she is unclean and uncared for, and was not to return until both she and her clothes had been washed.

"When was Cissie Dummott last in school?" she asks Miss Windley.

She knows that Cissie's attendance has always been erratic, as she looks after her little brother Ernie, whilst her mother is absent. There are some nursery places available for women doing war work, so their children can be cared for, but these places are few and far between, and are only for munitions workers. There are more than one hundred nurseries across the country, but there is no provision for women working in any other form of employment, and most rely on friends and family to help care for their children while they are at work. There are certainly no nursery places for the offspring of mothers who did the kind of work that Ivy Dummott does.

Miss Windley responds, "I'd need to check the register, but not for some weeks. Her mother leaves her small son in the girl's charge."

"Yes, to the detriment of the girl's education. The less said about her mother, the better," says Miss Garrett, with a sniff of disapproval. "The poor girl will never escape poverty at this rate. I need to do something about all the children missing school, including Cissie and Ernie, if they are to grow up and contribute to society," She gives a decisive sniff, and forgetting her tea, which Miss Windley is in the process of making, she returns to her desk to make plans.

*****

The Courthouse is in Bluetown, opposite the south dock gate. It pulls off a unique trick of being both squat and grand at the same time. It is squeezed into a corner, by a pub on one side in the next road, and the ruined shell of Gieves, the Gentleman's Outfitters, on the other. The outfitters was demolished by a bomb on the fifth of June 1917, killing the manager and a Chief Warrant Officer, who had only popped in to buy some handkerchiefs. The court then sprawls backwards into the alley behind, in order to fit in to its limited space, but comes up sharp against a house of ill repute, which stops it taking up too much room.

Inside, the heavy oak panelling is lit by high arched windows. The sun would have streamed in during the late afternoon had it not been for the twenty-foot-high dockyard wall that occupied the whole length of the street, on the opposite side, and blocks its rays.

Hattie asked for the morning off from school and is in the public gallery, along with John Phillips and several of the girls from the football team. Alice's mother is there too, but her father is at work. Maggie McDonald promised to come and tell him the verdict, ,as soon as the trial is over. The rest of the wooden benches in the gallery are packed with those looking to hear some salacious gossip, including several members of the local press.

Alice enters the courtroom with the constable and the police lawyer, who will be acting for the prosecution. She looks small and vulnerable as they direct her where to sit. The other witnesses are also in the courtroom. Alice knows Tilly and Reggie Symonds, who was the customer who came into the loan store straight after the assault. She also knows Mrs Eames and Mrs Blueitt, the supervisors from the dockyard, and Mrs Strike, the police matron, who examined her after the attack. But there are others she doesn't know, who have come in support of Victor, and she feels their hostility. He sits on the other side of the court to her, and he keeps glancing up at the gallery to where his mother sits. She, in turn, is trying to cultivate an air of being the victim of the piece, whilst radiating self-righteous anger that her precious boy has been wrongly accused of such a despicable crime.

Alice is pleased to see Reggie Symonds; she looks over towards him and gives him a tiny nod of acknowledgement. He has been very kind to her since the incident. He pops into the stores for a chat every day, and is really interested in her football. Reggie is not unpleasant to look at, but is not remarkable in any way. He is younger than she had first thought him, probably about twenty, although his hair is already starting to thin, but, like all the men in the yard, this fact is usually concealed by his work cap. But this lack of hair is on show today, as he has removed his cap indoors.

The magistrate, Mr Ranger-Jones, enters the court, and they all rise on command of the clerk of the court. He is a portly, pompous, florid man, who prides himself on his ability to know instantly if a person is guilty or not. Fortunately, as it is his job to refer cases to the higher court, those whom he misdiagnoses as guilty when they are innocent, get a second chance to prove themselves in front of a jury. Unfortunately, those he wrongly believes to be innocent when they are not, get away with it.

Alice's complaint is the first case of the day, so she is called to state her case. She looks up at Hattie in the gallery for support. Hattie gives Alice a reassuring nod as she starts to put her side of things to the court. Her mouth is very dry, and she smoothes down her skirt before relaying the events. She speaks quietly, so the people in the gallery lean forward as one to hear her clearly. When she gets to the bit where she has to say how Victor grabbed her and pushed himself against her, she starts to cry, and stumbles over her words. It is one thing telling those who care about her, but another to repeat it in front of strangers. She reaches into her pocket and finds her handkerchief; she wipes her eyes and blows her nose. Mr Ranger-Jones looks down on her from his elevated position, in an unsympathetic way, and motions for her to continue.

When she gets to the end of her testimony, Mr Herbert, Victor's defence, stands up to question her. Herbert is tall and thin, and has the habit of elongating certain vowel sounds, as he enunciates every syllable. He is also very astute in the use of the dramatic pause, which he uses to great effect when driving home a point.

"Miss McDonald, I'm sorry to have to ask you these questions… but I must," he opens with, in a way that suggests he is not sorry at all, but will enjoy examining the girl. "Are you… chaste?"

Fortunately, Miss Garrett has explained that the court will use unfamiliar words and has explained a number of them to her. This is amongst them, so she knows to answer, "Yes, sir, I am."

"Do you have… a boyfriend?"

"No, sir, I do not."

"Have you ever had… a boyfriend? Someone you have… kissed and cuddled with?"

"No, sir, I have not."

"But when Mr Banks tried to get your attention in the loan store… where you have told us you tried to ignore him… you immediately thought he is trying to…" He pauses to check his notes. "…interfere with you." He enunciates every syllable of the word "interfere," so it comes out as "Inn-terr-fear", drawing it out for the benefit of the gallery, and causing a ripple of shock around the room.

"He was sir. He put his hand up my skirt. I showed Mrs Eames, Mrs Blueitt, and Mrs Strike the bruises."

"I understand that you play in a… football team." He says the words "football team", as though this is something that nobody will have heard of. Alice again answers yes to this, before he continues. "I understand that football is a… physical game, not really suited for… young ladies to play. I understand you have training sessions and play regular matches. Is that so?"

Alice again affirms this.

"So, how is the court to believe that the bruises you say are inflicted on you by Mr Banks are not caused by your playing this… unladylike game?" Before Alice can answer, he continues. "And what do you… wear to play football?" He glances up at the men in the gallery, and raises his eyebrows.

"We wear what men wear, boots, shorts, jerseys."

"So, you show off your… legs to any man who wants to look?"

He again glances up at the men in the gallery, and raises his eyebrows this time with a knowing smile, man to man.

"No, sir, we wear shorts, so we can run around."

"But you did not," he pauses to smirk, "run away from Mr Banks. You said you tried to push him off. But surely, if this incident happened, you would have run away."

"No, sir, it wasn't like that. He came up behind me."

"No further questions," he says, dismissing her before she has the chance to explain further.

The other witnesses are called, but neither Tilly nor Reggie Symonds have seen anything. Symonds testifies that he heard a commotion, Victor had barged past him, and that Alice was upset, but Mr Herbert makes light of this saying, "Miss McDonald had tried to ignore him, perhaps Mr Banks was just annoyed at her…poor service."

Before Reggie can answer again, Mr Herbert continues. "Did you hear Miss McDonald say anything at all?"

"I don't think so," Symonds responds vaguely, inwardly cursing that he could not be certain; if only he had arrived a couple of minutes earlier.

"Well, you would have heard something if she had called 'Help!'" interjects Mr Ranger-Jones.

Mrs Strike is called next, and Mr Herbert asks for her evidence. Mrs Strike is well seasoned in court procedures and remains unflustered, as she reads her report aloud. When she says, "I examined Miss McDonald intimately and can confirm that her hymen is intact. She is a virgin," there is a gasp, and some tittering around the room. Alice goes bright red with embarrassment, and casts her eyes down to her lap.

"Are you… sure, Mrs Strike?" Mr Herbert asks.

"Yes, sir, I have been the police matron for ten years. I am quite sure," she answers, with a steady look at Mr Herbert, and it is he who looks away first.

Mr Herbert quickly dismisses her after that, without further questions.

Witnesses are then called to sing Victor's praises, including his mother. Finally, Mr Herbert calls Teddie Taylor. This is a surprise to Alice, as it is well known that Teddie bullies Victor regularly, and nobody will expect him to defend him in court.

However, Mr Herbert welcomes him to the stand and begins his questioning.

"Have you known the defendant long?"

"About four years, since I began my apprenticeship in the dockyard."

"I understand you call him…" He pauses to check his notes again. "…Verge. Why is that?"

Teddie is embarrassed, but at the same time can't resist a dig at Victor, "That's right," he answers, "it's short for virgin."

"Why do you call him that?"

Teddie begins to warm to the subject, "Because he is. He's twenty-eight and still a virgin. He never talks to girls. Never had a girlfriend."

"Never talks to girls? Never had a girlfriend? So, what is his relationship to….Miss McDonald?"

"He fancies her, but she isn't interested in him. He follows her about, he watches her play football, he hangs about outside her house, but he doesn't have the courage to ask her for a drink. He's never been known to ask any girl out."

"But we are being asks to believe that this man who never talks to girls….will be bold enough to go up to Miss McDonald and assault her at her place of work. No further questions!"

The magistrate then asks to hear Victor's evidence, and he enters the witness box. The clerk reads out the charge and asks Victor, "How do you plead, guilty or not guilty?"

"Not guilty!" he responds, loud and clear. He stands up straight and holds his best Sunday bowler hat between his hands, as he looks the magistrate directly in the eye.

Mr Herbert turns to the defendant and says, "Mr Banks, kindly tell us your side of this sorry story."

Victor nods, pulls himself up straight, and begins, "I went into the stores, as usual, to get some tools. My boss usually sends me, as I am always willing, no matter what the weather, nor how many times before I've already been." Victor looks around the court to try to emphasise his affability. "Miss McDonald is often rude to me, and can be quite surly as she fulfils the orders on the voucher. But I bear it with good grace. I was a little sweet on her, it's true, but I respected that this is work, and there is a war on, and we should all get on with our jobs. On this occasion, she was rude, as usual, and went out the back before I had given her the voucher. So, I went after her and touched her on the shoulder, to let her know I was still there. She still ignored me, so I left, rather cross, as I knew I would get an earful from my boss back at the loco shed. I'm sorry I bumped into Mr Symonds, but that is all that happened. There is no truth whatsoever in the lie that I sexually assaulted her."

Before Mr Herbert, or the prosecution, has a chance to ask any questions, Mr Ranger-Jones takes command, and asks Victor directly, "Do you swear that you did not assault her?"

"Yes, sir, I swear that I did not," Victor responds, wide eyed, and as innocently as he can. "I know that she often puts her arms round other men's necks when they go in the store, but they are too embarrassed to come forward and tell the court what she is really like, in case their wives hear of it."

Alice gulps at this lie, and Tilly stands up in the gallery, but Hattie shakes her head, and pulls her back down. Tilly realises the futility of any protest, and doesn't resist.

The magistrate asks again, "Do you swear no indecency took place?"

"No, sir, it did not."

Mr Ranger-Jones then says, "It is up to me to decide if a jury will convict the defendant, for the case to go forward to the crown court. I am convinced that no jury in the land will convict Mr Banks on the flimsy evidence submitted. The summons is dismissed." He bangs his gavel, to confirm his decision.

The clerk indicates that everyone should rise, and the magistrate leaves the court.

Victor's mother dramatically gasps and pretends to swoon, whilst those around her attend to her with smelling salts and by fanning her, before Victor arrives at her side, to be clasped to her bosom with joy.

"Thank goodness, my son is proved innocent," she cries, ensuring that everyone hears her. "What an evil girl to bear false witness against him. *Exodus, chapter twenty, verse sixteen!*"

The newspaper men in the gallery swiftly leave the courtroom to get their stories in to their editors. Each journalist races away, to be the first with this salacious story. They are all totally disinterested in the cases of petty thefts and lights left on during the blackout that are to follow.

The police sergeant and matron just leave Alice sitting where she is, bewildered and abandoned. Neither looks back to see if she is okay, but just carry on their day, as there are other cases to bring, and they can't waste time with a girl whom the court believes to be a liar.

*****

A Plan is Hatched

Alice's friends soon come down from the public gallery and surround her in the courtroom. Hattie and Tilly have pushed through the crowd and get to her side to reassure and comfort her.

Her mother follows in their wake to hug her daughter quickly, as she isn't given to displays of affection. "I'll see you at home," she says, then leaves abruptly to go and tell her husband the bad news that the magistrate has dismissed the summons. She knows he won't be pleased with the outcome.

John Phillips stops Hattie, and says, "Let's speak later. Come and find me in my office when you are free," then leaves the building to return to work.

Alice feels disorientated as she walks out into the cold overcast winter's morning, which is threatening rain. Tilly and the rest of the football girls gather around her on the pavement outside, and Hattie takes a deep breath as she searches for something to say before settling on, "Right, girls, let's find a tea shop. We can talk in the warm then." Most of the girls go back to work, disappearing through the dock gate opposite the court, and just Tilly goes with Hattie and Alice to the café.

A little way down the road, they find an almost empty café, as it is not yet lunch time. The net curtains are clean and white, and it looks inviting. Hattie orders three teas and some cake at the counter, then joins the girls at a table in the corner. Alice is white faced, and her lip is trembling, as she tries not to cry. Tilly holds her hand, and looks both concerned and angry as Hattie reaches across to place a comforting hand on Alice's shoulder.

"We knew it would be hard," she says. "I will ask Mr Phillips to move you to a job where you don't have to serve Victor Banks. He will probably avoid you now, as he has lied in court and people will be watching him."

"But it's me they think is a liar," Alice says, giving into the tears that have been threatening.

"Nonsense," Hattie says, dismissively, although she knows there is an element of truth in that. "Anyone who thinks that is a bigger fool than the magistrate. Men always stick together, even when they know someone is lying. We will just have to make sure that people know the truth."

Just then, the waitress came over with their tray of tea, and the group goes quiet as she places the cups and saucers on the table, along with the ginger cake. The cake is made without eggs, and with margarine instead of butter. Similar recipes are filling the newspapers, along with things like fatless carrot cake or potato scones, which uses left over mash, but as potatoes are getting harder to find, even this treat is becoming a rarity. Once the waitress returns to the counter, the conversation restarts.

Alice and Tilly think about the possibility of everyone blaming Victor, but without speaking, they both arrive at the conclusion that Hattie West is too idealistic for the real world of the dockyard, but don't say it; they just exchange looks.

"My Dad and my Uncle Ginger will give him a good kicking for this!" Alice announces defiantly.

"That isn't wise," Hattie responds sensibly. "They can end up in trouble themselves."

Alice knows that is true, and becomes even more deflated.

"The thing to do is look to the future," Hattie says brightly. "We have our first cup tie in two weeks, and we are going to win!" But this prediction doesn't achieve the result she hopes for, so, as an afterthought, she says, "And I will confer with Miss

Garrett and Miss Briggs to see if we can come up with a suitable 'come uppance' for Victor."

"Will you, Miss?" Tilly asks hopefully, seizing on the idea of some sort of revenge.

"Yes, something that won't get any of you in trouble!" Hattie smiles, and then thinks, goodness what am I promising?

*****

Maggie decides to go to the shops to buy some meat at the butchers for dinner, before going to tell Rab the result of the court hearing on her way home. She hates queuing, and there is so little on offer. Before the war, the butcher's window was filled with blood-red joints of lamb and beef, with plucked chickens hanging from the steel hooks above, and the streaky bacon ready on the slicer to be cut into rashers. Now, there is nothing but trotters or bristled pigs heads in the window, and tiny cuts of meat at exorbitant prices.

It has started to rain, and Maggie stands with her hat pulled down, her collar up, and her shawl wrapped tightly around her shoulders. She is small but feisty, and is inwardly seething as she stands outside Palmer's butcher shop. A few people who had been in court pass by, and Maggie can see them whispering and looking at her. They know Alice is her daughter, and her blood begins to boil. It is not fair that Victor had got away with his despicable behaviour, but she knows the courts are against women and the lower classes like them.

She has her suspicions that Victor's mother, Phyllis Banks, is the one who sent those interfering "*Befriending*" women round to her house, when her daughter Cathy fell pregnant. Those do-gooders pretend they have the unborn baby's best interests at heart, but really they are just too "holier than thou," she thinks. They wanted to send Cathy to a mother and baby home, but Rab McDonald had shown them a letter from the commanding officer of Cathy's young man, Wilf Kingston. It gave him permission to marry Cathy, once his current tour of duty was up and he returned to Sheerness.

"That wee bairn's got a father," he had told them on the doorstep, which he barred with all his five-foot four frame. Rab is not someone to cross, so the Befrienders had retreated on that occasion.

Mrs Jinks comes out the butcher's shop, grumbling about the lack of choice, when she spots Maggie trying to get under the shop awning to keep out of the rain. "How did your Alice get on today?" she asks, alluding to the court case.

"Not good, that Banks boy got away with it."

"Isn't that always the way?" Mrs Jinks says helpfully. "Men have always done what they pleased, and we women get the blame."

Maggie is about to respond, when she spots Phyllis Banks across the street. Mrs Banks is returning home from the court in triumph, the cords in her skinny neck taught, like the hawsers on the ships' anchors in the dockyard. She has left Victor at the dock gates, and is now doing a lap of honour around the high street. She is stopping to shake hands with her cronies, and smirking as she gives them the news, no trace of the fainting fit she had displayed within the courtroom. Maggie is torn between the desire to run across the road to slap the woman, and the possibility of losing her place in the queue if a scuffle breaks out. She settles for hurling abuse over the cobbles.

"Keep your son out of our way. My Rab and our Ginger will give him what for, if we see him in West Minster!" she yells, whilst waving her small fist in a threatening manner. Mrs Jinks folds her arms to enjoy the show, forgetting about the poor value of meat for the moment.

Mrs Banks ignores Maggie and sticks her nose, which is usually in other people's business, into the air, as she walks on. But Maggie isn't finished. "You sanctimonious old busy body!" As another customer comes out of the shop, Maggie shuffles along, keeping in the queue without pausing for breath. "If you had brought your son up right, to be respectful to women, none of this would have happened!"

The other woman can't ignore this jibe and stands her ground to shout back, "We all know how you brought your family up! Your eldest a mother before her wedding day, and the next one putting herself about inside the dockyard! We all know what she will be doing there when the war ends! Didn't that cousin of yours, Ivy Dummott, get done for soliciting and being nothing but a common prostitute, only the other week?" She marches off, leaving Maggie open mouthed. Ivy is not her true cousin; she is the stepchild of an uncle when he had married a widow, but she is dumbfounded that Mrs Banks knows there is a family connection, no matter how tenuous.

Mrs Jinks slinks off, show over, to repeat all of this to her neighbour, Mrs Lynmouth. The poor woman doesn't get out much, and this will cheer her up no end when Mrs Jinks tells her.

Maggie's face burns as the other customers whisper about her. She wishes she'd opted for the slap, but it is her turn next in the butchers, and she will buy some scrag-end to make a stew, and when she is chopping the vegetables, she will imagine they are Victor Banks' manhood!

*****

After leaving the cafe, Alice goes home for the rest of the day, where her mother is waiting.

"It would have been better if your Dad had gone out and thumped him rather than running to the police. They never help the likes of us," Maggie McDonald says, with her own brand of affection for her children, and keeping quiet about her encounter in town. "Now, you will have to go back to work and face them all."

"I don't know if I can, Mum," Alice responds, slumping into one of the kitchen chairs.

"You will have to. We can't do without your wages. By all means look for something else, but nowhere pays as well as the dockyard does."

Alice is one of eight children, but only six are still at home. Eight people, all living in Khartoum Road, and only her father and herself on a full wage. Her eldest brother Billie is twenty-three and is serving in the Kent Buffs, Cathy is married and has her own home.

Her younger brother, Walter, has turned twelve, and has a job after school and on Saturdays, where he helps the milkman with his horse, Polyphemus, a heavy shire horse, with a glossy brown coat, who has a way of looking at you through his forelock that suggests he knows what you are thinking. The horse is named after one of the ships built in Sheerness that saw service with Nelson at Trafalgar. Polly, as they call him for short, had previously worked in the dockyard. If the horse hears the end of shift siren from the yard, he will still turn around (whether harnessed to the cart or not) and set off for his stable. The milkman's afternoon route always starts near the dockyard, then extends as far away as possible, to prevent Polly from hearing the siren. Walter's job is to hold onto the horse and get him to stop before he manages to get too far away, if they are within earshot of the yard. He hands over his wages to his mother, and she gives him back a shilling to spend on himself. He always whistles *"Burlington Bertie"* in celebration, as he pockets his hard-earned money.

Nine-year-old Joe helps out by mud larking under the coal jetty near the gas works for any pieces of fuel and driftwood he can find, to supplement their supplies. He also runs errands for Mrs Schilling, who ran the Post Office. Sometimes, he takes the telegrams sent to tell people of the death of their son in action. He will whistle as he rides the heavy Post Office bike through the narrow streets, but he falls silent as he approaches the front door of the person the telegram is destined for, out of respect. Even though it is unwelcome news, the recipients will often tip him a penny or two.

All these contributions go to pay the rent, put money in the gas meter, and buy food and the odd luxury. Rent control, introduced in 1915, means that the cost of housing has stabilised, but their rent is still seventeen shillings a week.

"For once in our lives, we're not living hand to mouth," Maggie says. "That will all change, if you don't return to work at the dockyard. We can't afford to keep you."

Alice blurts out resentfully, "Not when we've got Ivy Dummott's two kids here every time she gets into trouble, or is too incapable to look after them, which is happening more and more!"

Although Cissie's father pays maintenance for her, the money goes on keeping Ivy's rooms in

Gordon Road, and so, when her cousin's children come to stay, Maggie has to find the money and the rations to feed them.

"I know, but I can't let them go cold and hungry," Maggie responds, with an air of desperation.

Alice knows her Mum is right; she can't just walk away from her job in the yard, and, apart from Victor, she likes working in the tool store and enjoys the camaraderie, and the money is so good. She will just have to see what tomorrow brings.

*****

Hattie stops by at John Phillips' office, after she parts from Tilly and Alice. She tells the soldiers guarding the dock gate it is football business, and they let her in, without question. She is becoming a familiar face around the docks and the Wellmarsh recreation ground, as she is often at the swimming pool or with the girls playing football. She is also to be seen on these occasions, stopping to talk to the stray cats and producing packets of cooked fish heads from the depths of her bag to tempt them with.

It isn't strictly untrue that she has business with the stores' manager, as she has arranged to talk to him about the cup tie against the *Foundry Foxes* in two weeks' time, so takes the opportunity to discuss how the court case had gone.

John's office is in the main office block, near the south gate, but as he needs to be in and out all the time to visit the Quadrangle stores, it is at the end facing the stores block, and so Hattie doesn't need to go into the building itself and walk the long corridor, past all the other managers; she is able to go in the separate door at the back, without causing gossip.

John is annoyed about the outcome of the court case, but again promises to ensure that Alice is not alone with Victor again. "I've already put a work order in for the counter in the tool store, Mrs West. There will be an internal side door that locks on the inside, and a sliding window hatch that can be closed when the girls go out the back. I said it is to stop the pilfering that was going on, even though we have got rid of the culprit a while ago. The Admiralty are slow to realise that there has been no thieving for some months, so are happy to pay for the alterations."

"Well, that is a comfort, Mr Phillips," Hattie responds.

"I will also revoke Banks' exemption from conscription. He will still be free to appeal at the *Military Service Tribunal*, but without the support of the dockyard saying he is doing work of National importance, he won't get far. I want to send a message to all the men that they can't "interfere" with the women workers and get away with it," he says, using the more delicate word than "assaulted," but even this word is mouthed rather than said aloud.

"Do you think the other men believe that Banks "interfered" with Alice?" she mouths back at him.

"I'm sure they do, but the grey area for the men is, did she encourage him? We need to remove any opportunity for the men to say that any girl did."

Hattie is reassured by what John says, so decides to change the subject back to football.

"Have you picked the team for Saturday week?"

"Yes," he replies, drawing a sheet of paper out of a buff folder, with all the flourish of a stage magician, and passes it across to Hattie.

"So, Coach, if you can accompany me to watch the *Foundry Foxes* this coming weekend, when they are playing a friendly against the glue works, we can see if we can spot their weaknesses."

"Yes, of course, Mr Phillips, that is a good idea. Right. Meanwhile, I'll get the team practicing their passing this week and we'll see how we get on."

*****

Hattie calls an emergency meeting that evening with Miss Garrett at Ena's house. Lucy Hardcastle asks if she can join them, as Hattie relates what happened in the police court that day. Lucy is still not quite one of the group, but they are including her more and more. She is not striking to look at, but has lovely silver gilt hair and is very musical; she can play a number of instruments including the piano and flute. Miss Garrett is considering asking her to help out with the Guides, as she is also very good at arts and crafts. It is another thing the headmistress will be able to delegate.

Miss Garrett gives one of her sniffs, to demonstrate her disapproval of the court outcome, before saying, "Well, we knew it would be hard for poor Alice to convince a room of men that Mr Banks is to blame, and that she did not encourage him."

Ena agrees, "And the worse thing is that people will think she lied."

"I'm not so sure they will," Hattie says, as she scoops Tibby the cat up for a cuddle. "I got the impression that other people in the court think that Victor must have done something, as Mr Symonds said he'd heard a commotion, and he also said that Alice was upset. It's a shame he didn't witness anything conclusive." The others nod as Hattie continues. "But I promised Alice that we will ensure that Victor gets his come uppance."

Miss Garrett and Ena gasp, as Hattie makes this revelation. Lucy listens, without saying anything. As a newcomer, she doesn't feel that her comments will be appreciated.

Miss Garrett shakes her head. "What were you thinking, Mrs West, to make that promise?" she asks, too taken aback to even punctuate her response with her trademark sniffs.

Hattie takes this comment literally, and answers, "Well, I don't know. Something to show him in his true colours. Something to humiliate him, the way Alice was humiliated in court. But it will need to be something that doesn't break the law."

"We need to catch him with his trousers down, as they say!" Lucy contributes.

"That's it Lucy! Catch him with his trousers down! Show him for the creep he is!" Hattie claps her hands together as she considers the prospect.

"But how?"

*****

Maggie has Rab's dinner ready on the kitchen table. The incident at the butcher's with Mrs Banks made her forget to pop into the gas works on the way home to tell her husband the outcome from the court hearing. She hopes he won't lose his temper. Although he has never raised a hand to her, he can be unpredictable, and may go out looking for Victor. She will need to think of a strategy to mitigate things.

Just then, Ginger puts his head around the door to wish her good evening, before returning to his home four doors down. She invites him to join them for dinner, hoping his more placid presence might calm Rab, if he takes the news too badly.

Ginger's real name is Angus, but nobody calls him that since his wife died two years ago of a tumour. Only she and his mother ever used his given name. Now, he lives alone; his two daughters, Maud, and Florrie, have both married and moved away. He keeps house for himself, and has converted one of the two upstairs rooms to a bathroom, a luxury in these back streets. Maggie suggested that he should move in with them, and that the whole family seek a bigger home together. However, Ginger's girls have counselled him against that, warning him that he will soon be helping to support all his brother's children, as well as Cissie and Ernie. Florrie had invited her Dad to live with her when she moved up to Scotland with her soldier husband. But Rab and Ginger had moved south over twenty years ago; two orphaned teenagers keen to see the bright lights of London, but they ended up fifty miles away in Sheerness, after hitching a free ride on a train full of soldiers, heading to the dockyard for a troopship, and from there out into the Empire. He has never been back to Glasgow since, and feels no connection to Scotland, beyond his accent, which he hasn't lost. That is unless whisky has been taken, then he will get maudlin and start singing, *"Roamin' in the Gloamin"*, or *"I Love a Lassie,"* or anything else sung by Harry Lauder, whom he had once seen at the local music hall.

Maggie sets another place and serves up a second bowl of the rich stew, made with the scrag end bought from the butchers and the hearty vegetables she has chopped, imagining they are Victor Banks. She carves another hunk of bread for Ginger, and sets the dish down in front of him.

"The magistrate dismissed Alice's complaint. Victor Banks walked free," Maggie tells them, without preamble, and giving no explanation as to why she hasn't told Rab at work, as she promised.

Rab stops eating for a moment, and exchanges a look with Ginger, before uttering some expletives under his breath.

"Where's my wee hen, now?"

"I sent her to bed. She is very upset."

"Aye, I bet she is. Well, he'd best nay come round here again. If I catch him, he's for it."

"Aye," agrees Ginger, between mouthfuls of stew. "His card is marked."

Maggie clears the plates. She doesn't tell anyone about her own brush with Mrs Banks, although she knows it won't take long to get around the small town.

******

Alice clocks on for her shift at the dockyard with trepidation. She has lost much of her confidence because of the incident with Victor, and has withdrawn into herself. She walks down the road with Tilly, whom she has met on the corner by the train station, as usual. Tilly chats about the cup game, to keep Alice's mind off the court case, but she isn't sure how much her friend is listening.

Mr Phillips is waiting for her with Mrs Blueitt and the colour loft supervisor, under the arch outside the Quadrangle. "Let's go for a cup of tea in my office," says Mrs Eames, and the four of them disappear up the stairs, leaving Tilly to get on with opening the loan tool store on her own, and getting the stove going so they can keep warm and brew their tea.

One of Mrs Eames' women makes the tea and brings it through. Alice's stomach is in knots, as she fears that Mr Phillips will dismiss her as a troublemaker.

"I wanted a quiet word with you before you started work today," he begins. "I know it will be very difficult for you to begin with, but we are making changes, and Mr Banks' supervisor has been told not to send him to the stores. And if there are any other issues, please come and see Mrs Blueitt, and she will tell me."

Alice murmurs her thanks, and keeps her eyes on her hands in her lap, as she sits uncomfortably with her work superiors.

"Mrs Bennington, the Superintendent's wife, has taken an interest in your case, and is keen that there will be no repeats for you or any other woman. Rear Admiral Bennington leaves all the welfare issues to his wife. She has asked to speak to you today at three o'clock. So, come here to Mrs Eames' office before half past two, and she will take you to see her."

"Try not to get too dirty, and make sure you wash your hands and face before you come," the colour loft supervisor says, in a motherly way.

Alice is not expected to respond, so she just nods, thankful that she isn't blamed for the incident. She barely drinks the tea, too worried that her hand will shake, and she will spill it. She will need to be extra careful to stay clean for Mrs Bennington.

"Mrs Eames will get one of her women to take you back to the stores now," says Mr Phillips, as he nods to the two supervisors, leaving them to finish their tea, and indicates that Alice is dismissed.

Peggy Watson, one of the younger women in the loft, walks with Alice back to the stores, whilst Mrs Blueitt remains behind to discuss the incident. Peggy is a thickset woman, with rosy cheeks, which belies her sour disposition. She is said to have an eye for the men, but none of the men seem to reciprocate. On the way, Peggy can't help but ask, "So what really happened? Did he assault you, or did you give him the glad eye?"

"He assaulted me, otherwise I wouldn't have gone to Mrs Eames," replies Alice, put out by Peggy's tone of voice.

"A skinny thing like you should be glad of a bit of attention, I'd have thought," continues Peggy, looking Alice up and down, "He's got a bit of money. You could have done okay."

Alice is mortified. She thinks the women will stick together, but clearly Peggy is more interested in gossip than her welfare. As soon as the stores are in sight, Alice says, "I'll be okay from here," glad to get out of the other woman's company.

"Suit yourself," Peggy responds, disappointed that she has gleaned nothing from her walk with Alice, and she sets off back to the Quadrangle and the colour loft with her nose in the air.

Tilly is on tenterhooks, waiting to hear what Mr Phillips has said to Alice, and thinks her friend looks uncomfortable as she comes through the door into the stores.

"What happened?" she asks, as Alice takes off her coat and hangs it up, before putting on her smock and cap.

Alice immediately tells her about Peggy's snide remarks, before finishing, "Those colour loft women are all the same. They think they are better than us!"

It takes a few minutes before she is calm enough to tell Tilly that Mrs Bennington wants to see her, although, after her experience with Peggy, she is a little concerned that the Superintendent's wife is going to judge her as well.

*****

Miss Garrett is in a very bad mood. She is so cross that she purses her lips into a line so thin, that they have disappeared. Added to that, a little tut keeps escaping, which is accompanied by her eyes being raised and a little shake of her head. The military doctor called into the school that morning, without an appointment, and has thrown his weight about, by saying that Susan Kelly and Vera Ditton are suffering from mumps. She is duty bound to send them home, although she considers he is mistaken in his diagnosis; neither girl feels unwell nor has any symptoms. She has sent for Dr. Worth, and asks him to examine the girls, as she wants a second opinion, and doesn't think the military doctor knows his business. If it is mumps, they may end up having to shut the school. She is especially cross, because the "military doctor" had come from the "military hospital", housed in the Broadway School, - *her* Broadway School. His concern is that the service men will become infected, and this could lead to infertility. But there are enough illegitimate babies being born in the town since the war began, she thinks, with a sniff of disapproval. One or two infertile men might be a good thing, as being infertile is not the same as being impotent, after all. Why are men so keen that sex should lead to babies, when they are not the ones that have to carry them for nine months, at the risk to their own health.

Mr Pope, the scout master, calls into school at lunch time. Having already asked her to swap her day for Girl Guides, from Tuesday to Thursday, he wants to ask if she could take her guides earlier than half past six.

"Why do you now need me to be earlier?" she asks him.

"Well, in addition to helping out with the men doing air raid patrols, I want to train my scouts in firefighting. You know that the scout movement's handbook, instructs all boys to *'be prepared to die for your country if need be*[1]*'*. I also want them to assist with air raid duties, including sounding the all-clear signal after an attack. I need the extra time in the hall for that."

She summons all her dignity and responds, "I can't possibly move my girls any earlier. We are rehearsing for a concert that Mrs Bennington is giving for the service women, to raise funds for them to build them their own recreation hut. We can't possibly change that, as the Rear Admiral's wife herself is coming to see how the girls are doing." She smirks to herself as she tells him, knowing that he won't cross Mrs Bennington;

---

[1] *Lieut. Gen. Baden Powell C.B., Scouting for Boys - 1908*

nobody in the town will dare, not even Miss Garrett. "Why not teach your scouts when you teach the men, and help with the war effort by saving fuel by not having the hall open late every evening?" she finishes, with as a *fait accompli*. Mr Pope leaves with his tail between his legs.

On top of all that, she is still annoyed about yesterday's court case. Whilst, in the past, her Christian faith led her to believe that women are the custodians of morality, recent experience has taught her that men should not only take responsibility for their own actions, but, more importantly, should be held responsible by society. She knows that the magistrate blames Alice for the incident, and knows that many people will think Alice in the wrong for making a complaint. Now, Hattie has promised Alice that they will ensure that Victor gets his come uppance, and she is concerned it will all go wrong. But she thinks a more long-term answer is needed, to improve Alice's lot in life. She will have to think of another way to help Alice.

*****

The day drags slowly, as Tilly deals with the men at the counter, whilst Alice stays out the back, fetching the items requested on the vouchers. Only one customer makes any comments, an older man who had been in the navy before swapping to work in the dockyard as a skilled labourer. He calls out loudly for Alice to hear. "Hope your mate has learned a lesson before she tries getting innocent men into trouble. She should keep both her mouth and her legs shut!" Tilly sends him packing, but it still stings.

At quarter to two, Mrs Blueitt comes into the loan store and inspects Alice, to ensure she looks presentable for Mrs Bennington.

"That smock isn't clean enough, you'd best borrow one from the stores," she says, as she appraises Alice, sending Tilly off to fetch one. She produces a hairbrush from the pocket of her apron and sets about ensuring all Alice's hair is tucked neatly in her snood. When she is satisfied, Mrs Blueitt walks her over to Mrs Eames' office, arriving a good quarter hour before half past two, so the loft supervisor can in turn inspect the girl a second time.

"Run a hot iron over Alice's smock, please" Mrs Eames asks one of her girls, "We need to remove the folds where it been laying in the stores chest awaiting requisition before she sees Mrs Bennington. Can't let her be seen like this."

"You should have seen the state of the one I made her change out of. You could grow potatoes on the front of it," Mrs Blueitt says, ensuring Mrs Eames knows she is responsible for the new smock.

Mrs Eames has already spent a good half an hour getting herself ready. Only when she is content with Alice's appearance does Mrs Eames consider it okay to set off for Admiralty House, but she still makes sure they arrive well before three o'clock for their audience. Mrs Blueitt returns to the stores, slightly miffed that she hadn't been invited too. She wastes no time in finding Mr Dennis in his private office, so that she can bemoan her lot to him.

******

The Superintendent's residence is set in its own grounds, away from the main dockyard, but within the walls. It is guarded by two sailors on the door, armed with rifles. Mrs Eames takes Alice to the office entrance, rather than the front door or tradesmen's entrance around the back. A clerk checks their names off a list of visitors for the day, before summoning another rating to take them to wait for Mrs Bennington.

After about five minutes, a maid comes to take them to the sitting room that overlooks the manicured gardens at the rear of the house. As they follow the girl, Mrs Eames again rattles out her instructions to Alice.

"Remember to stand up straight, don't speak unless you are spoken to, no backchat, and remember the privilege that she is bestowing on you." Alice isn't sure what kind of privilege it is to be asked to stand in a grand lady's presence, but she had started her working life in service, so knows better than to answer back.

Mrs Bennington is seated in a comfortable chair at a small escritoire, where she is writing her letters on monogrammed paper. A fire blazes in the marble fireplace, but Alice and Mrs Eames stand too far away to get the benefit of it, and Mrs Bennington is shielded from the heat by a fire screen, to save her complexion. She looks up when her maid gives a little cough, and introduces the colour loft supervisor.

"Ah, Mrs Eames," she says, smiling, "and this must be the girl from the stores."

"Yes, ma'am," responds the older woman. "This is Alice."

Mrs Bennington does not invite them to sit, but leaves them standing, as she moves slightly in her chair to address them better, arranging her dark purple silk skirts around her ankles as she does so; she is known for her lovely clothes.

"I heard about the court case. I'm sure we could have dealt with the matter without the need to call in the police," she says, looking directly at Mrs Eames, who colours accordingly. "I realise that justice must be done, but it so seldom is in these cases. We women end up shouldering the blame. My husband is responsible for so many men that it does not escape my notice that far too often they can end up scot free. If one of the girls comes to you again with a complaint, you must bring it to me first." She turns her attention to Alice. "I'm sorry that you had an unpleasant experience. Can you assure me that you did not encourage,... what is his name?"

"Banks, ma'am," Mrs Eames murmurs.

"Yes, that you did not encourage Banks?"

"No, ma'am, I didn't," Alice whispers.

"Right, well don't let it happen again. If anything like it does, we will deal with it in our own way."

Mrs Eames takes this for a dismissal and starts to chivvy Alice out of the room. She regrets that Mrs Blueitt brought the girl to her for help and had not dealt with it herself, as she had been made to feel in the wrong by Mrs Bennington. It is just the kind of thing that Ruby Blueitt would do, passing the buck so someone else takes the blame. But the Rear Admiral's wife is not finished.

"I am very pleased that the girls have a mother figure they can turn to in these circumstances. They are helping us to win the war, and we need to protect them too." Mrs Eames stops in her tracks, and straightens her drooping shoulders at this praise. "My husband has told me that you are to receive an extra ten shillings a week, and are to be made senior women's supervisor, so all the other women supervisors will now defer to you, and the pastoral care of the women will devolve to you. And any cases of difficulty you will bring to me."

Mrs Bennington ignores Mrs Eames' murmured thanks, and turns her attention to the girl. "I understand that you are one of the many female footballers in the dockyard, Alice. I am championing the women's cup, and have been tasked with giving it a name. Will you mind helping me decide? I've got the list down to just two. I thought about '*Munitionesses Cup*', as I'm informed there is already a '*Munitionettes Cup*', somewhere in the north of the country," she says vaguely, waving a hand in the general direction of where the north might be. "Or maybe the '*Sheerness Dockyard Ladies Cup.*' What do you think?"

Alice is taken aback for a moment. "Probably the '*Ladies Cup*', ma'am."

"Yes, I thought so too. How long have you been playing?" Mrs Bennington asks, then, after several more questions about the game, she inquires, "And when is the first cup match?"

"Not this Saturday, but the next one. You can come and watch us if you like, ma'am. Mrs West, our coach, can explain the game to you."

"I might just do that," she responds, turning back to her correspondence. The conversation over, the two women from the dockyard leave to find their own way out, before the maid once again intercepts them and takes them to the office door.

As they return to their workplace, both women are unsure if they had been reprimanded or praised by the Rear Admiral's wife. But they both feel she is on their side.

*****

The Tournament Begins

Hattie, Lucy, Ena, and Miss Garrett rack their brains trying to work out a plan of how to embarrass Victor Banks, and catch him with his trousers down, whilst they are knitting mufflers for soldiers one evening at Ena's.

"We need others to do the catching for us, if it's to be effective," says Ena.

"We could involve one of his colleagues. That young Mr Symonds might help," suggests Hattie. "He seems nice."

Miss Garrett dismisses the suggestion with a sniff. "That won't do. The dockyard men will just view any kind of embarrassing situation as horse play."

"What about the kind of scenario used in divorce cases?" ventures Ena.

"No, the logistics are just too much. We'd need a hotel room and private detectives, and then where will the embarrassment be to Banks, as he is an unmarried man," Miss Garrett says, emphasising the impracticality of the suggestion with a little shake of her head, which came hard on the heels of the more customary sniff.

"Yes, and he'd probably revel in it, as that Taylor boy told everyone that Victor is a virgin in court."

"That kind of scenario with a woman of the night will build him up before men like Taylor," Miss Garrett says, full of horror that it might end up doing Banks a good turn.

"We can ask the women's football team to debag him," contributes Lucy, from her position just outside the circle that the other women are occupying in Ena's parlour. She is allotted the task of unpicking old woollen garments, then rolling the yarn into balls, ready to be knitted up into scarves. All "comforts" are meant to be knitted in khaki, so the finished items will be dyed, using onion skins. It will fall to her to be the one with sore eyes from that operation.

"No, that will reflect badly on the girls," says Hattie, wanting to protect the *Naval Stores Ladies* team from untoward criticism.

"We need Victor to have removed his trousers voluntarily, for some reason, and to be caught without them in front of someone of note," summarises Ena.

"The obvious person will be the Rear Admiral, but I have no idea how that can be managed. I can perhaps confide in Mrs Bennington," Hattie proposes. "Alice tells me that she is interested in the case, and is now championing the women's football."

Miss Garrett sniffs. "That will never do. She will probably tell her husband our plans, and that will bring it all to an end."

"Why not enlist Mrs Eames? She might help," Lucy says. "She must know when the boss is coming, and she is the only woman with any real authority in the dockyard."

Once again, they are all in awe of Lucy's insight. Hattie promises to sound Mrs Eames out the next time she is in the yard.

*****

"How come we haven't seen Cissie or little Ernie for a few weeks?" Alice asks her mother one morning, as she helps get the younger ones ready for school. Ever since her outburst on the day of the court hearing, she has done her best to help her cousins.

"I've been avoiding Ivy for some weeks," Maggie explains to her daughter. "She was summoned for soliciting, and found guilty of being a common prostitute. I hope that if I'm not around, Ivy might realise that she has to take more responsibility for her own children, and not rely on me to bail her out."

Ivy's children often fend for themselves, and her daughter, Cissie, acts as a mother to three-year-old Ernie. At just eleven years old, she is quite confident in her dealings with money and the responsibility of the household. The small family only rent two rooms in Gordon Road. Most of their income is from the maintenance payments made by Cissie's father, Eli, as Ivy is still legally married to him. Cissie collects the money from the Parish Office in the workhouse, on her mother's behalf.

"It's a good thing that the Parish Office is at the top of the hill, otherwise if Ivy was the one to collect it, you can be sure there will not be enough to pay the rent before she returns home, as there are far too many pubs for her to pass on the way," Alice says, as she brushes and plats her sister Dolly's hair, giving it a sly pull every now and then, just to annoy her sulky sister.

"Cissie is such a good little mother. Each week, she goes straight to the rent collector and pays what they owe, so she can keep a roof over their heads and somewhere for her mother to sleep, when she eventually rolls home," Maggie recounts to Alice. "Cissie has a complete routine to make the money go as far as it can, without her mother getting her hands on it and drinking it away."

When Ivy is drunk or with a customer, her friend Pearl Bidgood looks out for her and, in return, she looks out for her friend. Pearl has long since lost any semblance of prettiness that she might have had in her youth. Several of her teeth have been knocked out by the kind of customer who enjoyed a little casual violence to gain satisfaction. She smokes a pipe, which she wedges into the gap in the front of her mouth, and keeps it there, lit or unlit. On her right cheek, she bears a scar from a client, who, it was later discovered, had been too handy with a knife. Another working girl had been found murdered down a back alley, her throat slashed, and a similar scar carved into her face, only a day after he had maimed Pearl.

It's Pearl who comes knocking at Maggie's door later that day to deliver some unwanted news. As soon as Maggie opens the door to her, she launches off with, "Ivy's got seven days inside.

They'll take the kids away if you don't do something."

"Why me?" asks Maggie. "She's got other family. We're not real cousins."

"But you're the only one who cares, and she trusts you."

"Why has she gone inside this time?" asks Maggie, knowing this is not Ivy's first brush with the law for being a prostitute.

"She was summoned under DORA, for having an unmentionable disease. The military doctor examined her and said she was clean. Gave her a certificate an' al', which is good. But, as she was convicted a few weeks ago for soliciting, the magistrate decided she ought to go away to teach her a lesson."

The War Office is attempting to control people's lives in a number of ways under DORA – the *Defence of the Realm Act*; and this includes restricting drinking, imposing curfews, and banning suspected prostitutes from the vicinity of military and naval establishments. Soliciting had become a crime in 1916. In a town like Sheerness, where there is both a naval dockyard and army barracks, the police have their work cut out keeping track of all the women they think are flouting the law. Ivy has fallen foul of these changes.

The regulations also seek to limit the cases of venereal disease (VD), which is a big problem in the services, leading to almost as many men being unfit as there are casualties from the front. Some prostitutes obtain health certificates from doctors, stating that they are free from infection. They show these to potential clients, as well as to the police. It is this certificate that the military doctor has given to Ivy, and which Pearl is pleased (and a little envious) that her friend has obtained.

"You best get round her place before the police get there," Pearl says, turning on her heel, and heading back to the pubs to earn her own drink, as she won't have the more attractive Ivy to do it for her.

Maggie wonders how Pearl has not been brought before the magistrate herself, but the entire system works on accusations made by the servicemen, once they are found to be infected. Soldiers and sailors hospitalised with VD find themselves facing a fine, as they are deemed to have been admitted to hospital because of their own actions. They are quick to shift the blame to the women they consort with, to try to alleviate the penalties they receive. But Pearl is so ugly that even the most desperate serviceman may not wish to admit he has been with her in front of his colleagues.

Maggie says, "I'll get my coat. Dolly, look after little Rab, and wipe that sulk off your face," and sets off for Ivy's rooms in Gordon Road, as quickly as she can. The smell of tar, sea breezes, and coke fumes fill the air, whilst the pigs on the Co-op Dairy farm, across the railway, do their best to add to the particular fragrance of West Minster.

Cissie is off school again and attending to her little brother Ernie, when Maggie arrives. "Pack up quick," she says, "your Mum's gone inside for seven days. You're coming home with me till she's back out."

Whilst Maggie doesn't need another two mouths to feed in the house, she won't see her cousin's children in the workhouse, because once they are admitted, Ivy will never be able to get them back out. Ernie will be put in an education institution for imbeciles. They may never see the child again.

Cissie knows this too, and quickly packs up their scant belongings. Before she locks up, she writes a note to pin to the door, directing any callers to their temporary home. Maggie wonders what her

Rab will say when he finishes work, and finds two more children at the dinner table, but he'll probably just grunt, as it is only for the week, or so she hopes.

******

The foundry is no place for a woman, but here they all are. It is dark, hot, and dangerous. There is little daylight, as the blacksmiths need to judge the temperature of the fire correctly, or the metal won't respond. The women are employed to fetch the coal, stoke the fires, and generally do the labouring. When a larger item is being forged, a gang of them are needed to carry and manipulate the item in and out of the steam hammer, whilst the blacksmith directs them in what to do. Sparks fly, and the women are covered in tiny burns where they get hit, their heavy smocks only giving limited protection. Last summer, Emmy Latimer had her arm broken by the hammer, and had to go to the Naval Hospital at Chatham Dockyard to get it seen to. It is mended now, and she has transferred back to light duties.

Ruth Pamplin, the foundry supervisor, has never been interested in sport, but when different areas of the dockyard start forming women's football teams, she sees it as an opportunity to get in with the management, as they are encouraging these pursuits. She calls the girls together during their tea brake to announce that she has entered them as a team in Mrs Bennington's *Sheerness Dockyard Ladies Cup*.

"Right, girls, I need eleven of you to volunteer to be in the team. Tom Foster, the blacksmith's son from the brass foundry, has kindly agreed to train you."

A couple of girls put their hands up, and Ruth writes their names down, "Come on, I need more than two!" she bullies. "It will get you noticed by the management. Mrs Bennington herself is championing it."

"Are there any handsome men playing?" asks one girl, to the giggles of the others, Ruth ignores her and looks over her head for volunteers. She is used to supervising workers, having previously been a charge hand at the tile works, in Queenborough. She was employed there as a girl, then when she was widowed, she went back to work there. She isn't really a widow; her husband had gone to India with the railway, at the turn of the century, not long after they were married. Within months, he had written to tell her he had met someone else, and won't be returning. She had packed up her home in readiness to follow him out, but found herself deserted, and in need of means to support herself. So, she told everyone he had died of malaria, and asked for her old job back. The marriage had never been consummated, and it was whispered that Jim Pamplin was queer. But she will never know if that is true. She doesn't know if he is alive or dead, but she no longer cares anyway; she has cried her tears long ago.

Alice and Tilly's friend Kitty puts her hand up to ask a practical question, "What will we wear?"

Ruth notes the use of the word "we" and adds the girl's name to the team sheet. "I've begged and borrowed football boots, for those girls who don't have any, which will probably be most of you, and I've negotiated the use of some kit, so you can look like a team. Mr Foster, your new coach, plays for one of the dockyard teams, and his teammates have agreed to lend their blue shorts and blue jerseys. There is a slight catch, as in return they ask that we wash their kit for several weeks, by way of payment." There is a slight rumbling at this, but as the number of girls willing to play increases, Mrs Pamplin takes satisfaction from it.

When Ruth had seen a vacancy advertised for a women's supervisor in the dockyard, she had applied straight away. The pay is better than at the tile works, and some of the jobs are cushy little numbers. But not the foundry. It had been hot at the tile works around the bottle shaped kilns, but they are in the yard, and the factory itself is cold, as the clay is machine rolled, and pressed and cut into squares by sharp automated blades before firing. The factory doors are opened and closed so frequently, that all the heat inside escapes, so the warmest place is outside near the kilns.

"Come on, girls, I just need three more volunteers. You will get time off to practice," she promises. She enjoys getting one over on the bosses, and will do what she can to ensure the girls are treated well. When she had been at the tile works, a girl had lost two fingers to the cutters, a couple of years ago; she had been trying to remove a stone that had somehow ended up in the clay, but wasn't quick enough to avoid the blades. She had been to court for compensation, and the company had to make up her wages each week to that which she earned on piece rates. But the management had tried to claim she had never been a fast worker, and that she didn't earn what she told the court she had earned previously, so as to reduce what they had to pay her. Ruth had been the girl's charge hand, and had been asked to lie in court by her boss, and say the girl was slow. It was fortuitous for her that the dockyard advertised the supervisor jobs at that moment. So, she tells the truth in court, that the girl had been the fastest worker, and leaves her job before her manager has a chance to victimise her for it. She'll have to find something else after the war, when the men are demobbed and want their jobs back in the yard, but that is in the future, so she won't worry about that for now.

A few weeks later, the first cup tie is almost upon them, and Mrs Pamplin has worked hard at getting the team ready. All the girls are very excited; what they lack in talent; they make up with enthusiasm. They are looking forward to a friendly match against the ladies from the glue factory, this coming Saturday. Unlike many of the dockyard teams, this will be their first proper game. Tom has helped them considerably, not least because he is sweet on Violet Cathcart. And, if they lose, it doesn't really matter to Ruth; at least they have tried their best, and she will have been seen by her superiors to be participating.

*****

Saturday arrives, and the *Foundry Foxes* run onto the glue factory's pitch, with some confidence in their blue jerseys. *The Queenborough Glue and Fertilizer Ladies* (to give them their full name) are wearing a hooped black and white strip. Hattie West has abandoned her own ladies team to the care of Mr Phillips. They are playing a friendly against a team of *WRAF*s, from the aerodrome at Eastchurch. Hattie has dodged the rain showers to cycle to the glue factory's recreation ground, at the Halfway Houses. She stands on the touch line, with her coat buttoned up against the March weather, and studies the two teams intently.

There are one or two skilful players in the foundry team, girls who are taking it seriously. The rest are just running around, not really able to control the ball, or do much more than boot it from one end of the pitch to the other. Hattie is about to leave, when Dotty Cox scores for the *Foundry Foxes*, taking them into the lead.

Ruth Pamplin cheers and shouts encouragement, and the foundry girls seem to rally. They then start to attack with some purpose, remembering the training they have received from Tom Foster, who is standing on the touch line with Ruth, waving his arms and shouting his instructions to them, caught up in the excitement of the game.

The second half shows the foundry girls in a better light. They defend almost skilfully, as one of the glue factory players hits the post. They tighten their formation and stop any shots on target from the opposition, to win the game, one - nil.

Hattie makes notes during the game, including descriptions of the better players and the number on the reverse of the jerseys they wear, so that she can tell her team. She is just putting her notebook away, when Mrs Pamplin walks over to her.

"Are you with the *Sheppey Star* or with the *Sheerness Advertiser*?" she asks, wrongly assuming that Hattie is a reporter. "None of the women's games ever seem to make it into the paper. But you're the first female journalist I've seen, so hopefully you can change that."

Hattie has a moment of indecision; should she lie and pretend to be there from one of the local papers, or admit she is spying for the *Naval Stores Ladies*? But she is saved by Lily Hancock, Miss Briggs' housekeeper's daughter,. Lily is one of the players for the glue factory team.

"Mrs West, I thought it was you. How is Miss Briggs? Mum said you are interested in football. It's really kind of you to come and watch me. Mum will be thrilled that you came," Lily says, as she comes running over to Hattie.

Hattie takes advantage of Lily's misunderstanding and says, "Yes, your mother said you played now." (Although Hattie has forgotten until that moment) "I'm trying to learn all the rules, quite different from cricket." Mrs Pamplin loses interest in Hattie and drifts away to congratulate her girls on their win, allowing Hattie to make good her escape on her bicycle.

*****

Miss Garrett does not enjoy Sunday school like she used to, now that the Napier Hall building is also her normal place of work. She is beginning to hate the place. At least during the week, there is relative calm as her staff teach the girls the three R's. But on a Sunday, the place is invaded by raucous boys, who the moment their Sunday school teacher turns his back, are prone to run around shouting and generally being disruptive. How can they hear the Lord's words, when she can't even hear herself think?

On top of that, there has been a thick fog for a couple of days, which hangs heavy across the town, like a pall cloth on top of a coffin. It muffles all sound, and she had nearly been run down by Polly, the milkman's horse, who is convinced the foghorn that wails out every few minutes to warn shipping, is the siren for the end of the shift in the dockyard, and has abruptly decided to return to his stable. The boy holding him is dragged off his feet. It is only because two young sailors have grabbed her and pulled her back from the road, that she has lived to tell the tale. But she had been shaken, and it has left her feeling out of sorts for the rest of the week.

She gathers her Sunday school class closer in their circle, as she tells them the story of the *Widow's Mite*. But she becomes increasingly cross with the hullaballoo, until she stands up and loudly rebukes Mr Pope. "Will you please keep those boys in order, otherwise I will do it for you!"

"Boys will be boys," Mr Pope responds infuriatingly, having none of the skills to control a class of children that Miss Garrett has, "They have to let off steam."

The other women Sunday school teachers take their lead from Miss Garrett, and gather their girls closer to continue with their lessons. Meanwhile, some of the male teachers attempt to bring order, but without Mr Pope putting his foot down, the boys run riot. Small scuffles break out, which distract the girls from their learning.

Just then, there is an almighty bang. Timmy Halfpenny has produced a detonator he has picked up from the railway line. The device is to warn the locomotive drivers of any obstructions when it is too foggy to see, and must have been left behind after some incident over the last few days, whilst visibility was poor. Timmy had found one where the level crossing at West Minster crosses the line, and has been carrying it about since then. The bedlam that is taking place at Sunday school that morning has encouraged him to retrieve the item from his pocket to see what will happen if he sets it off. He hadn't banked on it blowing half his hand off, and showering those around him with shrapnel and gobbets of flesh and bone.

All hell is let loose, as Timmy wails for his mother, and three or four other children who are injured (thankfully superficially) join in the cacophony. The children who are hit with Timmy's blood and tissue, scream in horror, whilst Miss Garrett starts shouting commands. Those trained in first aid are called into action to treat the wounded. Timmy's hand is attended to, but requires more than just a bandage. Fortunately, Mr Pope's car is outside, and he, together with one of the other teachers, takes Timmy to St Barts Hospital in Rochester, to be properly cared for.

There is no damage done to the building, but Mr Moss the caretaker is less than pleased at the amount of blood on the floor, not to mention some parts of Timmy's fingers that also require clearing up.

Miss Garrett eyes the mess, and thinks how her teachers will need to be able to carry on with their classes if a permanent stain is left tomorrow, when the building returns to being the Broadway School. It will certainly unsettle some of the more delicate ones. She is also concerned about how upset everyone at Sunday school will be because of the incident; she doesn't want them leaving the congregation and joining some other non-conformist sect, or worse, the Church of England. Last, but not least, she hopes that Timmy will recover from his injury, although she is often heard to say, *"The Lord does not pay all his debts with money,"* but, on this occasion, she swallows the words whenever they threatened to rise to her lips.

The other casualties are taken home to their mothers by two other Sunday school teachers, who have to explain what has happened to the injured infants. The rest of the Sunday school is dismissed for the day, and sent home to disturb parents who are trying to enjoy a little privacy for once, whilst Mr Moss and the remaining teachers scrub the floor and walls of blood, under Miss Garrett's supervision.

Miss Garrett is so cross with Mr Pope for allowing the boys to run out of control, that her usual sniffing in annoyance nowhere near calms her nerves. She has to go home and have a lie down, as soon as she feels the hall is clean enough to pass muster. Her lodger, Lucy, is kind enough to make her some tea, and draws the bedroom curtains before offering to fetch Ena to sooth her friend.

"That Mr Pope is such a buffoon," Miss Garrett declares, as Lucy tucks her in to bed. "It's not just Victor Banks who deserves a come uppance!"

*****

Nothing untoward happens in the dockyard stores for the rest of the week, and it is almost as though the incident with Victor Banks never happened. Tilly serves the customers and Alice fulfils the vouchers.

It isn't till the Saturday morning of the cup tie that either girl sees Victor. He has obviously been keeping a low profile in the dockyard, and Rab McDonald has put the word out that if he is seen in West Minster, then he will get a pasting, courtesy of Rab and Ginger. But as the girls leave work and head towards the recreation ground, they spot him lurking behind one of the sheds.

Tilly loops her arm into Alice's, and both girls put their heads down to avoid eye contact with Victor. They pass him without a word, and he pretends to be reading the newspaper, but too late Tilly spots it is the local weekly news. Just then, Victor darts out and leaves the paper open on top of a coil of rope ahead of them, before creeping back into the piles of timber, like a wood louse. The newspaper headline reads, "*AN UNSUSTAINED CHARGE,*" and immediately below it says, "*Girl Accuses Dockyard Worker of Indecent Assault.*" Alice's eyes are immediately drawn to it and her stomach knots. Tilly grabs the paper and, as soon as they pass a rubbish bin, she throws it away.

"Don't think about it," Tilly advises Alice. "Keep your mind on the game."

But the damage is done; by the time they reach the changing rooms, Alice is in tears.

"Whatever is the matter?" asks Hattie, full of concern when she sees the state of Alice. Tilly starts to explain what had happened as she tries to comfort her friend, and also change into her football kit, but before she can finish, there is a knock at the door, and Mrs Bennington sweeps in, wearing a sable fur coat and ostrich plumed hat. She is carrying an enormous fur muff, in which she could have concealed quite a large baby, (should she have ever needed to) in readiness for the game.

"I thought I'd pop in to wish you luck!" she starts to say breezily, before stopping abruptly. "Alice, what has happened?"

Hattie quickly updates the Rear Admiral's wife, who in turn looks thoughtful, and says, "That young man needs to be taught a lesson!"

"I think we can all agree on that. He needs to be caught with his trousers down, as they say," says Hattie, "but we can't think how we can execute such a plan."

Mrs Bennington puts her hand up to stop Hattie saying anymore. "Please, don't say anything else. I cannot be a party to it. But my thoughts are with you. Dry your tears, Alice, and show everyone that you are made of sterner stuff, there's a good girl."

Mrs Bennington's concern goes a long way towards making Alice feel she is not alone, and she gets changed ready for the match, as Hattie and the Superintendent's wife exchange some pleasantries about the coming game. Then, abruptly, Mrs Bennington calls out her best wishes to all the girls and leaves, carrying the "baby smuggler" muff under her arm.

The Rear Admiral's wife also goes to wish the *Foundry Foxes* luck in their changing room before kick-off. Mrs Pamplin is surprisingly unctuous in her reception of the superintendent's wife, offering her some tea from a billycan that she has brought with her. But Mrs Bennington declines, saying, "My husband kindly bought me one of those new thermos flasks before the war. It's jolly good at keeping the tea hot," before she swans out in a flurry of ostrich feathers.

When she returns to the Lanchester car, Mrs Bennington's maid swaddles her in blankets to keep out the cold in the enclosed rear of the vehicle, whilst the girl does her best to keep warm in the open fronted driver's cab, in just a woollen coat. She wraps a shawl over her head, so as not to disturb her cap, and end up in trouble with the housekeeper when they get back to Admiralty House.

Mrs Bennington's chauffeur is a navy driver, who, to everyone's surprise, is a woman, one of the new *Women's Royal Naval Service*, which had been formed the previous year. She looks very smart in her *Wrens* uniform, and some of the dockyard girls think about joining up when they see her. It is said that some girls are posted overseas to naval bases elsewhere in the Empire, which makes her seem very exciting.

The two women don't talk, as the maid is not permitted to speak unless spoken to, and the Wren, in turn, is not permitted to unless granted permission. So, they sit silently frozen in the front, as Mrs Bennington sits in the relative warmth of the back of the car. She doesn't watch the game, but reads a penny dreadful book that she has concealed within a secret pocket in her giant muff, along with a small hip flask of medicinal brandy, to keep out the cold.

The two teams run out onto the pitch that is yet to be touched by spring, and the referee blows his whistle for the game to start. Hattie has briefed the *Stores Ladies* about how the foundry girls play, and Dotty Cox finds herself more closely marked than she had ever been before. This leads to some frustration from the foundry girls, and a number of fouls start to creep in.

Tom Foster has taught his team to play dirty, which Hattie has never seen before (it isn't cricket after all), and several girls pick up bruised shins while being tackled. As the time ticks away towards the final whistle, the score is still nil - nil. Both teams are tiring, and the foundry girls play dirtier. When Alice takes a pass from Gladys in the penalty box, and is in line to shoot, one of the vixens from the *Foundry Foxes* chops her legs from under her. The referee awards a penalty and Alice remembers her training: side of the foot for accuracy, and laces for power. She opts for power and drives the ball into the top left-hand corner of the net. When the final whistle goes, the *Stores Ladies* have won.

Mrs Bennington emerges from her cocoon of blankets to congratulate the winners, and commiserate with the losers. She has sent her two daughters off to watch another match, the *Rigging Shop Roses* playing the *Wrens*. Next week, it will be the *Colour Loft Ladies* playing the dockyard office staff (who have yet to think of a catchy team name), and the *Torpedo Amazons* against the *Women's Auxiliary Army Corps* (*WAAC*s). The *Stores Ladies* will find out who they will play in the semi-final, from the results of next week's matches.

As she is going, the Rear Admiral's wife shakes Hattie's hand and says, "If there is anything

I can do to help with the other little matter, I will do my best. I'm not sure if its common knowledge yet, but the Thursday before Empire Day, His Majesty the King is visiting the dockyard to inspect the service men and meet the workers. I understand he intends meeting several of the women employees. It would be dreadful if anything untoward happens then. But sometimes justice has to be seen to be done." She holds Hattie's gaze, each understanding the other. "When we meet again, at the semi-finals, I will know the timing of the King's route through the dockyard, and we will talk again."

Hattie nods, her mind racing at this fresh news about the King's visit. She will need to talk to the others, but would there be a better day to deliver Victor's come uppance than the day of the King visit?

*****

Watching the Opposition

Easter has fallen at the end of March, which makes April a long month, and it seems to drag on. The date for the semi-final cup match is set for Saturday the twenty-seventh. Things have returned to normal in the stores; the new layout is in place, and Alice stays well away from the front counter.

Victor has stopped going to fetch the tools from the store, but he hangs about outside the dock gates in the evening, and follows Alice down the road at a safe distance, as far as the railway station. He doesn't go further, as he isn't keen to bump into Rab McDonald, or his brother Ginger.

The dockyard empties swiftly once the end of shift siren goes, as hundreds of men stream out the gates. Some are on their bicycles, whistling as they go, their caps pulled down tight to their ears, or marching out *en masse*, lighting up their cigarettes and pipes as soon as they are through the gates, as smoking is prohibited within the yard. But Teddie Taylor has still managed to spot Victor lurking outside, spying on Alice, and spreads this tasty bit of gossip around the other dock workers.

Mrs Banks takes Victor to task when she finds out he is hanging about after work. "People will start saying that you really did assault that girl, if you keep following her," she warns. But he can't help himself. He is convinced that Alice is to blame, that she has led him on, and she is laughing at him. He has written insults about her on the walls of the dockyard latrines, calling her names, and alleging that she is promiscuous.

Teddie catches him doing it once, and ribs him mercilessly. "Oi, Verge! Still waiting to lose your virginity? She won't want you after you denied having your hand up her skirt. No girl wants to feel rejected!" he laughs, believing his own rhetoric.

This just adds to Victor's sense of being hard done by, and the next time he follows Alice down the road, he shouts out, "You think you are too good for me! Your family is nothing! Your sister is a slut, giving birth to a baby out of wedlock!"

Alice walks faster and catches up with a neighbour going the same way home. Her eyes prick with tears, but she refuses to give in, and chats as brightly as she can to Horace, from three doors down from her home.

"How is your allotment and your pigeons?" She knows that Horace will rattle on for ages about his birds, and she will be able to walk safely with him away from Victor.

"If only the army would ask me for a couple," he muses, glad to have someone to listen to him. "They would be excellent carriers. I've already presented two pairs to the Royal Navy Air Service at Eastchurch. You see I read in the *Illustrated London News* about how every sea plane carries two birds. They are there to send duplicate emergency messages back to base. The paper explains that they replace the wireless in small vessels, and some sea planes. I'm confident that my birds will be heroes one day and save the lives of the pilots on some mission or other."

Alice listens to his story again without interrupting him, as she knows Victor will stay away from her whilst she is in the company of someone else.

After the first time, Victor feels emboldened to shout out obscenities at Alice whenever there is no one else around. She does her best to always leave with Tilly or Horace, or she will try to get into a group of other workers walking towards West Minster. Sometimes, she walks with Reggie Symonds as far as the beginning of her road. Other times, if she sees Reggie out walking his black and tan Manchester Terrier, Patch, he will offer to escort her home, whether it is a workday or not. When Reggie sees Victor, he warns him off. However, often Victor appears out of alleyways, the moment she is left on her own.

Alice tells her mother, who keeps it from her father, as she knows this will set him off. He and Ginger will knock at Victor's door and drag him out for a pasting if they find out; they have done it before, when Ginger's daughter Maud came home pregnant by a married man. Although she later found out she was not expecting, the damage was done. They had also gone to find Cathy's boyfriend in the army camp, as soon as he came back from his tour of duty, to ensure he married her and gave their baby a name, before being sent to the front, back in 1914.

The two Glaswegians are well known for their short tempers, and the police will waste no time looking for them if they go after Victor. Maggie is worried that the two of them will be sent to prison, as Victor will be bound to complain, unlike Maud and Cathy's men friends, who accepted the beatings as their just desserts.

*****

Victor's mother follows the court cases avidly in the local paper. She circles the most interesting ones to read aloud to her son when he returns from work. She has relished the report that had exonerated Victor, with its headline *"AN UNSUSTAINED CHARGE,"* and subheading; *"Girl Accuses Dockyard Worker of Indecent Assault."* She has cut it out and put it into a frame, almost obscuring the photograph of her late husband.

It is with glee that she spots that Ivy Dummott has once again been up before the magistrate, and is serving seven days in prison. Because of the timing of the weekly paper coming out on a Monday (so it can capture the weekend events), it is almost two weeks since her case was heard, and Ivy is already back out on the streets again, as her week in jail is up.

As soon as Victor gets home, his mother starts to regale him with the story. "That Alice is no better than she should be," Mrs Banks begins, her neck taut like a hangman's rope. "Her Aunt Ivy is nothing but a common prostitute. It's right here in the paper. Seven days inside!"

She passes the newspaper to Victor to read for himself, pointing to the ringed item, in case he misses it.

"How do you know it's Alice's aunt?"

"Well, not her aunt exactly, but her mother's cousin. Well, cousin by marriage, but it's all the same. That Ivy is always hanging about with the sailors in Bluetown, until she is paralytic and has to be carried home or sleeps in the gutter."

Victor is enjoying the story, until his mother says, "You have probably seen her. She used to be very pretty when she was young, but she looks a bit raddled now, close up. You must have seen her, she is missing the bottom of her ear, so only wears one earring."

He realises it is Ivy whom he propositioned on the day he had got his mother to complain to the local police that the newsagent was selling pornographic postcards. At first, he feels sick to his stomach, then he comes to the realisation that Alice is just like her aunt. She must have led him on, it is all her fault, and he is being made to feel an outcast at work, despite the magistrate saying there was no case to answer. Alice and her Aunt Ivy deserve all they get.

*****

Reggie Symonds finds himself looking forward to meeting up with Alice to walk her home. She is always pleased to see him, and he feels he is doing her a service by deterring Victor from speaking to her. Patch, the Manchester Terrier, with his one tan pirate's eye, has never had so many walks, and is now as pleased to see Alice as Reggie is.

"How was football practice?" he asks her, as he catches up with her one day.

"Oh, really good. I'm getting so much better at passing the ball now. You should come along to watch, you might learn something," she jokes, "Where are you off to today?"

"Oh, you know, just popping in on Uncle Horace. There's a pigeon race coming up, and he wants my opinion on which bird to enter." This isn't strictly true, the race is ages off, but Reggie doesn't want Alice to know he hopes to bump into her when he takes Patch out.

When he gets to Horace's house, he and Patch say their goodbyes and leave Alice at the gate.

Horace appears out of his pigeon loft when he hears Patch's excited bark, "You again?" he says, pleased to see his nephew. "Have you walked down with Alice?"

"Yes, I just happened along the road at the same time." Horace gives him a knowing look; he isn't fooled by Reggie's nonchalance.

"She's quite pretty, that one," Horace says, as he fusses Patch's ears, much to the dog's delight.

"Yes she is, but not like on a magazine cover, such as *Woman's Own.* Those girls all look soppy, with rosebud lips and dewy eyes. No, she's livelier than that. She's more like Edna Purviance, from the Chaplin films. More ready to laugh and have fun. Although that Victor has robbed her of some of her sparkle, I can see it coming back every time I chat to her."

If he can pluck up the courage, he will ask Alice to go to the pictures with him to see the latest little tramp film.

*****

Hattie goes to visit her friend, Rosie Harris, one day after school, to keep her up to date on events. Rosie was quite keen on playing tennis with Hattie, before she became a wife and mother, and she now enjoys hearing about her friend's sporting triumphs, as she doesn't get the opportunity to participate herself. When Hattie arrives, her friend, Maisie Barnes, is also there.

"How lovely to see you Maisie," Hattie says. "Where is Albert?"

"He's at home with his nurse. I can be a lady of leisure," her friend responds with some irony. Her husband Peter's family manufacture *Barnes Best Pickles,* and Maisie initially found herself struggling to occupy her time as she is no longer able to teach as a married woman, but she is also unable to assist at the pickle factory, which her two sisters-in-law run so well, and her limited office skills are not required. She and her husband had briefly lived near them in Southwark, but returned to Sheerness, as Peter is permanently assigned to the *Naval Flying School* in Eastchurch, and is now part of the newly formed *Royal Air Force.*

Hattie smiles, knowing that Maisie has thrown herself into a number of organisations set up to help with the war. "How's the *Linen League?"* Hattie asks.

"It's getting harder to get enough clean white rags to make bandages, as the war drags on," Maisie replies. "We've had to use our stock at the *St John Ambulance.* There have been so many wounded civilians in the recent air raids that we've almost run out. Still, at least I can ensure that we keep our own supplies for use on our own people."

"Maisie has recruited me to the *War Work Depot*," Rosie says, as she busies herself making tea for her friends.

The *War Work Depot* makes, sorts, and sends garments to the front. Maisie ran the collection of items, like knitted socks and mufflers. These are made by the schools and various organisations, like church leagues and girls' recreational clubs. The depot then packages them for despatch to the soldiers overseas. These items are affectionately known as *soldiers' comforts*. There is a mass knitting frenzy across the country that has started as a response to the gaps in uniform supply. But the War Office is nervous about the colourful, quirky garments reaching soldiers at the front, and making them look like ragbags to both their allies, the French, and to their enemies, the Germans. So, they issue official knitting patterns, and warn the well-meaning women to limit the types of garments made. As an added restriction, they stipulate that only khaki wool should be used. Finally, the War Office introduces the *Kitchener stitch*, to improve the comfort of knitted socks for the men in the trenches. The *War Work Depot* ensures that only acceptable items are despatched to the front.

"I help with collecting monetary donations," Rosie explains. "Lots of people are willing to contribute, as the wool for a pair of socks costs one shilling and eight pence, and its nine pence for a pair of mittens, and not everyone enjoys knitting."

The two officers' wives are keen to do their bit and as these ladylike activities are considered suitable for married women, they busy themselves helping out. But the two women also love to catch up with Hattie, and keep in touch with their former school colleagues.

"Anyway, that's enough about our war work, I'd rather still be teaching. It's madness when there are such staff shortages that we married women can't," Maisie says.

"Tell us more about the football team you're coaching, Hattie. I do miss playing tennis with you in the summer. Tell me more about what independent women like you are able to get up to!" Rosie jokes.

The three of them settle down around the table with their tea for a chat. Rosie's four-year-old son, Sammy, plays with his toy ships in a large enamel bowl of water, on the back step, under the supervision of his nine-year-old cousin, Alberta.

She is Rosie's sister Betty's illegitimate daughter, whom their mother is raising as her own.

"It's all very exciting, we are entering the *Ladies Dockyard Cup* and there's a new cricket league starting, just for ladies!" Hattie brings them up to date, then moves on to what is happening with Victor. Their plans for his come uppance are still a bit nebulous. They intend to trick Victor into removing his trousers, and to be confronted by the Rear Admiral, but the "how" remains uncertain. Just then, there is uproar from Sammy, as he knocks over the bowl in an attempt to stop Alberta playing with the boats, and the water goes all over his little sailor suit. The child howls with all his might, as the water soaks him to his skin.

"Mama, Mama, pants off, pants off!" he shrieks, as he pulls at his wet clothing.

Hattie, Maisie, and Rosie exchange looks. "That solves part of the riddle," says Hattie, as Rosie reaches out to divest Sammy of his wet things, "We just need to work out who and where now!"

*****

"I'm not really interested in the football the girls are playing, but feel I have to show willing,"

Mrs Eames confides in Mrs Jinks, when she finds herself cornered by the town gossip in the High Street. "The ladies from the loft haven't been playing as a team prior to Mrs Bennington inviting us to enter the cup she is championing. Two of my girls, Mabel and Bessie, were previously in other dockyard sides, and it's fallen to them to try to knock the rest of the girls into shape and make a team."

"Aren't your ladies a bit older than most of those girls?" Mrs Jinks queries, "I hear some of the teams are getting quite good. My Alfred went to watch them at the Wellmarsh the other day."

"Well, yes, Iris Deadman is thirty-eight and Lizzie Wade's forty, but they are willing to play." She doesn't say that she thinks Iris is a little too hefty, and will have been better suited to rugby. But she is good in goal, blocking a fair bit of space.

Mrs Eames has gone along to a couple of practices, but doesn't understand the rules. During a friendly, one girl is sent off for a foul, and she naively asks, "When do you go back on the pitch?" much to the derision of her colleagues. But the senior managers are keen for all the areas where the women work to have teams, so she stands in the spring rain and watches a bunch of women chase the ball around.

"Our first match is against the *Office Staff Ladies*," she explains. "They are even less of a team than my girls. They are a bit more stuck up. The men in the offices are no help, as they are the sort who played cricket or hockey, or the kind of sports played at grammar schools or posh public schools. If it wasn't for the local men who worked their way up from messenger boys through the dockyard exam system, there would be nobody in the offices to give them any coaching."

But, fortunately for the *Loft Ladies*, the efforts of the male office workers turn out to be a fruitless exercise and the *Office Staff Ladies* lose by two goals to nil. Mrs Eames finds herself facing a second cup match against the *WAAC,* who have played a hard game against the *Torpedo Amazons* and have scraped a one - nil win.

"It seems a little unfair that the *Loft Ladies* played the *Office Staff Ladies*, as neither side is a serious team. I've heard grumblings that they should have both been eliminated in the first round," Mrs Jinks says, eyeing Mrs Eames to see if she will rise to the implied insult to her girls.

"Well, that is because some people don't know how fixtures are arranged. Mr Phillips and the other senior staff did a blind draw, and that's just how the matches fell," Mrs Eames responds, as though she is knowledgeable about such things, when she too had hoped her ladies would be out of the cup, so they could forget all about football till next year.

The semi-final match between the *WAAC* and *Loft Ladies* is set for April 13th, at the recreation ground, and the loft is filled with trepidation as a result. Mrs Eames takes the opportunity of Mrs Swift coming by to escape Mrs Jinks, and goes back to her objective of seeing what she can buy on the ration.

The government had started to ration sugar in January 1918. They will introduce rationing of meat, butter, margarine, and cheese by the end of April, but these items are already hard to come by. Everyone is issued with ration cards, and has to register with a local butcher and grocer. Mrs Eames has registered at the International Stores, in the High Street, and at Mr Palmer's butcher shop, on the corner of her road. She has chosen the International, as they are advertising that they are now employing two thousand women across the country, to release men for the front. It is also common knowledge that Mitchell's Grocers had been prosecuted for selling margarine and calling it butter, as well as adulterating the milk; in a small town, that kind of news spread quickly. But, added to that, the International Stores are also opening later in the evening, until nine o'clock, to accommodate working women. So, she stops off on her way home to buy some cheese and macaroni, which is promoted as a good substitute for potatoes, and is only fourpence ha'penny a pound. She plans to make macaroni cheese to Mrs Beeton's recipe, but substituting margarine for butter, and doing without the extra cheese and breadcrumbs for a topping.

She joins the inevitable queue, which inches slowly along in front of the plate glass windows that still proudly display larger than life empty packages of items no longer available to buy without a ration card: tea, coffee, sugar, butter. As she nears the doorway, Victor emerges from the store, carrying his mother's shopping for her. Mrs Eames can hear Mrs Banks remonstrating with her son, who is sporting a painful looking black eye.

"I told you to keep away from West Minster. You know those two mad Glaswegians, Rab and Ginger McDonald are looking for you. Though, why that man hasn't taken a hand to that slut of a daughter, where it's deserved, I don't know."

"Shush, Mum. Someone will hear you," Victor responds, eyeing Mrs Eames with his good eye. "It wasn't them, just leave it!" he hisses.

Beryl Eames watches the couple retreating down the High Street, and she can feel her hackles rising. After Alice's court case, one of the loft ladies, Bessie Smart, has told her that Victor followed her home a few times. He cornered her and asked if she was lonely at night, as she is a widow, and tried to push his way in through her front door. He only stopped when one of the dockyard chippies, who lived next door, heard Bessie's cries for help, and came out and threatened him with a hammer. He has left Bessie alone since then, but now she is afraid to walk home alone. It is only playing football that has rebuilt the girl's confidence again.

As she watches him walk down the road, Beryl sees Hattie West emerging from Mr Bartlett the greengrocers, opposite. Hattie waves and crosses the road to speak to her.

"Hello, Beryl, that greengrocer weighs more mud than spud," she says, tutting at the contents of her shopping basket. "How are your footballers coming along?"

209

"Fine," Mrs Eames responds, still distracted by seeing Victor. Hattie turns to follow the other woman's gaze.

"Ah, Victor Banks," Hattie says, her eyes narrowing.

By now, Mrs Eames is at the front of the queue and about to go in.

"Can you wait for me a moment, I'd like a chat," she says, placing her hand on Hattie's arm.

"Certainly, I just need to buy some fish heads for Tibby, if the fishmonger has any. People are making fishcakes from cod cheeks, and it's sometimes hard to get enough scraps for the cat."

When Beryl comes out of the shop with her purchases, she exchanges some pleasantries with Hattie about how she has bought some "evaporated" fruit salad, on an impulse. It only cost five pence a pound, and promises it equals five pound of fresh fruit. "I'm not sure how much water to add, and how long to soak it so the pieces become plump fruit again, but I can take out a few slices at a time for my dessert, and the rest will keep for ages," she explains, eyeing Hattie's tinned peaches that the greengrocer is stocking now, through want of fresh fruit. "I've bought margarine instead of butter, as it's in such short supply, but even that cost seven pence a pound," she tuts, before she suggests, "Shall we pop into the snug of the *Rose and Crown*? We can be private there."

Hattie agrees and Beryl leads the way to a side door down an alley, hoping they won't be observed. The smell of beer and urine is not welcoming, but once inside, the snug bar is cosy enough.

As the October 1915 *'No Treating Order'* means that any drink ordered has to be paid for by the person drinking it, each woman orders and pays for her own refreshment. Hattie asks for a glass of lemonade, whilst Mrs Eames buys half a pint of beer.

They sit at a small corner table, and Mrs Eames gazes into her glass for a moment, before saying, "One of my girls was hassled by Victor before he turned his attention to Alice. It is only after the court case that she told me." She fills in the details, whilst Hattie listens.

"Tilly tells me that he is following Alice outside the dockyard, but she won't complain again, as she doesn't think anyone will take notice," Hattie reports back to Beryl.

"He's got a black eye. I heard from Mrs Pamplin that he tried rubbing up against one of the foundry girls behind one of the sheds, but she is made of tougher stuff, and she belted him one." The two women laugh at the image.

"He really needs teaching a lesson," says Beryl, locking eyes with Hattie.

Hattie takes a breath, and says, "We have a plan, maybe you can help. We need to work out where and when."

Hattie goes over their scheme so far, and says, "If we can arrange for someone to spill something on his trousers in the colour loft, you can offer to dry them, and lend him something to wear."

Beryl's face brightens, "Count me in," she responds.

******

Ruth Pamplin marches into John Phillips' office without knocking. John is reading a memo, and looks up in surprise.

"That Victor Banks touched one of my girls," she announces, before he has a chance to speak. "He got Vicky Watts behind the coke store. He told her there is an injured kitten there and asked her to help. When she went to look for it with him, he tried to pin her against the wall and touch her bosom! He picked on the wrong one there. She's from bargee stock, and gave him a left hook."

Afterwards, the other women tell Ruth that, in her youth, Vicky's grandmother once fought the female prize fighter Hattie Madders (*The Mad Hatter*), at a side show of a travelling fair. Madders was the only woman to hold the boxing *Heavyweight Champion of the World* title. Apparently, the grandmother almost had the better of her opponent, but caught her foot in her long skirt and had been knocked out. It is she who had taught Vicky to box as a child.

"Victor tried to whine that he would report Vicky for assault. She's only told us today because she heard he still follows that little Alice McDonald about. He needs to be stopped!" Ruth finishes, and thumps the desk to emphasise her point.

Mr Phillips sits open mouthed. He has heard that Victor is harassing Alice from Hattie. He has withdrawn Victor's category of doing *"work of National importance"*. However, until the next military tribunal, he is stuck with Victor on the work force. It isn't helped by the fact that Victor's uncle is part of the Tribunal Board. Victor will need to be seriously discredited before he finds himself in khaki.

"I'm sorry to hear that Mrs Pamplin, Ruth," he says, trying to calm her. "Let me think on it."

"And apparently, one of the loft ladies was assaulted before Alice, but has only just told Mrs Eames," she says, over her shoulder as she leaves. "He should be locked up!"

*****

After work, John meets up with Hattie for football practice. Hattie is desperate to tell him about the latest revelations about Victor, but can see that John is preoccupied. The next cup game against the *Rigging Shop Roses* is the following week, and this game will be harder. *The Roses* have beaten the *Wrens* quite convincingly, and have their sights set on the final. However, after about half an hour he says, "I hear Banks is up to his old tricks, and has a black eye for his trouble."

"Yes, I've heard that too. He thinks he is invulnerable."

"My plan to get him out is too slow. I need to get him discredited."

Hattie looks at her friend, and decides to include him in the plan. He will be a great asset. "Can I tell you something in confidence?" she begins.

When she finishes, Mr Phillips thinks quietly for a moment. Then, he says, "Right, you have a plan of what to do, once Victor is in the colour loft. We need to work out how to get him in there, and how to keep him there when the King arrives. This could be treason, but I have an idea!"

******

The Saturday cup match between the *Naval Stores Ladies* and the *Rigging Shop Roses* arrives in no time. Mrs Bennington's daughters, Amelia and Daphne, are despatched to fly the flag, and they arrive at a quarter to one, for the one o'clock kick-off. It is a fine spring day, but a squally breeze keeps the temperature down.

Gladys and Gertie have been practising their passing skills and feel that they are now really playing football, rather than just chasing the ball. Alice is small and nippy, and can often evade attempts by the opposition to tackle her. Before the game starts, they feel that with Gertie and Gladys making goals for Alice to score, they should do well. However, the *Roses* are a thorny bunch, and are not afraid to use their elbows for a sly dig, when the referee is looking the other way.

By half time, the *Stores Ladies* are two - nil down. They traipse into the dressing room, feeling that they have lost already. Hattie has some oranges, and gives them all a half to suck on. They are sharp, but still sweet. Oranges are a war time luxury, but she asked her friend Maisie for help as her husband, Peter, is part of the *Barnes Best Pickles* family. When he was wooing Maisie, he had bought enough oranges, so that every girl in the school could have one, all just to impress Maisie. As requested, he has popped in with some on his way back to the *Royal Naval Flying School* in Eastchurch, after visiting his sisters at the pickle factory in London. He had acquired a dozen oranges from Covent Garden. This rare treat is a great pick-me-up, and starts to lift the girls' spirits.

John knocks on the door of the girls' dressing room and enters when they all shout in unison, "Come in." He calls them together for a team talk. "Games aren't won out on the pitch. They are won up here," he says, tapping his head. "The moment you think you have lost, you have. You need to think like winners. Picture yourselves next month lifting the cup. Press forward and you can outrun them. You are quicker than they are, nippier.

You are more skilled than them. You have more stamina. So, they will be tired in the second half. You can run rings round them and whenever you are in line with the goal - shoot!"

When they prepare to run back out onto the pitch, Mr Phillips passes them each a second half of an orange. "Suck on this as you go out there, and their mouths will go dry. They will be thirsty for the whole forty-five minutes," he says, tapping his nose conspiratorially.

When the whistle goes, signalling the end of the game, the *Stores Ladies* have turned it round and finished three - two. They are through to the final. Amelia and Daphne Bennington come over and shake all the girls' hands.

"We are so looking forward to the final," says Daphne, as she walks down the line.

"Although I have applied to be a nurse with the Red Cross, and am looking forward to being a VAD. I may well be posted before then," the older sister, Amelia adds. "But if I'm not, I will be there."

Daphne gives her a look; Amelia is not yet eighteen, and won't be called upon to serve until she is. "When do you find out who you are playing?" Daphne asks, ignoring her sister's attempt to appear grown up in front of the girls from the yard. Even though several are no older than they are, they have more experience of life.

"Next week, the *Colour Loft Ladies* are playing the *WAAC*," says Tilly. "*The Stores Ladies* will find out who we are playing in the cup final from the result of that game."

Amelia nods politely and returns to the car, without another word, leaving Daphne to run after her to catch up.

*****

Hattie and John both go along to watch the other semi-final, and are surprised at the discipline shown by the *WAACs*. When the *Naval Stores Ladies* aren't playing, the couple have got into the habit of going to watch a rival team together, to pick up tactics and assess the opposition. Afterwards, they will stop for a cup of tea together so they can discuss what they have learned about the opposition. But they find they enjoy each other's company as much as anything. John has never known a woman to be as sport mad as Hattie is.

The *WAAC's* coach is a PT instructor with the *Royal Garrison Artillery,* based at the Wellmarsh. He has trained the women in the same manner as he has trained the men, and they play well as a team. The *Loft Ladies* don't stand a chance, and the game turns into a bit of a rout, with the *WAAC* winning by seven goals to one, and even that was an own goal.

Mrs Bennington is there and comes across to speak to Hattie and Mr Phillips. "What an exciting game," she says politely, even though it is obvious that she has been reading a magazine in her car whilst the match was played. "I'm looking forward to the final between the *Naval Stores Ladies* and the *WAAC*. There will be a garden party at Admiralty House afterwards for all the teams, so please tell your girls. It will start at four o'clock, to give them time to change."

They thank her, and she continues, "It will be a busy few days, as the King is visiting the week before. Have you received a copy of his itinerary yet, Mr Phillips?" She produces a copy out of her bag and looks at it. "He is visiting the women in the colour loft, the rigging shop, and the foundry. I'm sure your girls will be keen to wave to him on his route. I will, of course, be with Queen Mary, so that I can make sure that she doesn't come across any of the rough types one sometimes encounters in a dockyard. I notice that, unlike when the King passes through the foundry and the rigging shop, he will exit by a different door to the one he enters by when he visits the colour loft, before his next appointment in the Quadrangle. I believe that it can be very confusing in there, as there are several large cupboards in the loft, and the doors all look the same. Mistakes sometimes happen, don't they? It will be dreadful if someone innocently comes across something they shouldn't there. Heads might roll, especially if someone is hiding there for whatever reason," she says meaningfully, as she takes her leave.

Just then, Mrs Eames emerges from the changing rooms and seeing Hattie, waves to her. Hattie beckons her over and says, "Mrs Bennington has been updating us on the King's visit. She says that he will be coming into the colour loft. Mr Phillips and I think we can finalise our plans for the day now."

*****

Miss Windley dreads handing Miss Garrett the post every day. The headmistress writes copious letters every week, both at home and at school, and will spend ages talking about her current pet hobby horses. She writes letters to the national newspapers about world affairs and to the local ones about smaller issues. Only that week, she has written to the *Sheerness Advertiser* about the plight of the female scavengers. Poor Miss Windley finds herself listening to Miss Garrett talking about the women who are sweeping the roads and collecting the rubbish. No men are willing to apply for such lowly jobs, in a time of labour shortages, despite the better pay of four shillings a day, plus twelve shillings a week war bonus.

"Do you know that on wet days, the women are sent home, without pay, whilst the men are given wet weather clothing or found work indoors?" Miss Garrett says, "And the poor women suffer abuse from men passers-by, which their male counterparts don't." The headmistress is incensed by this unfair treatment, and has begun some correspondence with the Borough Surveyor and the Editor of the local paper on the matter.

She writes to many of her former lodgers and colleagues, even when they still live locally. And, of course, she writes to her star pupils, especially anybody who has gained a place at a teacher training college.

That morning, there is a letter from Miss Metcalf, who was one of her outstanding students. Miss Windley has, of course, already read the letter. She has to decide what post is handed to

Miss Garrett and what she has to deal with herself. Letters about why a child is sick are her domain, but letters from the School Attendance Inspector about the same child, are Miss Garrett's.

"Miss Metcalf has written to me to say that she is training to teach Pitman's and typewriting, and that she hopes that the Broadway School might look into buying some typewriting machines after the war. She would love to be able to return to Sheerness to teach some of the brighter girls this skill, should there be a vacancy at the school. How wonderful, when the school leaving age is raised to fourteen, later this year. It will be a real boon if the school can teach a modern trade to the older girls."

Miss Windley usually says nothing, but for once she can see the potential and says, "The dockyard donated three old machines to the school. They are currently in storage, due to lack of space in the makeshift classrooms. We can start with those."

"Yes, why didn't I think of that before?" Miss Garrett asks herself, even though it's Miss Windley's idea. "If we can teach Alice McDonald to type, she can apply for work that takes her away from the naval stores, and it will help her to get away from the likes of Mr Banks!" She thinks for a while, then says, "It will be summer before Miss Metcalf graduates from college, but Mrs Barnes took private secretarial lessons whilst she lived in Southwark, and helped her sisters-in-law to run the pickle factory. I will write to Mrs Barnes and ask for her help to teach Alice some secretarial skills."

Miss Windley nods with resignation at having the credit for her idea stolen, and says, "I'll get the caretaker to look at the machines."

*****

Cissie and Ernie

"Next week will be a very unsatisfactory one for trying to teach the children," Miss Garrett says to Miss Windley, as she paces restlessly up and down the small school office like a caged animal. The room is so small that the headmistress can't build up to her normal brisk walking speed and this just adds to her annoyance. Even when she stands still, she is shifting her weight from one foot to the other.

"Monday is Bank Holiday, as it's Whit Monday, and Tuesday is an additional holiday given by the Education Board. So, school returns on Wednesday, only to close again the next day for the King's visit. It's ridiculous!"

"But it will be lovely for all the children to see the King's party pass by as a special treat," Miss Windley ventures, only to be ignored.

"Then, Friday is *Empire Day.* The timetable will be made up of special lessons on the *Growth and Greatness of the British Empire*, and at twelve o'clock the children will be dismissed for the remainder of the day. We won't get any real work done at all," she sniffs.

At assembly, Miss Garrett stands at the front of the school once again, and goes over how the girls are to behave at the King's visit to inspect the dockyard. "Right, girls, what do you say if one of the Royal party asks you about your school activities?"

Several hands shoot up and Miss Garrett points to one of the cleaner looking girls, as she believes they are also more intelligent.

"We're to say that we are busy knitting socks to send to the soldiers at the front."

"Good girl. And what else do we say?" She selects another child.

"'We are giving our pocket money to the fund for soldiers comforts."

"That's right. Anything else?" She points to another student to answer.

"We are to say we are very brave during the air raids."

Miss Garrett gives a frozen smile, because she hopes that neither the King nor the Queen will ask about the air raids. Many of the girls have nightmares and, as a result, some families have moved away. Typical of men, Miss Garrett thinks, they invent a flying machine, and just a few years later they use it to try to kill innocent people by dropping bombs on them. Even before the war, a

Zeppelin had flown over the town one day, and questions were asked in Parliament. It was believed it was the German's testing out the possibility of staging air raids, but they never admitted to it, and what other country has Zeppelins?

Over the length of the war, there is much damage to the town. Two houses in Invicta Road were blown up with everyone in them, as well as the various military targets. Nearly a dozen service men and half a dozen local men were killed, as were two innocent women, leaving their children motherless.

One of her staff, Miss Watson, has not been well since the last air raid. She has injured her back and hand where some debris hit her, knocking her to the ground and pinning her there until she was rescued. But she has been pluckily attending school, despite her ordeal. The doctor says she is bruised internally. Still, there are a lot of air raids where there are no casualties, so we should be thankful for small mercies, Miss Garrett thinks.

When the air raids take place during the day, you can see the Hun air men leaning out of the Zeppelins to throw the bombs down on the town. Luckily, they don't play cricket in Germany, Miss Garrett muses; their skill at throwing a hand bomb is limited, and they miss more times than they hit their targets. But it was a shame that time they killed a number of horses in that field. The wounded horses screamed and screamed in pain, and had to be shot. All senseless.

After assembly, Miss Garrett returns to her office to complete the school log. She scratches her narrow nose, as she considers what to write, but beyond the attendance numbers she can't find much to say.

"Is there any news from the Education Board about filling the vacancies?" she asks Miss Windley. They are short staffed, as some teachers have not yet been replaced when they leave. Miss Young is the latest person to leave the school's staff. Her worries about the air raids led to her resigning, and she moved away. It is going to be difficult to fill her vacancy, as it is almost impossible to get teachers to come into Sheerness, which is seen as a "War Area."

"Not today, but we can ask for one of the married ladies back, until there is a suitable candidate," Miss Windley suggests.

The Education Board is forced to relax the convention that, on marriage, women resign from teaching posts. However, they are only employing married women where there are staff shortages, and it is accepted that appointments are liable to be terminated at a month's notice, if suitable unmarried alternative candidates can be found. This means some women are working a few months, then are replaced by the Board by a spinster or a widow, only to be re-employed again a short while later, when another vacancy occurs.

"I suppose we will have to do that, but it can be disruptive to the children, to keep changing teachers. I can't see why they don't do away with the silly rule altogether. Nobody asks the men to resign on marriage."

At the end of the school day, she holds a staff meeting to discuss the preparations for the Royal visit. She feels she has just enough teachers to be able to organise the day. Her friend, Ena Briggs, has been helping her. Ena is usually practical, but the prospect of seeing the King and Queen has gone to her head.

"The girls can make some little cakes to offer the King and Queen, should they stop to speak to any of them," Ena suggests, full of enthusiasm.

Miss Garrett points out the impracticalities, with a little dismissive tut. "That won't work, as the students will need to stand for at least an hour holding trays. They will attract wasps and flies, and, if it is hot, the buttercream will melt, that's if we can get enough butter off the ration!" she finishes, dismissively. Ena sulks after that for a little while, but she comes back into the conversation later with more sensible ideas of how to make flags out of old sheets and red and blue ink, for the girls to wave.

Hattie West has been drilling the girls to march smartly to their allotted space along the road from the dockyard railway station to the main gates, and then to stand up straight whilst waiting. "I tell them they don't want to look like the back end of a Yankee destroyer. I say they need to smarten up and be a credit to their mothers and fathers working in the dockyard," she says, straightening her own swimmer's shoulders. She pours herself more tea from the big tea pot that they have brought with them from the Broadway School to the Napier Road Hall, where the small kitchen is also serving as their staff room.

"We need to ensure they are all dressed in their best clothes," Ena suggests. "I've been making new pinafores for those girls who don't have decent ones, so if anyone has any old sheets for use for flags or pinafores, please bring them in for me."

Miss Garrett makes a list of materials needed and a list of volunteers. Several teachers offer to get the girls ship shape for the big day. Miss Beswick proffers starch for a crisp finish; this is also hard to come by, as it is a by-product of the food industry and there is no food to spare. Miss Derby promises a supply of hair ribbons from her brother's drapers shop. Other teachers offer an assortment of items to make the day go well.

Organisation matters, the headmistress thinks, whilst her teachers know she has no practical skills to offer. They just smile behind her back, knowing that making the day a success will be down to them.

******

Beryl Eames needs to enlist the help of some of her ladies with the plan to embarrass Victor Banks. She takes Bessie Smart, his previous victim, to one side and outlines their plan to her. When she finishes, she says, "I need some assistance to pull it off. Are you willing to help? You will get the satisfaction of knowing that he has got his come uppance."

"Count me in," Bessie responds enthusiastically. "I will ask Lottie Payne and Mabel Taverner to help as well. I know that he has been seen watching Mabel at football, and Lottie had a run in with his mother when she was expecting her last baby. His mother said it can't be Lottie's late husband's as the dates don't add up. But she was just overdue, and anyone could see that as the baby came out as dry and cracked as an old shoe."

Beryl knows that Mrs Banks can be quite poisonous when she puts her mind to it, and can see how upset the new widow would have been at that accusation. It could have jeopardised her widow's pension, as well as her reputation.

Bessie has a debt to repay, and her friends in the loft are happy to help her. Sarah Knowles is keen to help when Lottie approaches her as she lives next door to Bessie, and it was her brother who chased Victor off.

Beryl's boss has asks her to choose six women to meet the King. She doesn't tell the girls this, as she doesn't want any to feel like favourites, and at the same time, the girls involved in the scheme with Victor will need to be excluded from meeting the Royal party, as they can't do both.

The four conspirators hold a planning meeting in Mrs Eames' office one evening after work to decide the best way to catch Victor.

"I suggest we pour hot tea over him – not too hot, but enough so he can be persuaded he needs attention," suggests Mabel.

"Yes, then I will offer him first aid to treat his injuries. We will need to clear a space in one of the big cupboards to be a first aid room," Lottie adds. Everyone is keen on first aid since the air raids began. Within the first six months of the war, St John Ambulance had twelve thousand trained volunteers, and Lottie was amongst them. It was Princess Christian, Queen Victoria's daughter, who had championed the subject back in 1882. This royal seal of approval elevated the matter in everyone's mind.

"I've managed to get some basic supplies from stores, now that the dockyard has started to see the benefits of first aid. But I've had to improvise other items from what's available," Lottie continues.

"It's going to be a juggling act to be ready for the King's visit and also produce a normal day's work. Everyone will need to look like they are busy. And, at the same time, your smocks will need to be as clean as possible, and the loft needs to stay pristine," Mrs Eames realises. "His Majesty is due to arrive at half past ten at the dockyard station, and from there he will be visiting the various workshops to meet the staff. Our shift starts at eight o'clock, so everyone will need to stay smart that long. And all the time, we need to make sure Victor gets his come uppance."

She runs through the plan to the assembled women. "Mr Phillips is going to send Victor to me with a note at ten o'clock. Victor will no doubt dawdle and arrive at quarter past." The women nod agreement at this, as Victor is a well-known skiver. "We will need to delay him further, and keep him here until around quarter to eleven."

"We can offer him a cup of tea then, ready to pour it on his trousers, and get him into the first aid room," schemes Mable.

Mrs Eames nods agreement, then continues. "When the King comes into the loft, Mr Phillips will be part of the party, and he will discreetly open the door to the first aid room, and ask Victor what he is playing at with no trousers on."

"And sack him on the spot for spying on us girls, the creep," Bessie says.

"The other officials will never know, as the King will move on through a different door to exit the loft, and from there, visit the foundry where Mrs

Pamplin will be waiting, without needing to pass back to where Victor is hiding. What can possibly go wrong?"

******

Miss Garrett wrote to Maisie, and set out her idea of teaching Alice to typewrite, and has received a pleasing reply. Maisie is keen to get involved, as she misses teaching, and can spare a few hours once a week to help train Alice. Miss Garrett has got the caretaker to fetch the machines out of storage and fix up the best of the three. A new ribbon is purchased, along with a sheath of appropriate paper and some carbon sheets, so that Alice can learn how to make duplicates.

Maisie pops in to look at the machine one afternoon, after school. After a quick inspection, she says, "I'm a bit rusty, but I'm sure I will be able to teach Alice the basics. What's her grammar like?"

Miss Garrett sniffs, as she remembers Alice's absences from school once her sister Cathy was expecting. But, before that, Alice enjoyed English in class. "She isn't bad at grammar. Her handwriting isn't neat, so maybe once she can typewrite, she will come on leaps and bounds."

Maisie sits down at the typewriter, inserts a sheet of paper, and does a few practice sentences, clattering the keys in a staccato rhythm. She isn't fast, but she is accurate, so makes less mistakes.

"Right, the next thing then is to make arrangements with Alice," she says, looking satisfied at her attempts. "I remember how sad I was to find she had been taken out of school to work for Miss Dobbs. I was so upset that she was denied her education. I'm really looking forward to teaching her. It will make such a difference to her employment choices."

******

Miss Garrett wastes no time in seeking Alice out. She goes to her home one evening, after she knows that football training has finished, and knocks on her door in Khartoum Road. Rab comes to the door, freshly washed, after his shift shovelling coal all day at the gas works. He is smoking one of his hand rolled cigarettes that has turned his fingers yellow, and makes all his clothes smell of tobacco. He knows Miss Garrett by sight, everyone does, and knows her reputation of being a busy body. He wonders if she's come to check up on Cissie. She and Ernie had returned to their rooms in Gordon

Road, the day after her mother Ivy had been released from prison.

"Is Alice there, please?" Miss Garrett enquires.

Rab looks surprised, as he eyes the severe looking woman in her itchy looking tweed suit. "Aye, she is. I thought you were here for Cissie," he says, getting ready to retreat behind the door to fetch Alice.

"Cissie Dummott? Is she here? She hasn't been at school for a while."

"No, she's back with her mammy. We only see them when they need something." He slips away, and Alice comes to the door.

"Hello, Miss Garrett, can I help you?" Alice asks, surprised that the headmistress has sought her out. She has not been in contact with her since the court case.

"Now, Alice, I have been thinking about you and your place in the dockyard stores, and I have decided that you should learn how to typewrite. Then, you will be able to apply for a job in the office, away from the likes of Mr Banks." This is said as a statement, rather than a suggestion to help improve Alice. "Mrs Barnes, (you will remember her as Miss Kendrick) has kindly offered to teach you. So, you will come every Tuesday to the Napier Road Hall, as soon as you finish work. We will go into the office, and be out of Mr Pope's way when he is leading the scouts."

Miss Garrett is about to turn and walk away, her instructions delivered, when Alice says, "But Tuesday is football training with Mrs West."

"Oh dear, well, you will have to give that up. Tuesdays is the day that Mrs Barnes can do."

"No, Miss Garrett, I'm sorry, but I can't do Tuesdays. Thank you very much, and please thank Mrs Barnes, but I can't give up football. We're in the cup, and I can't let the team down."

Miss Garrett isn't used to being contradicted, but she listens to Alice and says, "Very well, I will see if Mrs Barnes can do Wednesdays."

"Thank you," says Alice. "I'd like to learn typewriting, so I can work in the dockyard offices. Can Tilly come too?"

Miss Garrett gives her the briefest of nods. I will need to get the caretaker to set up a second machine, she thinks. She then asks, "And can you take me to see your cousin Cissie, whilst I'm here?"

*****

Cissie answers the door, holding Ernie's hand tightly, as he is frightened of strangers at the door. His mother's customers are usually drunk and can be aggressive. If the visitors are sober, their mother usually owes them money, so they shout through the letter box and thump the door, until something is paid to them on account. Cissie is horrified to see Miss Garrett, who is known for her nosiness, standing on the doorstep. She almost wishes it was one of her mother's callers. She is only mildly reassured by the sight of Alice.

"May I come in?" asks the headmistress, moving towards the door, without waiting for a response.

Cissie stands back to allow her to pass. Alice is in a dilemma whether to stay or go. The Dummott's are not really their family, but everyone treats them as though they are cousins. She knows her Mum will be cross if she returns home without finding out what Miss Garrett wants, but, at the same time, she is keen not to add another two mouths to be fed from the family income, now that she contributes to it. But since her outburst on the day of the court hearing, she is doing what she can to help her cousins, so, in the end, her mother's curiosity will need to be satisfied, and Alice follows Miss Garrett in.

Cissie does her best to keep the two rooms clean, but it's hard. She is concerned that Miss Garrett will judge her on what she sees there. One room serves as a bedroom for the children and their mother. It contains one big bed, covered by some threadbare blankets and an old coat. Sometimes, it serves as Ivy's place of work when she has sailors to stay on extended shore leave. She keeps a green silk kimono style wrap to wear on these occasions. She bought it from Cissie's school jumble sale, a couple of years ago. Most other mothers were buying second hand coats and clothes for their children, but Ivy spotted the kimono and had to have it. It is beautifully embroidered, with exotic birds in colourful silks, and when she wears it, she feels that she is a courtesan in a palace, rather than a common prostitute eking a living from sailors. The kimono must have belonged to someone "well-to-do" in the past, as it is such fine quality, and even after all this time, Ivy fancies that an expensive perfume still lingers in the seams.

When Ivy has clients staying over, the children have to sleep in the scullery, which consists of an open fire with a trivet for cooking, and a battered table with a couple of stick chairs. A three-legged stool doubles as a table for an oil lamp. There is a gas mantle to give light in the scullery, but not in the bedroom. However, the meter usually needs feeding, so, most of the time, the rooms are lit by candles. They share a privy at the end of the yard with two other families; an outside tap is nearby to provide the family's water supply.

Miss Garrett sniffs and looks down her narrow nose at what she finds.

"Where's your mother?" she asks Cissie, looking around for any sign of the woman.

"She's popped out to the shops. She must be stuck in a queue at the butchers again. She is always buying us chops or steak for dinner," responds Cissie, thinking on her feet.

Miss Garrett looks at her and knows this is untrue. Just then, the front door flies open, and Maggie McDonald bursts in. Rather late in the day, Rab has alerted her that the headmistress is snooping. She is annoyed that he didn't call her when Miss Garrett first knocked, nor did Alice tell her where she was going before she brought Miss

Garrett round to Ivy's rooms. She will give her daughter a piece of her mind later.

"Cissie's just tidying up before coming back to ours for her tea with little Ernie," says Maggie, under pressure. "I keep an eye on them when their Mum is out." She starts chivvying Cissie into getting Ernie ready to return to Khartoum Road and directing Alice to help.

"I expect to see you in class tomorrow," Miss Garrett says, as she opens the front door to leave, giving both Cissie and Maggie a hard look that brooks no disagreement.

As soon as Maggie feels Miss Garrett is out of earshot, she looks at Cissie and says, "We can't keep on like this. I will have to tell Rab that I'm taking you in, or else you will end up in the workhouse."

*****

Maggie packs Cissie off to school the following morning with Mary and Dolly. She has missed so much schooling, but is certainly bright. She wonders if it is too late for the girl to catch up. Maybe she can find her some work to do. Children younger than the school leaving age of twelve often work in factories or on farms. Alice was working before she was twelve, while Dolly and Walter have been working every day, as well as going to school for a couple of years. The children's earnings are a helpful addition to the family's income. She knows that Miss Garrett will be back if she doesn't send Cissie to school. Once that woman decides to help, you will be helped, like it or not. The Minister for Education, Herbert Fisher, claims that over half a million children have been 'prematurely' put to work. A bill has been put before Parliament to raise the school leaving age to fourteen, and will be law by the summer. For many families that will be two year's lost earnings from the child. Maggie knows that Miss Garrett will want Cissie to be in school now, so that she can catch up by the time she is fourteen.

Ernie stands at the door and watches Cissie disappear up the road with her cousins. His bottom lip trembles, and his eyes fill with tears. A big snot bubble forms and pops, as he calls after his sister, "Issy, Issy."

"Cissie will be back for lunch, and you will see her then," says Maggie. "Why don't you play nicely with Little Rab, and I will find you a biscuit."

Ernie's face brightens at the prospect of a treat. There are never any biscuits in their rooms in

Gordon Road. Only his Auntie Maggie gives him anything nice to eat. She sits him down on the rag rug and finds him some wooden bricks to play with.

"Do you want to help me with the bunnies?" Maggie asks, a little later, taking Ernie's hand and leading him out the back, ducking under the full washing lines that criss-cross the yard. There are a dozen hutches now, as the rabbits breed prodigiously, and the family can sell the meat and skins. Maggie even boils up the entrails to sell for dog food to the neighbours. The children are sent to collect grass and dandelion leaves daily to supply the rabbits' needs. Ernie sits happily with one on his lap, whilst Maggie cleans out the hutches, and Little Rab changes the water.

That evening, Ernie sits with Cissie, as Maggie prepares to dish up some stew, with big hunks of bread for everyone. It smells delicious, and the broth contains chunks of onion and carrot, as well as fat blobs of pearl barley, that look like little grubs.

Ernie and Cissie are squashed up the end of the table, where a plank of wood is balanced across two chairs to make a bench. Ernie eyes the stew hungrily. His belly is never full at home, and he loves being at Auntie Maggie's, where it feels warm and safe, and he loves looking after the rabbits. He'd like to live here all the time, if only his own Mum could live here too.

"I don't want rabbit stew!" cries Little Rab. "I love the bunnies!" He stands up from the table and folds his arms in defiance.

"The left half is rabbit, and the right half is chicken," Maggie replies, indicating which is which in the big stew pot with her ladle, "You can have chicken for your dinner."

Little Rab sits down next to Ernie, and now looks expectantly towards his mother as she lifts the ladle in readiness. Maggie plunges the utensil into the pot. "I'll just give it a bit of a stir," she says, swirling the stew around, so that any demarcation of which meat is which is lost before serving a big spoonful up for her youngest son. But he eats it without questioning, accepting that the fictitious chicken is mixed up with the factual rabbit.

"How was school, Cissie?" Maggie asks, as she gives a plate to her cousin's daughter.

"It was good, Auntie Maggie. Miss Briggs is my teacher, and she says she will give me extra lessons at her house on Saturdays, to catch up."

"It will have to be in the afternoon, after you finish your chores."

"When will I be able to collect the maintenance money from the Parish, if I'm at school?"

"Don't worry about that," responds Maggie. "We will sort something out."

She hasn't yet told Rab that she is keeping the two children, so doesn't want any talk of permanent arrangements discussed at the table. And there is still Ivy to think of; some of the money is also for her keep from her husband. She will have to talk to her too.

*****

Reggie Symonds goes to the stores, just as a delivery has arrived. The carter has deposited a number of boxes outside the door, and left the girls to it; he is of the opinion that if women want to do a man's job, then they should do all of it, not just the easy bits. So, Reggie offers to assist Tilly and Alice carrying in the supplies to the storeroom at the back. He slightly regrets offering, as his dodgy foot pains him as he carries the boxes through. He is surprised that the girls can lift the heavy crates between them, and with his help, they make short work of it.

"Thanks, Reggie," Tilly says, as she reaches for the gemmy to get the lid off one of the boxes and reveal the contents.

"I just popped over to see if you are okay. I hear that Victor tried to touch up one of the foundry girls and got a black eye for his trouble. If I had been able to say something more helpful in court, he wouldn't have been able to do it again, and you wouldn't have to put up with him keep following you," Reggie explains to Alice, as he draws her aside.

Alice smiles at him, and says, "Thank you for walking me home. When you're there, he leaves me alone. I'm really grateful."

Reggie blushes. Although he has chatted to Alice many times since the incident, it is never directly mentioned. Tilly makes herself scarce behind the racking, pretending to record the delivery into the stock book, so Reggie screws up his courage and says, "Would you like to come to the pictures one evening? There's a new Buster Keaton and Fatty Arbuckle film on. I think it's called *Out West*."

"I like Buster Keaton, he's so funny."

"I love a western! Did you go to that Wild West show that came to town just before the war? It was fantastic! I remember there was this one cowboy in a white hat, who rescued this saloon girl. Even though he was tied up, he got out of his bonds, then he lassoed the Indian Chief and tied him up. He was such a hero!"

"I was working for Miss Dobbs back then, so I couldn't go. She let us go to the parade through the High Street though, so I did see the elephant and the midget horses."

"I'll take you to the Wild West show after the war, if it comes round again. I bet all those midget horses are at the front now pulling tiny howitzers!" he jokes.

A day and time are agreed, and Reggie leaves the stores with a spring in his step.

Tilly emerges from the racking, "A date! Wait till I tell the others!" she teases, laughing, and hugging her friend. She hopes this will help Alice put the Victor incident behind her, once and for all.

******

At football that Saturday, the *Naval Stores Ladies* beat the *Sheerness Dockyard Sparklers,* (as the electrical department women now call themselves) two - nil. Triumphant at scoring a goal, Alice showers and changes after the match. She loves the hot showers available at the Wellmarsh changing rooms. At home, she only gets a bath once a week, and that water is shared with her sisters, so nobody wants to be last in. Normally, she lingers and chats, enjoying the luxury of hot water on tap, but she slips away from her teammates, without them knowing about her date with Reggie. Tilly has kept quiet, despite bursting with excitement for her friend, as she knows that Alice is nervous.

Reggie is waiting on the corner outside the recreation ground, as he watched the game with a group of chums, and has taken great pride in Alice's performance. "That was a great goal you scored!" he says, as they walk towards the Picture Drome. "You must be pleased." They chat about the game, all the way up the road.

When they get to the cinema, Reggie pays for Alice's ticket to see the film. She has never walked out with a man before, and is a little wary of what he will expect, but Reggie is the perfect gentleman. He buys her a fish supper and walks her home afterwards. He doesn't try to kiss her or touch her, and parts with a cheery wave saying, "See you Monday at work." Reggie makes Alice feel safe.

*****

The Day of the King's Visit

Everything goes into overdrive ahead of the King's visit in the dockyard. Any outstanding repairs to the buildings from the January air raid are finally finished. Anywhere His Majesty is due to pass is repainted, corners where weeds grow are rooted out, windows are cleaned, and the roads swept.

The dockyard railway station was also hit during the same air raid, and men and women from the yard are sent to help spruce it up, ready for the Royal train. A set of steps is commissioned from the dockyard carpenters, so that the King and Queen can step down easily from the train to the awaiting car. The Royal railway carriage is being attached to the London, Chatham, and Dover Railway's charcoal grey locomotive, together with other carriages in their orangey brown livery for the lesser visitors.

The Dockyard Superintendent, Rear Admiral Bennington, is at pains to ensure everywhere in the yard is spick and span. All the managers and supervisors of the workshops that the King and Queen are due to visit have been given a stiff lecture on protocol, and told to deliver it to their staff. Nothing is to go wrong, and, if it does, heads will roll.

Within the workshops, Mr Phillips, Mrs Pamplin, and Mrs Eames, amongst others, have their work cut out polishing machines that are meant for industrial use and not just for display, keeping the war effort going, whilst keeping the equipment pristine. They have set-to folding and tidying away all manner of items, and scrubbing and sweeping corners that no one saw and are unlikely to see on the twenty-third of May either.

The smocks and overalls of all the staff, both male and female, are inspected, and any that need repair or replacing are rejected, and new ones issued. Boots are cleaned, and hands and fingernails scrubbed.

All staff are ordered to wear their "*On War Service*" badges. Back in 1914, after some members of the public tried to shame men not in uniform to enlist by handing out white feathers, the Admiralty issued round gold and blue enamel badges to all workmen who are indispensable for the completion of His Majesty's ships and armaments. This proved that, although the man is not giving service in the armed forces, he too is doing his bit for his country, and the dockyards won't lose their skilled workers which would slow the war effort. The Ministry of Munitions, in turn, issued a bronze triangular shaped badge in 1916 for women engaged in urgent war work; the women in the dockyards have been awarded them too. These badges are worn with pride, and all the workers in the yard ensured the insignia gleams, and are pinned somewhere visible on their chests.

Fresh signs for the women's washroom facilities are put up, so the Queen can be confident that the female workers are well cared for. One block of men's latrines and one of the women's lavatories are designated as out of bounds at the beginning of the week, and each receives a facelift and extra cleaning, should they be needed if one of the Royal party is caught short. The dockyard women wonder how the Admiralty will cure the acrid smell of urine that hangs heavy in the female toilets. as their lavatories have been man free for about a year, but still smell like a Parisian street urinal.

All the local schools and community organisations who have been invited, are notified of the times the King is arriving and departing, so that they can line the route to and from the dockyard. Each school is allocated a space along the road on the dockyard wall side, so the children can see the motorcade as it goes by. The townspeople are allocated the opposite side of the road, and will fit in where they can, many taking to the top of the sea wall near the station, to gain an elevated view.

At ten o'clock, Miss Garrett leads the march of the children from the Broadway School's temporary home to their allotted space on the pavement outside the dockyard. She sets a brisk pace that leaves the smaller children running to keep up. The teachers then arrange the girls in order of height, so the smallest are at the front and the tallest at the back. Each row is staggered, so that the girls can see over the child in front's shoulders.

"Stand up straight, girls," Hattie commands, and Ena does another check on pinafores and flags.

The local police cancel all leave for the day, and the special constables are asked to obtain leave from their normal employment, so that they can assist in controlling the crowds.

The Boy Scouts are pressed into service and are put in charge of controlling the school parties. Mr Pope, the scout master, is beside himself with the responsibility, and orders are given to his troop to ensure they are as smart as Mr Baden-Powell would want. Added to this is the glee that Miss Garrett's Girl Guides are not privileged with guarding the King. As she is lining up the school children, the scout master comes across to her allotted pitch to gloat.

"I am so honoured to be included in the safety and security procedures for His Majesty's visit today."

Miss Garrett bares her teeth, in what she hopes might pass as a smile as she seethes inside. "I suppose the police think it will be better to give the boys a role, otherwise who knows what they might be throwing and shouting at the King!" she replies, scoring a point, which she punctuates with one of her sniffs. There has been a recent spate of stone throwing in the town, and one boy has lost an eye. Whilst none of the Boy Scouts are directly implicated, during an affray one boy has received a cut to his head which needed stitching, which suggests he may be involved in the stone throwing too. And that's not to mention the incident with the fog detonator at Sunday school, which she has not forgotten, and you can be sure she will not let others forget either. Mr Pope backs off to find an easier target to lord it over amongst the other schools.

The St John Ambulance Brigade also stand ready should there be an emergency. There was an air raid call on Sunday night at nearly eleven o'clock, but there has been no attack locally, although Southend and Shoeburyness directly across the Estuary were targeted. A bomb exploded in a marsh at Graveney, on the Kent mainland, just the other side of the Swale; the enemy's Gotha plane crashed on Sheppey, near Harty. There was also a single bomb dropped on the Isle of Grain, just across the River Medway from the dockyard, but without causing any damage. Elsewhere across Kent, London, and Essex, forty-nine people are killed, and one hundred and seventy-seven are injured. The fear is that the Germans will target the yard with another air raid whilst the King is visiting. The St John volunteers prepare their first aid kits in readiness, whilst sincerely hoping not to be required.

All the shops in Bluetown deck themselves out in bunting and swags in patriotic colours. They take deliveries, war restrictions permitting, of windmills and flags for children to wave, as well as extra treats and other fripperies that people might want to buy when in a holiday mood. Anything that bears the King's image is snapped up as a souvenir of the day, including some old coronation memorabilia from 1910 that had been dusted off and set out as new.

As the Royal train pulls into the station, the band of the King's Royal Rifles strikes up the National Anthem. King George V and Queen Mary step onto the platform. The King is wearing the uniform of the Admiral of the Fleet, in honour of the dockyard and the Royal Navy. A host of military dignitaries are there to meet him, along with the local bigwigs. A guard of honour is drawn up inside the station yard for the King to pass between, before going out onto the street.

As a young man, King George served in the navy for many years ,under the command of his uncle, Prince Alfred, Duke of Edinburgh. He was stationed in Malta, and is very keen to inspect the fleet and the Royal dockyards, whenever he can. As a result, he is rather quick to depart the station and begin the tour, giving a cursory wave to his subjects before getting into the awaiting car.

The Commander of the Nore, Admiral Sir Doveton Sturdee, is aware of the King's naval interest and is doing his best to impress the monarch. His own car has been overhauled to ensure its efficiency to drive the mile and a half from the station into the dockyard, and it is polished within an inch of its life. The Admiral is even more conscious than usual about the need for his men to pass muster, as the King is going straight on to

Chatham Dockyard afterwards, and comparisons will be made. Much to his chagrin, at the last minute, although in reality some days before, it is decided to use the Royal Air Service car from Eastchurch, and the Admiral's car takes the second division dignitaries, including the Mayor.

As the Royal party leaves the railway station, the crowds go wild, cheering and waving to King George V and Queen Mary as the motorcade passes by. The Royal party wave back, as do all the naval and town dignitaries. The Broadway School girls forget all their discipline and shout until they are hoarse, and their arms are about to drop off from waving their home-makes flags so hard.

Rear Admiral and Mrs Bennington follow in the third car, driven by the wren who regularly drives the superintendent's wife to the football. There is another officer with them in the vehicle, wearing the uniform of the newly formed Royal Air Force, Wing Captain Barnes, and his wife, Maisie. She keeps an eye out for her former pupils from the Broadway School, and waves back enthusiastically when she spies her former students, now four years older, and standing at the back, as they are now the taller senior girls.

"Look, it's Miss Kendrick," a couple of girls shout, not using her married name. "See how beautiful she looks!" Maisie is every inch the lady, in her fashionable hat and matching outfit in her favourite colour, a soft lilac. Hattie and Ena wave to their friend too, as the car disappears into the crowd.

"I didn't know Maisie was in the Royal party, she never said!" Hattie muses, a little put out that her friend has not confided that she will be enjoying the privilege of being part of the motorcade. "She was always Mrs Bennington's favourite. Even when the Rear Admiral's wife visited the school, it was Maisie's pupils she praised."

The cars sweep through the garrison, before entering the dockyard gate, where the troops greet the King with enthusiasm. Just inside the yard, the principal officers of the dockyard are assembled and wait to take the party around the workshops. Mr Phillips is in the second row, behind the naval officials. His stomach knots as he thinks about the plan he agreed to with Hattie and Beryl Eames to embarrass Victor, and wonders why they had ever thought it will be a good idea; but it is too late now to stop it.

The Royal party disembark from the vehicles and introductions are made to the awaiting VIPs. Queen Mary's party split away from the King's, as the two royal personages have different routes to follow. This is a last-minute change to the plans for the day, as it has been decided that the visit to Chatham dockyard should be brought forward. It will now include a visit to the naval hospital, where there are still some injured men from the Zeebrugge Raid, which had taken place on the twenty-third of April. The Royal Navy had attempted to blockade the Belgium port of Bruges-Zeebrugge with block ships, as it is an important base for German U-boats. The raid is only partially successful, but is an important propaganda victory. As the King is in Chatham, it is thought a further visit to the wounded will be good for morale. He visited on the day following the raid and has spoken to many of the men, but as the King is a naval man himself, he has expressed an interest in those men who are still injured, so the whole day's programme is changed, to enable the King to visit the hospital.

John Phillips has only received the updated itinerary as he joins the assembled dignitaries to await the King, and hasn't time to warn Mrs Eames that they need to abandon their plan to expose Victor Banks. He had given Victor a note to take to the colour loft at ten o'clock and, unbeknown to the messenger, this starts Victor's own downfall. John thinks he has started a chain that could instead bring about his own demise. He wonders if it wasn't for Hattie West, would he be doing this. What is it about her that makes him so willing to take the risk? It's Hattie who put this plan in place, but she is outside the dock walls and playing no part in its execution.

As Rear Admiral Bennington takes charge of the King's party, he divides up the yard officials and says, "You're with me, Phillips."

John responds, "Perhaps I should go with Her Majesty's party, as she is touring many of my areas of responsibility."

But Mrs Bennington comes over, gives him a slight dismissive nod of her head, and says, "I can take charge from here."

John knows she is aware of their plans, but how much is another matter. He hopes the sight of the Queen's party will stop Mrs Eames in her tracks. He can only pray so.

******

As planned, at quarter past ten, Victor goes to Mrs Eames' office with the fictitious note from Mr Phillips.

"Please wait a moment, in case I need to reply," says the colour loft supervisor, as she opens the envelope to read the note inside. "Hmmm, it seems they need some of the smaller ensigns to decorate one of the outbuildings. It has been added to the route at the last minute, and hasn't been decorated already. Would you mind waiting whilst I sort some out, then take them back to Mr Phillips, please? You can wait over there in the workroom." She indicates a spare chair next to a small table, away from the sewing machines, in the main room in the loft.

Victor thinks they are leaving it a bit late, as the King is due to arrive at about half past ten, but agrees to wait. Mrs Eames starts bustling about, poking in and out of the various pigeonholes, inspecting and rejecting flags as she goes.

After about ten minutes, she asks, "Would you like some refreshment, it may be some minutes before I can assemble what they need?" She doesn't wait for a reply, but says, "Bessie, can you make this gentleman some tea whilst he waits, please?"

Bessie Smart is waiting to play her part, and some minutes later returns with a hot drink. As she gets near to Victor, she gives him a vengeful look, as she pretends to trip and throws the contents of the cup over him.

Victor yells as his legs are scalded, and two other ladies of the loft jump up to help. "You must get your trousers off and put some cold water on the burn," Mabel Taverner says, pouring a jug of cold water that happens to have been left handily on a side table, over the hapless Victor's groin.

"I'm trained in first aid with the St John Ambulance," says Lottie Payne. "I can treat a burn. Come into the first aid room." Between them, the three women hustle Victor into the walk-in cupboard, to which Lottie has pinned a notice saying, "First Aid", with a hand drawn red cross on it.

"Off with your trousers," she says, tugging at them with the aid of Mabel and Bessie, so Victor is left standing in his wet, knee length drawers and shirt tails, for modesty.

"I'll rinse the tea off and dry them," says Bessie, leaving the cupboard, with Victor's trousers over her arm.

Lottie starts rummaging through her first aid supplies and pronounces, "I don't have the right cream here for burns, so you will need the air to get to the scald to cool it down, before I apply a dressing. Just wait here for a few minutes and we will be back. We will put your trousers in the hot press, so they should be dry by then."

The two women leave the First Aid room, and lock the door behind them. They quickly clear up the spilt tea and water from around where Victor was sitting, before they throw his trousers into one of the cupboards, without the care they have promised.

Outside the Quadrangle, Mrs Bennington is escorting Queen Mary to the colour loft. Maisie Barnes and some other officers and dignitaries, together with the Queen's Lady-in-Waiting, follow at the rear of the group.

Sarah Knowles is stationed along the corridor, near to the stairs, to give the nod to Mrs Eames that the Royal party is approaching. Beryl is feeling triumphant that their scheme is going to plan, but she notices that instead of indicating the arrival of the King, Sarah is gesticulating and drawing an imaginary knife across her throat. Beryl doesn't know what the issue is, and says, "Stand up straight, girl," as Mrs Bennington sweeps into the corridor, with the Queen in her wake.

"This way, Your Majesty," the Rear Admiral's wife says, indicating the direction the party should take.

Mrs Eames's stomach turns over unpleasantly, but she summons a smile to greet the deputation, and drops a curtsey as they approach.

"Ah, Mrs Eames, I trust all is well in the colour loft," says Mrs Bennington, in a voice that carries into the workshop.

All the women stand up ready to drop a curtsey, as the Queen comes into the room. Bessie, Lottie, and Mabel hastily return to their places by their machines, and eye each other with concern; they hadn't factored in that their Royal visitor might be the Queen, with Mrs Bennington leading the party. They hope Victor will have the sense to keep quiet. The last thing they want is for him to be exposed whilst the Queen is there; it is not what they had planned at all.

Mrs Bennington introduces Mrs Eames to Queen Mary, and begins to explain what work is carried on in the loft. Meanwhile, Maisie's attention is caught by the first aid cupboard, as most workplaces have little by way of equipment, and she is curious to find that provision has been made. She wanders over towards the door and hears a funny noise coming from inside. She turns the key and opens the door, and before she can stop herself, she exclaims, "There's a man in here, with no trousers on!"

Every head turns, as poor Victor tries to cover his embarrassment with the Royal Navy's White Ensign, and retreats to the farthest corner of the cupboard. "Lottie was treating my burn, but she didn't have any cream, and had gone to fetch some as the Queen arrived," he tries to explain, in the hope of making his appearance seem more normal than it is. However, Mrs Bennington cuts across him with, "Is it that Victor Banks spying on the girls again?"

There is a ripple of laughter, which quickly takes hold of the whole party and the women in the loft. "You had best finish tending the wounded," Mrs Bennington says to no one in particular. Lottie scuttles off to the first aid cupboard and Mabel follows, quickly retrieving Victor's still wet and tea-stained trousers, as she shuts the door behind them. Mabel flings the trousers in Victor's direction, and Lottie quickly applies a dressing to his wound.

"Lottie does first aid with me at the St John Ambulance," says Maisie, to the group escorting the Queen through the loft. "It's very kind of the girls here to use their skills to treat their work colleagues."

The party agrees, and the Queen nods in approval. Mr Reynolds, one of the senior dockyard officials says, "Well done, Mrs Eames. I didn't realise that you had taken it upon yourselves to run a first aid post. I must commend you. I will ensure that you receive some supplies, including the right cream to treat burns."

He nods to the ladies of the loft, and follows the rest of the Queen's party out to visit the rigging shop, on the second floor of the Quadrangle.

*****

Back out on the pavement, the school children are getting restless. They are facing a long wait for the King to return to the train station, whilst he and the Queen tour of the dockyard. It is thought to be unpatriotic for the crowd to disperse and for the King to come out of the yard to no one, so they have been asked to remain until the Royal party depart. The children have brought packed lunches, and the teachers run around taking their charges back and forth to the toilets in the station and in the

Court House, who have kindly opened their doors to the crowds.

Ena has partially got her way, and has made a great many fatless carrot cakes and eggless ginger buns to go around the girls. Other teachers have also made tea loaves and sandwiches filled with cheese, pooled by the whole staff to ensure every child has enough to eat. There are also crates of ginger beer and lemonade, paid for by Mrs Barnes, as a gift for her former school pupils.

The children sit down on the pavement and eat their picnic in the May sunshine, after which they play guessing games that don't involve running about and sing patriotic songs. All the other schools, stretched out along the pavement, do the same.

Hattie nervously checks her watch, wondering how her scheme to embarrass Victor Banks is going, but powerless to do anything about it. She hopes that it all is going to plan, and that nobody ends up in trouble.

A signal is given that the King has reached the Garrison and is inspecting the troops stationed there, under the command of Major General Herbert Mullaly, and that the Royal tour will soon be at an end. The police and scouts begin requesting that the schools and townspeople return to their positions on the pavement, in readiness to cheer His Majesty, when the cars sweep back out of the dock gates.

Mr Pope, the scout master, begins chivvying the lines of school children back into order, when Ellie Masters announces to Miss Garrett that she feels sick. The child has eaten more than her fair share of the goodies, plus what her mother packed for her, and it is all threatening to come back up with the excitement of the day.

Miss Garrett breaks ranks with the girl to quickly use the station toilets, when Mr Pope blocks her way.

"You can't go now; the King will be out at any moment!" he says, holding his arms out to stop Miss Garrett crossing the road.

The headmistress draws herself up and responds, "Don't be ridiculous, Mr Pope, the child is going to be sick. Would you rather she soiled the road, so the King has to drive over it?"

"Find her a paper bag! I can hear the band striking up *God Save the King* in the Garrison!"

"It will only take a moment. He has still got to inspect the Royal Garrison Artillery men in the dockyard fort, according to the itinerary. That should give us ample time." Miss Garrett's demeanour becomes increasingly waspish, and a more sensible man would back away. She draws Ellie Masters in front of her, seemingly to hold her tenderly by the shoulders, but in reality she is taking aim, and like a Vickers machine gun, without further warning, the child sprays vomit over the scout master's pristine uniform.

"Oh dear," says Miss Garrett, without a hint of sincerity, "now look what has happened. I'd best take her to the toilet to clean her up." She leaves Mr Pope standing in the middle of the road; his uniform ruined. "*The righteous will rejoice when he sees the vengeance; Psalm 58,*" she thinks, and she smiles to herself the whole way to the station toilets, holding Ellie's hand and slipping the girl a sixpence, much to the girl's surprise.

****

Later, after the Royal party has departed, the Superintendent calls a meeting of all his officials and managers to discuss how the day went.

"Well done, all of you," says Rear Admiral Bennington. "The King and Queen had nothing but praise for the workers."

"The Queen was impressed that we take first aid so seriously," mentions Mr Reynolds. "However, it was a little embarrassing that the injured man was hiding in the cupboard when Her Majesty came to view the colour loft. Good job Mrs Barnes opened the door, and not one of the Royal party. It's very confusing in there, as there are a number of doors to choose from, and they all look the same. If someone hadn't pinned a notice saying, "First Aid," I'm sure the Royal party would have blundered in on him trying to find the way out."

"Yes," responds the Rear Admiral, "isn't he the one that was the subject of a recent complaint to the police? Do we know what he was doing in the loft, Mr Phillips? Mrs Bennington tells me that he spies on the women from secret places."

"Unfortunately, Victor Banks is known for running the errands to anywhere that the women are working. He will offer to get tools from the stores, or take messages. If another man is asked to take a note, he will take it off him, so he is the one that is always going where the ladies are. I think there have been a couple of other complaints about him, since the court case, but the women aren't willing to come forward, after the first girl was made to look a liar in court."

"Well, we can't have that," says the Rear Admiral. "What can be done about it?"

"I've removed his status as doing work of national importance, but he still has some time to run on his exemption, before he is called up to the Military Service Tribunal again."

"I'll transfer him elsewhere, in the meantime. We'll commend him and despatch him to Pembroke," the Rear Admiral says, looking around at the assembled group, and nodding to his ensign to make a note. "That should be far enough away. I'll get the paperwork drawn up. We'll say something about his keenness to assist and recognise the Queen's attention. We'll have him out in a couple of weeks."

John Phillips can barely conceal his glee at this sudden turn of events, and can't wait to tell Hattie. He grins widely and exposes his crooked tooth. It isn't the outcome they hoped for, but Victor will be gone, and that will be enough. And none of the women will be in trouble either. Now, he just needs the *Naval Stores Ladies* team to win the *Dockyard Cup*, and all will be right with the world.

*****

All the children are dismissed and given a half day holiday from school, after the Royal visit ends. The McDonald children return home to West Minster and, together with their cousins, Cissie and Ernie, decide to go mud larking at the coal jetty next to the gas works, for the afternoon. The weather is fine, and it is low tide, ideal conditions. Spring and summer are good times to go, as the numbers of other kids is smaller as some families have left the area to start fruit picking on the Kentish farms; the competition to find lumps of coal that have fallen overboard from the unloading colliers is a good deal less. They will also collect driftwood from the beach for kindling, and sometimes there are other items washed up, like lengths of rope or empty bottles, which they can sell to the rag and bone man for a penny or two.

Usually, Cissie stores the coal and driftwood that she collects for the winter, if she can. During the summer, she only lights a fire for a short time each day, to boil water for washing and making tea. Otherwise, she and Ernie eat cold meals of bread and jam, and drink cold water, saving their fuel for heating food in the autumn and winter; quite different to the lovely hot dinners their Auntie Maggie gives them. But now, her finds of coal will go to Auntie Maggie's store, to keep them all warm this winter. She is happy to be able to contribute.

Ernie can't tell coal from stones, and brings Cissie all sorts of useless items, which she pretends to praise and put into her basket, before discreetly tossing them back into the mud left at low tide. She has done well, and nearly has as much as she can carry, before the tide turns and comes rushing back in. Suddenly, a shout goes up. Ernie is stuck in the glutinous brown mud near the wharf. It is sucking on his feet like quicksand. The water is already starting to return and is around their ankles.

Cissie shouts to her cousin, "Joe, go and get help," as she tries in vain to pull Ernie out with the help of her cousin, Mary. The two girls are beginning to be sucked down themselves, as their weight disturbs the mixture of mud, sand, and water, making it become more liquid, and causing their bodies to sink down further. As the water reaches their skirts that are tucked up above their knees, their clothes become heavier, pulling them even further down. Buried in this muddy concoction, they need a lot of force to loosen the mix enough to escape, which the three children can't generate, as the tide rapidly creeps up.

Joe runs straight into the gas works and finds his Dad shovelling coal in the yard. "Dad, Mary and the others are stuck in the mud and the tide is coming in!" he shouts to his Dad and Ginger. The men drop everything, and along with several colleagues rush down onto the beach. The tide at West Minster will reach over twelve foot at the sea wall, and will be at least twenty where the children are stuck. It is already touching the bottom of the sea defences.

Rab takes charge of the operation. He knows you have to spread your weight across the mud, but the rising tide makes this impossible. Ginger runs for a small boat tied to the bottom of the wharf, and begins to paddle it across to where Mary, Cissie, and Ernie are. The boy has sunk to his belly, whilst the girls are still just thigh deep.

Rab ties a rope to his waist, and his colleagues anchor him like a tug of war team, as he wades out into the cold sea.

"Keep still," he shouts, knowing that by struggling the mud will suck them deeper. Cissie and Mary comply, but Ernie is in a full-scale panic as the water reaches his chest. Cissie is crying and shouting to her brother to not move, as Rab inches closer, but the noise around him means the partially deaf child can't hear her instructions, and he thrashes about, causing the mud to suck him down further.

Rab reaches Mary first and pulls her out by sheer strength, and passes her backwards down the line. Maggie has arrived on the sea wall with Dolly, alerted by Joe that Mary is in danger, along with the Dummott children. She has grabbed a spare shawl and wraps her daughter Mary in it. Dolly carries some towels from the waiting laundry and sets to rubbing her sister dry.

"Save Ernie next!" Cissie pleads, as Rab wades towards her.

"You are nearest," Rab says, trying to grab her as she fights him off in an attempt to get him to rescue Ernie. His colleague, Buster Clarkson, wades into the water to help pull Cissie out and drags her to the shore. As Cissie is passed up the line, Maggie removes her own cardigan to place round the girl's shoulders. Cissie struggles to return to the water, but Maggie and Dolly hold on tight to her, not letting her go.

By now, Ginger has got the boat to where Ernie is. The child is now up to his neck, and is flailing about and being steadily sucked further down. Ginger is trying to grab Ernie, but can't get the leverage he needs to be able to pull him upwards and out.

Rab and Buster wade across and hold the boat steady, as Ginger tries to squat before standing, to pull Ernie up and free.

There is a commotion from the sea wall. News spreads fast in the small town, and someone has gone to fetch Ivy from the pub. She staggers down the road, as fast as she can go, under the influence of the gin she had consumed, and is almost hysterical by the time the sea comes into view, where the men are struggling to extricate Ernie from the sucking mud. She arrives just in time to see the boy's head disappear under the water.

"No," she screams, and climbs over the wall to reach her son. The steep gradient sends the drunken woman catapulting into the water, and the weight of her long skirts pulls her under, even though it is less than two feet deep at that point. The alcohol in her blood disorientates her, and she too is soon in danger of drowning. Two of Rab's colleagues are able to grab her and haul her back up the steep sea wall, as Ginger finally manages to get a firm enough grip on Ernie, and gain the purchase he needs to pull him out. But it is too late, the child is already dead.

*****

When Alice returns from the dockyard, following the King's visit, she finds nobody is at home, and no note to say where everyone has gone. She is desperate to tell her mother about how Victor had been caught in the cupboard without his trousers on. It is rumoured he is being packed off to another dockyard, but she hasn't heard anything officially. She goes out onto the street and sees Horace walking down the road.

. "Hi, Horace," she says, "have you seen my Mum? I want to tell her all about the King's visit."

"They're all at the sea wall. There's been an accident. Little Ernie Dummott has drowned," he tells her bluntly.

Alice races to the shoreline, where a large crowd has now gathered. There is a police officer taking statements from those involved. The undertaker's cart rattles over the cobbles, ready to take the small body away, and the crowd parts respectfully.

Rab and Ginger are giving the facts to the constable, who writes the details in his notebook. The local doctor, Dr Penneyweight, has arrived to check on the two girls and Ivy, and to pronounce Ernie dead, as it will need to be reported to the coroner, and an inquest held to determine the cause of death. Dr Penneyweight gives Maggie a sedative to give to Ivy, but apart from being cold, the two girls are okay. Poor Cissie can't stop crying and blaming herself.

"I should never have let him wander off on his own. It's all my fault," she sobs.

"Don't be silly," soothes Maggie. "It's just an accident. You mustn't blame yourself."

"Aye, that mud is like quicksand," Rab says, surprised at his own feeling of loss for the little boy. "He's not the first to be caught like that." He lays a comforting hand on the girl's shoulder.

Once the formalities are completed, they all return to Khartoum Road, and Maggie puts the kettle on to make tea. She takes Ivy upstairs, strips off her wet clothes, and puts her in the girls' bed with a stone hot water bottle. Ivy has sobered up, but is still in shock.

"Here, the doctor gave me this medicine for you. It will help you to sleep," Maggie says, as she spoons out the liquid for Ivy to take.

"He was my baby," Ivy sobs into the pillow, as Maggie strokes her hair, whilst the draught takes effect.

"I know," Maggie whispers, brushing away a tear. "And he was mine too."

Cissie and Mary also strip off their clothes, and between the girls they find a clean set of things for Cissie to put on. She has lost her boots when the incoming tide reached the spot on the shore where she left them, so they give her a pair of Alice's that are too big.

Rab has gone to Ginger's house for a bath and clean clothes. His brother has installed a gas geezer to heat water, now that there is no one at home to boil it up for him at the end of the day. The men can change on their own, whilst the women can have Rab's house to themselves for a short while.

Nobody has much to say, and Alice tries to cheer people up a little with her tales of the Royal visit, and how Victor has got his come uppance after all. The dockyard had laid on a tea party afterwards for the staff to celebrate the event. She has secreted some cakes in her pocket, along with some scones to share with her family. These titbits are bite sized and dainty, and they barely touch the sides as they are solemnly consumed. Everyone appreciates how Alice is trying to bring comfort to them.

Maggie doesn't feel like cooking, as she deals with her own grief at losing Ernie. So, when Rab returns with Ginger, they find a couple of shillings between them to send Joe and Walter to get some chips for everyone. The men also find some coppers to get some beer from the off licence in the *Duke of Clarence.* It is quite a forlorn party that sits around eating the hot meal from the newspaper wrappers.

"Cissie will have to live here with us now," Rab announces, without preamble. "We can't have the lassie fending for herself any longer. When Ivy is better, we will pack her off on her way. She has other family she can call on."

Maggie doesn't try to argue with him; she had already decided this some days ago, before the tragedy, but didn't tell Rab of her decision. It is her usual practice to make him think it is his idea, but this is not how she had planned it. It is too late to save Ernie, but they must save Cissie from a life of misery.

*****

Beryl Eames stops off at Hattie's lodgings after work, to tell her the news about Victor. Hattie invites her friend in for some tea, so they can discuss all the day's events; she is desperate to hear all the details first hand.

"The Rear Admiral was true to his word. He has already got his staff to draw up Banks' dubious commendation. All the necessary paperwork is in the process of being prepared. Milly Kitter from the office told me so. In just a few weeks, he will be gone," Beryl says, as Hattie leads the way through to the parlour.

"I know it's not justice, but Mr Phillips has managed to get him out of our hair," Hattie says, as she pours the tea that the housekeeper, Mrs Hancock brought in. She strokes her ageing cat Tibby's ears. The cat is sat on the back of an armchair in the sunshine, watching the women's activities. It no longer goes out searching for lovers and returning pregnant with half a dozen kittens.

Ena has become reconciled to the animal being in the house and sleeping on her lodger Hattie's bed, although she still goes mad if she finds a flea.

"I just pity the women in Pembroke," says Hattie, settling down to nurse her cup and enjoy the gossip. "But he might have learned his lesson."

"Yes, it's all round the dockyard that he was spying on the loft ladies with his trousers down. The part of the story about being scalded is hardly repeated, as the tea wasn't hot enough to cause him any real damage, so he has nothing to prove he is injured. Plus, it doesn't make such a good story! I think everyone has put two and two together, and knows the real reason he is being moved," responds Beryl Eames.

"Has anyone told Alice, or the other women he pestered?" asks Hattie, as she picks up Tibby from where she has jumped down onto the floor. She sits the cat on her lap, whilst they chat.

"I have spoken to Bessie, and Mrs Pamplin has spoken to Vicky Watts. They are both relieved he is going. Alice has yet to be told."

"Well, I hope that no longer having that burden to carry will help Alice play well in the cup final next week. Are you going to tell her tonight?"

"That was my original intention, but you may have heard about that little boy drowning at West Minster. It was her cousin, Ernie. I don't want to disturb the family tonight, so will tell her first thing tomorrow."

"Oh dear," says Hattie, "I had best go round and see her tomorrow evening."

******

Ivy soon recovers and returns to her rooms in Gordon Road. However, she is not the same as before Ernie drowned. It's as though her soul has died, but her body still lives on. She still goes to the pub with Pearl, and still entertains customers, but she just goes through the motions, seeking to get as drunk as quickly as possible, and staying that way for as long as she can.

Cissie visits her, but Ivy barely acknowledges her daughter, blaming her for Ernie's death. "You were supposed to look after him," she says with bitterness. Poor Cissie is grieving not only for Ernie, but for the loss of her mother's love, such as it had been. Maggie does her best to treat the girl as one of her own, but she is not demonstrative herself, and does not know how to comfort the girl.

At school, Cissie works hard to catch up; she knows that if she is unable to read and write well, then her chances of leading an independent life will be slim. She doesn't want to end up like her mother, for all that she is mourning the loss of Ivy's casual love. But Ena Briggs makes it her business to give Cissie extra tuition on a Wednesday after school, whilst Alice and Tilly learn how to typewrite. There are also extra lessons on Saturday afternoons, after Cissie has finished her chores. Ena finds that Cissie's numerical ability is excellent. It has been honed keeping house on the limited income they receive from her father via the Parish. As she is good at arithmetic, Ena soon has the girl learning rudimentary bookkeeping.

Ivy never comes to see Cissie, and the rooms in Gordon Road are exchanged for one above a pub in Bluetown. Ivy pays the rent by sharing the money she gets from the sailors with the landlord, but as she drinks more and more, she is earning less and less. Her disinterested response to her potential clients leads them to seek satisfaction elsewhere. Those that still seek Ivy's charms are often brutal, leaving her bruised and battered in the morning. Pearl still hangs around with her, but is spending more time in the company of other working girls, who are willing to share what they earn, in return for Pearl keeping a look out for them. Maggie wonders how long Ivy can go on like this.

*****

The Cup Final

On the evening before the women's cup final, Maggie McDonald makes Alice's favourite tea of saveloy and pease pudding. Even though meat is rationed, making it hard to get enough for everyone, she has put together a feast. Maggie has planned this celebratory meal for some days, and it becomes a double celebration, when it is officially known that Victor is on his way to Pembroke. The yellow split peas need soaking overnight, so it requires some preparation. They are then boiled in a cloth for three hours. It isn't a meal you can rustle up in ten minutes. As she stirs in the tart malt vinegar, with lots of salt and pepper to the pease pudding, before adding a generous knob of precious butter, she feels the atmosphere in the room lift. Everyone is still grieving for little Ernie, but at last they feel there is something to look forward to.

"I hope we can put this business with Victor behind us now," Maggie says, as she places great dollops of pease pudding onto the stack of dinner plates.

Rab nods at Alice. "If you had let me deal with it, he would never have come back!" he says, as he tucks into the biggest plate with two saveloys, whilst the smaller children shared one between two.

"It's over now," Maggie says, closing the subject down. "Let's just look forward to Alice's cup game tomorrow."

*****

Alice sleeps well for the first time since February, and wakes up feeling that a weight has been lifted from her shoulders. She is so excited that she doesn't know if she will be able to concentrate on work that day, and can't wait for the morning to end. When eventually the lunch time siren sounds, she and Tilly can't get to the recreation ground fast enough.

Their football kits are washed and ironed. Alice has polished her boots till they almost shone. She secures her hair as tightly as she can under her cap, and waits for the signal to go out onto the pitch.

Hattie is there already, as excited as the girls. She does the rounds and speaks to each of them in turn, giving them encouragement. Then, Mr Phillips joins them and gives them a run down on the strengths and weaknesses of the *WAAC*. "They are good at set pieces, but they don't think independently. Too used to taking orders," he jokes. "If you can separate their best players by marking them tightly, then they won't get the opportunity to score." He looks around at the girls, who are absorbing this information, before he continues. "But they are also aggressive. Egg them on till they lose their tempers in front of the referee. But don't retaliate," he cautions, holding his finger up in warning, "We want the ref to send <u>them</u> off, not you."

As it is the cup final, a large crowd has gathered to watch the game. The money from the ticket sales is going towards the fund to provide recreation huts for the service women, and there are many uniformed girls there on the touch line, along with players from the other teams in the tournament, all keen to enjoy tea at Admiralty House afterwards. The *Wrens* and the *WRAFs* are cheering the *Naval Stores Ladies* on, as the competition between the different military organisations is strong.

When the game starts, the *WAAC* initially run rings around the *Naval Stores Ladies.* Their fitness is much higher than the dockyard women, even though the stores women have been training hard for months. But, steadily, the game play that Mr Phillips has instilled into them comes into its own. One of the *WAACs* is sent off for foul language in front of the referee, the kind of language that won't even be tolerated in the trenches, after one of the *Stores Ladies* has continually obstructed her. Another is sent off in the second half for pulling on Gertie's jersey, until a seam rips. But the score remains nil - nil. Then, in the eighty-fifth minute, Alice picks up the ball from a cross outside the penalty box, and has a clear view of the goal. Side of the foot for accuracy, laces for power, she thinks – as she propels it into the top right-hand corner of the net; the goalie doesn't stand a chance. The dockyard women just have to keep a clean sheet for five more minutes to win. The *Stores Ladies* throw everything at defence, and when the whistle goes, they are victorious. The *WAAC* captain walks off the pitch without shaking the *Stores Ladies'* captain's hand, and is visibly sulking, until it is time for the cup presentation.

The two teams line up, losers first, to shake Mrs Bennington's hand, and that of her two daughters, Amelia, and Daphne. As it is a lovely early summer's day, the trio have sat at a table provided for them to drink some refreshing lemonade, as the players sweat in the warm sunshine. Mrs Bennington remains seated as the women file past. The *WAAC* girls remember their manners, and each salutes the Superintendent's family as they take their losers' medals, passed to Mrs Bennington by the chairman of the dockyard's sports club. Next, comes the *Naval Stores Ladies* to accept their winners' medals and Agnes Beard, their captain, takes the cup from Mrs Bennington and holds it aloft. The crowd roars with approval and Alice is lifted onto the shoulders of her teammates, as they do a lap of honour.

When the furore has died down, the chairman retakes possession of the cup, to get it engraved with the winning team name and the year. He has been twitchy the whole time the girls have been handling it. The cup is already emblazoned with the words "*Sheerness Dockyard Ladies Cup*," its original purpose as the "*Plunge for Distance*" swimming gala cup, now forgotten. The teams return to their changing rooms to shower and change into their Sunday best clothes for the tea party at Admiralty House.

******

Alice is euphoric; she has never won anything before, and she scored the winning goal. And, best of all, Victor is being despatched to Pembroke. Her teammates slap her on the back and give her the compliment of calling her "Alice

Kell," the captain of the *Dick Kerr's Ladies* who play in Preston, Lancashire, and are the most famous women's football team in the country.

As they walk back from the recreation ground to Admiralty House in their finery, Alice sees Victor lurking by the dock gates. Her teammates see him too, and close ranks around her.

"Happy now that I've been sent away?" he shouts. "Think of my poor mother left on her own."

Suddenly, Alice breaks through her protective ring and squares up in front of Victor; she feels quite her old self again. "Your mother is nothing but a wicked old gossip! She isn't happy unless she is making someone else miserable! Maybe, without her on your back, you can become a nicer person too!" And with that, she hitches up her skirts, and kicks Victor where he will feel it most.

The *Naval Stores Ladies* cheer her for the second time that day, and Victor skulks away.

"Come on, let's go hobnobbing with the Navy!" says Tilly, linking her arm through Alice's, as they walk in the sunshine towards the formal gardens of Admiralty House.

******

The day nominated as the *King's Birthday* holiday is Monday the third of June. The dockyard shuts for the day, and the whole town celebrates. Reggie and Alice are planning to go for a ramble on Minster cliffs and catch one of Mr Stanton's omnibuses there. They can celebrate the *Dockyard Stores Ladies'* win in the cup, and Victor leaving the town for Pembroke. He also hopes that it will cheer Alice up a bit, as she is still understandably sad over the death of little Ernie, whom everyone loved.

But the day before, Reggie's older brother, Fred, came home unexpectedly on leave for a few days from the front. He has somehow managed to borrow a motorcycle with a sidecar, and has ridden through the night to be with them first thing. The plans for the outing are changed to include Fred, who will take Alice in the sidecar, and Reggie will ride pillion.

Alice has never been in a motor vehicle beyond an omnibus, and is very excited. She badgers her mother into making a picnic for them, consisting of ham sandwiches and some egg free cake. The boiled ham is obtained off the ration by swapping a couple of rabbits at the butchers. It isn't a big joint, but there is enough for a taster for everyone. Ginger has given her some strawberries and a handful of just ripe tomatoes from the cold frame he has in his garden. The tomatoes are still slightly green on one side, but they add a little summer freshness to the fare. Alice is really pleased to be able to offer this feast to Reggie and his brother, Fred, whom Reggie hero worships.

When the motorcycle roars into Khartoum Road, everyone comes out to look. Small boys are fascinated by Fred, as he has served in France and is wearing his uniform, complete with stains from the trenches. He is slightly taller than Reggie, and his cap hides his thinning hair, a family trait. He looks quite dashing, and Alice is a little shy of him. The local children are all enthralled and cluster around the vehicle to question him about his exploits.

Reggie's uncle Horace comes out to chat and shake his nephew's hand. "Where are you going?" he asks Reggie, as Alice climbs into the back of the sidecar with her small hamper, which she places in the footwell. She is wearing her Sunday best skirt and the blouse that Ena had made her for the court case back in February, and is very conscious that she doesn't want to trip on the hem of her skirt in front of Fred, as she clambers over the lip of the sidecar. She has secured her best straw hat to her head with a scarf against the wind, in case the speed of the motorcycle should cause it to blow away, and has used the ostentatious hat pin that Miss Briggs gave her to pin the whole confection to her hair. She also carries a blanket to wrap around herself on the journey, to keep the wind out. When they arrive, they can sit on it to eat their picnic.

"We are only going up to Minster cliffs," responds Reggie, dismounting to help Alice.

"Come in, lad, I have something you can take on your trip."

Reggie disappears round the back of Horace's house for some time, leaving Fred to help Alice. He reappears with a large hamper, which he installs into the small boot of the sidecar. He takes some care as he does so, as his Uncle Horace stands over him supervising.

Alice is now slightly embarrassed by the size of her picnic, compared to that donated by Uncle Horace. She wonders what he has given them, as the war means shortages of many tasty delicacies. Maybe it is just a fancy hamper, complete with crockery and cutlery. She has only brought a couple of napkins and a bottle opener for the three bottles of beer which her Dad contributed. They will have to eat the sandwiches out of the paper, but if Horace has provided china plates, it will be like a real picnic, the sort of picnic that Mrs Bennington goes on.

Eventually, Horace is satisfied that the hamper is safely stowed, and he stands away to allow them to drive off. He waves his hanky and shouts, "Don't forget the time," which seems a little odd to Alice, as they have all day.

Fred drives at some speed and uses the heel of his boot when he needs to slow down around bends. The sparks fly off his "Blakey Boot Protector" steel caps to the amusement of Reggie and consternation of Alice. They reach the clifftop in no time. Alice feels slightly wobbly, but exhilarated. Fred helps her out, then takes the small hamper from the foot well. Alice spreads the blanket on the ground, whilst Reggie extricates Uncle Horace's large hamper from the boot.

"That is kind of your Uncle Horace to give us a picnic," says Alice, as she reaches for the large basket.

"Don't touch it," shouts Reggie, shielding it from Alice's hand, and causing her to draw back. "I've just got to do this for Uncle Horace." He turns the basket, so that it faces towards West Minster, and undoes the straps, throwing open the lid. Two pigeons fly out and head for home.

"He asked me to release them from up here, so they can get used to returning home from any direction," Reggie explains. "Now, what have you got in that picnic hamper for us? I hope it's something nice."

Alice is crestfallen that her dreams of a feast are shattered by Uncle Horace's pigeons, especially as Reggie and Fred seem more interested in logging the time of their release and discussing potential arrival times. They don't notice her disappointment.

Later, after eating the picnic which Alice provided, the three of them go for a ramble across the cliff tops, and stand on a high point to look down at all the naval ships clustered around the dockyard.

"I wonder when the war will end?" Alice says, as they all remember those they have lost, and those still fighting.

"Now that the Yanks are committing their troops on the Western Front, we should see some progress," says Fred, lighting up a cigarette, and offering one to Reggie. The Americans first military engagement had occurred the week before, on the twenty-eighth of May. The First Infantry Division had attacked and captured the German-held village of Cantigny, France. They all agree that the end can't come soon enough.

They sit on the blanket, drinking their beer and smoking their *"Cup-Tie"* cigarettes, whilst looking out to sea to try to spot U-boats. Fred says, "I'm going to climb down the cliffs to see if I can find any sharks teeth amongst the fossils. I want to find a big one, if I can, to take back to show my chums at the front. They won't believe me that you can find such things turned to stone just lying on the beach."

"I'll come too," says Reggie, getting ready to stand up.

"You stay here with Alice. This is supposed to be your outing," Fred says tactfully, not wanting to be a gooseberry.

When they are left alone, Reggie reaches out his hand to stroke Alice's hair, as she has removed her hat. "How are things at home after the death of Ernie? He was such a little character."

"Everyone is so sad. Although he and Cissie aren't really family, Mum did more caring for him than Ivy ever did. I'm surprised how much we all miss him."

Reggie takes her in his arms to comfort her. It is the first time he has held her so close. She smells so nice; the sea breeze is caught in her hair. Suddenly, they are kissing, and Alice knows this is the right thing to do. When it is over, she thinks to herself, how can I explain away the grass stains to Mum when we get back?

At the end of the afternoon, Fred and Reggie drop Alice back to Khartoum Road, and return Horace's basket to him, with a note of the time the birds were released. The two pigeons have been back some time, and Horace is pleased with how the time trial has gone. They then return home to a wild greeting from Patch the dog, who feels that he should have gone along, as he is Reggie and Alice's best friend. Fred turns to Reggie and says, "You're going to marry that girl one day, I can tell."

*****

The Tuesday after the long weekend created by the *King's Birthday,* is the day designated for Victor to travel to Pembroke. His travel warrant is prepared, and he has lodgings arranged. No one has said to him if it is a temporary or permanent move, and he hopes to return home once the war ends and things return to normal. The men at the front will come back to their jobs, and the women will once more be housewives and mothers.

Mrs Banks bemoans the loss of her son for some days, as though he is dead. "I might never see you again," she wails, the sinews in her neck as tight as a jailer's shackles. As she packs his work clothes, laying out his best to travel in, she laments, "You'd have thought they would have given you a first-class ticket, considering the commendation you got!"

"I will do my best to come home once a month," he tries to reassure her, as she polishes his father's pocket watch, so that he can proudly display it across his waistcoat.

"I've spent all our meat ration on a joint of beef for Sunday. I will make you beef sandwiches for the journey. Things will never be the same again!" She brushes his bowler hat, then folds his cloth cap, putting it in his work jacket pocket, as though laying it to rest.

On the holiday Monday evening, Victor decides to visit the *Shipwright's Arms,* to say goodbye to his colleagues. He isn't well liked, and in turn, liked few people, but it is the done thing to buy a round of drinks before you depart for somewhere new. The "*No Treating*" order means it is prohibited to buy a round of drinks, but this can be circumvented simply by everyone asking for another drink at the same time, and all appearing to place fourpence each into a pile of coins on the bar.

The pub is crowded for the holiday, and Victor has to push his way in. Teddie Taylor is at the bar with a group of his cronies, and shouts across at him, "Oi, Verge, come and join us."

Victor manoeuvres himself across to where Teddie is standing at the counter, ready with his cronies to order another pint. It is obvious they have been there for some time.

Victor adds enough coppers to the pile on the bar to pay for all of Teddie's companions to have a beer, and accepts one as it is passed over to him. What he hasn't spotted is that a double tot of whisky is added to his glass. As he drinks it, he thinks, "This is strong stuff," but as beer has been watered down for the duration, he just thinks it must be how strong beer normally is.

"Have another," Teddie orders, before Victor's glass is empty.

"I've got to get up early tomorrow," Victor tries to reason with him, knowing it is pointless. He rarely drinks, and now regrets the decision to go to the pub.

"One more won't hurt!"

More coppers are added to the pile on the bar, and another pint of whisky-laced beer passes to Victor.

This continues until Victor has nearly drunk his third pint, which includes his sixth whisky, and he is beginning to feel the effects, as he is unused to strong spirits. He is slurring his words and is unsteady on his feet.

"I've got to go," he protests.

"Just one more for the road!"

Teddie wraps an arm around his shoulder, and says conspiratorially, "The lads have clubbed together for a little farewell present for you."

The befuddled Victor can't imagine what they might have bought him, and is overcome at their kindness.

"No, you shouldn't have, you're too kind," he mumbles at Teddie, who is much more sober than he should be, if he has drunk as much as Victor. But, of course, he hasn't. He's only drunk two pints of the weak beer, in the same time that Victor has drunk four pints of the whisky fortified beer.

"It's no trouble," says Teddie, steering Victor towards the door with the aid of Alex McKinley. "We've got a lovely surprise waiting for you, make a man of you."

As they reach the door, the fresh air hits Victor, and he really doesn't feel too good at all. "I need to go home," he protests, as he weaves from side to side between his two companions.

"Just round the corner for your big surprise," says Teddie, directing the swaying Victor along the road to the *Dockyard Arms*. They go in through a side door down the alley, where a sailor is enjoying the charms of one of the many working girls. Victor can't work out what is happening, as the man grunts and groans. The girl looks at them with dead eyes over the man's shoulder, whilst making encouraging noises to her customer; the night is still young, and she can perhaps manage another client or two before calling it a day.

Teddie ascends the creaking stairs, pulling Victor after him, whilst Alex bars his escape back down. When they reach the top, Teddie gives a cursory knock on one of the closed doors, before opening it to reveal a squalid bedroom. There is just a bed and a chair, with an oil lamp on it, in the room. There are some hooks on the wall for the resident to hang her clothes. A tattered curtain is drawn across the window, blocking out the mid-summer's evening light, and the lamp is lit to try to create a romantic ambience, or maybe just to make the resident look more attractive in a softer light. On the bed sits a woman, wearing a green silk kimono that has seen better days, covering her nakedness beneath. She has a half-drunk bottle of gin in one hand, from which she takes a sip, before focussing on the client that has been brought to her.

"We'll wait outside," says Teddie, propelling Victor towards the bed, as he places some half crowns on the chair. "Make a man of him," he adds, before leaving, taking Alex with him.

Victor is horrified; he doesn't know what to do, and the beer and whisky are not helping nature to lead him to do the necessary.

"Come here, handsome," the woman says, loosening her wrap to reveal the soft curve of her breast.

Victor can smell her animal scent, and it begins to have the required effect upon him. He feels a stirring in his groin and sits down on the bed beside the girl. She must have been pretty once, but is past her best. He notices there is a blueish tinge to one of her breasts that had been handled roughly by a previous client.

She leans backwards, so that her wrap falls open, and places her hand on Victor's thigh. Victor unbuttons his fly with one hand, whilst reaching for the girl with the other. She leans all the way back on the bed and reaches up to Victor's shoulder to pull him down. But Victor is having difficulty getting beyond the first stage of desire.

The girl puts her hand into his fly and tries to coax some life into Victor's unresponsive manhood. But nothing happens. She smiles encouragement. "Come on love, it's what we both want," she says, without meaning it, but is conscious of what might happen if Victor can't perform. If he blames her, he might turn nasty.

She tucks her loose hair behind her ear, in readiness to offer oral sex to the customer. As she does so, Victor sees that her ear lobe is missing, where a violent customer has bitten it off in the throes of passion, some time ago. He recognises Ivy, and remembers her laughing at him in the street, when he had last thought about consorting with a prostitute. Despite his befuddled state, he recalls that she is Alice's cousin, and that all his troubles are down to her, and something within him flips.

"You bitch!" he says, as he grabs Ivy by the throat, and begins to throttle her. The bed bangs against the wall, and she is gasping noisily as she struggles for breath. Victor grunts with the exertion, as he shakes the life out of Ivy.

Teddie and Alex are waiting outside, and can hear the sounds of "noisy love making" coming from inside. and grin at one another. When Victor emerges, they will slap him on the back in congratulations. But suddenly there is a crash, as Ivy manages to kick over the chair at the moment of her death. The oil lamp smashes on the floor, and the flames engulf the bed and Victor's clothing. Ivy is slumped lifelessly on the bare floorboards.

Teddie and Alex run up the stairs, and throw open the door to see Ivy lying dead, with livid marks on her neck, whilst Victor blunders about, consumed by fire. Alex runs for help in the pub, whilst Teddie attempts to beat out the flames, only to be driven back by the heat.

The landlord and the burly bar man run up the stairs, carrying buckets of water, whilst other customers prepare to form a chain. Alex runs to the police station to raise the alarm, and report that it looks like Ivy has been murdered by Victor.

Soon, the fire is under control, and the building saved. The landlord has done his best to beat the flames out, but it is too late. Victor has succumbed.

*****

The stench of scorched flesh fills the air, together with the smell of burnt wood. The reek causes Teddie to vomit into one of the buckets used in the chain as he sits on the kerb outside. The police constable asks the lad, "Are you with this man? Who is he?"

Teddie manages to splutter, "Victor Banks, I worked with him in the dockyard," before vomiting again. "He was going on a transfer to Pembroke tomorrow. He said he wanted to visit a friend to say goodbye before he goes home, and Alex and I walked with him here, as he was a bit drunk. He said he wouldn't be long. We waited down the stairs for him, as we promised to get him home safely. We heard a commotion, but we didn't think much of it, until we heard a crash. When we got up there, the girl was dead on the floor, and Victor was on fire. There have been some complaints from the women in the yard that he tries, I mean tried, to touch them up. One went to court over it. Maybe he tried it on with the one upstairs, and it got out of hand?"

"Yes, I remember the case, but the magistrate thought there was no case to answer," responds the constable.

"Other girls have come forward, but none want to make a formal complaint. It's rumoured that's why he is being packed off to Pembroke. Looks like he just doesn't know how to treat a lady."

"Indeed, sir," responds the constable. "Do you know the woman?"

"No, never seen her before," lies Teddie, as he and Alex had made the arrangement with Ivy earlier in the day. They had to pay her some money in advance, so that she would wait in for them to arrive with Victor, with the promise of more money when they appeared. Teddie feels some remorse that both Ivy and Victor are now dead, as he is the one that has instigated Victor's visit. However, he reasons that Victor would have done it at some time anyway; the signs were there, no one can lay the blame at Teddie's door.

The constable asks the landlord, "Who is the woman?"

"Just a woman who rents a room from me. Her little boy died a few weeks ago, and the poor wretch has turned to drink. Very sad. She can't bear to live in her rooms in West Minster, and see all the things that reminded her of the child, so I offered her a roof over her head till she got herself straight. I don't know how she knows Mr Banks, or why he was visiting her. She usually just kept to her room. I think her estranged husband gave her money, and that's how she got by," the landlord says, being economical with the truth, as he doesn't want to find he is being prosecuted for keeping a bawdy house. The constable accepts this explanation, as he had heard about Ernie's death from a colleague. He will have to report it all to his sergeant and the coroner. It looks like an open and shut case. Victor Banks visited the poor woman in her room, though no one knows how he knows her, then he flips and strangles her. The lamp got kicked over, and Victor died in the fire. It will save the hangman's noose.

Pearl is found in *The Jolly Jack Tar,* and despatched to fetch Maggie to formally identify her cousin.

******

The Women's Day

Hattie feels bereft after the *Dockyard Ladies Cup* is over. She had become so wrapped up with the desire to win, as well as with the players and their lives. But the cricket season has begun at Easter, and Miss Marchant, a wealthy landowner in Eastchurch, has turned one of her fields into a cricket pitch to start a ladies' league. Fixtures have been agreed against the *WAAC*, *WRAF* and *Wrens*, and Hattie enjoys playing for the *Eastchurch Ladies* team. She has always played as twelfth man for the male teachers' team, but there are often disputes as other men's teams object to her being a woman. It is good to be able to play without that added stress.

The *Eastchurch Ladies* have been practising in the long summer evenings every week, and she enjoys riding her bicycle to the sports ground through the dapple of the elm trees that line the lane. But somehow, she feels something is missing from her life that she can't quite put her finger on. For once, her sport is not enough.

That evening, when she arrives at the sports ground, several of the women are talking about a "*Women's Day*" carnival that is planned in town to celebrate the contribution to the war effort that they are making. There are going to be floats, featuring famous women such as Boadicea, Queen Elizabeth, and Cleopatra. The service women will march along with the Girl Guides to the music of the various military bands stationed in Sheerness and the RAF band stationed in Eastchurch. It is rumoured there will be other events, such as cricket and football matches, where the teams will be mixed men and women, plus there will be sideshows in the Beachfield Park, next to the Pavilion. Mrs Bennington is organising the day's events, along with a couple of her husband's officers. It promises to be a jolly day.

"Do you think we should host a cricket match, or make a float on a cart, perhaps cricket themed?" suggests Miss Marchant.

"We really ought to do something," says Miss Riviere, a local firebrand suffragette, who also owns a lot of land. Hattie knows her of old, as Miss Riviere once organised a firebombing of some haystacks, and had been prepared to let Hattie and her friend Maisie take the blame, whilst all the time, Miss Riviere protested that she wanted to be jailed like the more famous suffragette women. Miss Riviere doesn't even play cricket, but sees her friendship with Miss Marchant as a way in.

"We can have a float dedicated to the suffragettes, in celebration of the passing of the *'Representation of the People Act'* back in February."

"How about a cricket match, women against the *Royal Naval Flying School*?" suggests Hattie, only to be poo-pooed that the men won't play them.

"I think they will. If Mrs Bennington is organising it, they will all want to please her," Hattie counters.

But Miss Riviere has her way, as usual. Plans are drawn up, with Miss Riviere being the central figure of *"Justice,"* whilst other women will represent *"Democracy, Equality, Liberty, and Sorority."*

You didn't show much sorority in the past, Hattie thinks, as Miss Riviere outlines her plans. Hattie is so annoyed that she almost gives a Miss Garrett sniff, before making her excuses to go home, with no cricket being played at all that evening.

As she cycles back down the lane, she thinks to herself, just wait till I tell John Phillips. He would have opted for a cricket match between the *Eastchurch Ladies* and the *Royal Naval Flying*

School. But she hasn't seen John for some weeks, as she no longer has the excuse to pop into his office to discuss the football. It is then that she realises what it is she is missing in her life; it is John.

As she passes All Saints Church, she sees it is only ten past seven by the clock on the tower. She can cycle the six miles in just over an hour, and stop at John's house. They can organise a football match instead, between the *Naval Stores Ladies* and another team of men from the dockyard.

******

John Phillips is still running the ladies football, but the new season doesn't begin until late August. He has been trying to think of an excuse to meet up with Hattie West, but can't think of a plausible excuse to do so. He has glimpsed her a couple of times, leading her crocodile of swimmers back and forth from the dockyard swimming pool, But he is just too shy to go out and chat to her, without good reason. His colleagues will tease him, and she may not welcome him. But, now that school has broken up, he doesn't even have that to look forward to. Although the annual swimming gala will be soon, and he has already bought a ticket in the hope of seeing Hattie there.

He sits in the parlour of his house in Trafalgar Parade, and pretends to read the newspaper, in his shirt sleeves and Fair Isle sweater. His sister, Biddy, is making new school pinafores for their brother's two daughters, ahead of the school term recommencing after the summer harvest holidays, even though the girls have only just broken up for the summer. The papers are full of the death of the air ace, James McCudden VC. It is the talk of the whole town, as the McCudden family lived only a few streets away. The war is so cruel; two of his brothers have also been killed, William back in May 1915, and John only that March. How does their mother cope with losing three sons? And their sister Mary's husband, Arthur Scott Spears, was one of the dockyard workers killed when the troop ship *Princess Irene* exploded during a refit, also in May 1915. What a burden for one family.

Just then, there is a knock at the door. "Who can that be, it's gone eight o'clock?" Biddy gets up to peer through the lace curtains, and exclaims. "It's that teacher, Mrs West. She must be here for you." Biddy sits back down and picks up her needle work, and looks expectantly at John. Her brother stands up, flustered, smoothing his hair with one hand, and taking his reading glasses off with the other. He goes to open the door.

"Mrs West."

"Mr Phillips."

They both speak together, then laugh.

"Do you want to come in, Coach?" John asks.

"Well, just for a moment," she responds, smiling at his use of his pet name for her, as she crosses the threshold. John leads the way to the dining room, where he invites Hattie to sit down.

"Tea?" he asks awkwardly, as he hears Biddy moving about in the room next door.

"I'll do it," his sister calls, as she passes the open door and goes into the kitchen.

"I wanted to talk to you about the *Women's Day* that Mrs Bennington is organising. Have you heard about it?"

"Yes, it's the talk of the dockyard."

"I thought we might organise a women versus men football match. What do you think?"

"Great idea," he responds. "We will need to sound out the girls and draw up a plan. I heard that the St John's men are looking to organise such a game. I can find out about that."

John stops talking as Biddy returns with the tea tray. His sister notices how much he is blushing, as she serves the tea.

"I'll leave you to your sport," she says, as she starts to withdraw. "He won't tell you this himself, but he has missed your company."

Hattie also blushes, and nearly knocks over the teacup in her embarrassment. She takes a deep breath, and says, "I've missed you too."

Biddy just catches this, and smiles to herself as she shuts the parlour door.

*****

Alice watches the younger children go out looking for dandelion leaves for the rabbits, whilst Dolly is helping with the laundry by ironing shirts in the back room. School has broken up for the summer, and the children are able to go further afield foraging. Walter has left school and is now working full time for the dairy, and is up early to help with the morning's delivery. Alice goes into the scullery to find her mother.

"I feel like it's me that's been put through the wringer, just like the washing I take in," Maggie says to Alice over her shoulder, as she feeds the shirts through the rollers, turning the handle backwards at the right moment to regurgitate the items and not crush the buttons.

"First, we lost little Ernie, and had to use most of our savings to pay for his burial. I wouldn't let them put him in a pauper's grave. Then, we lost Ivy, and in such tragic circumstances." She empties the water from the tray under the mangle, and picks up the next item. "We didn't even get a say in Ivy's funeral, as Eli claimed her body and made all the arrangements. He was happy for us to look after her all these years. But he wanted the rest of his church congregation to see him as the grieving widower."

"Mrs Jinks says he's been wooing one of his parishioners," Alice says.

"Huh, that doesn't surprise me. Mrs Jinks is always first with the gossip," Maggie responds, raising her eyebrows. "No wonder he's reclaimed Cissie. His congregation will think less of him if he'd left her with us. I tried to reason with him that the girl had been through too much, and that she will be best left here, especially as she is getting to the age when a girl most needs her mother."

"I saw Cissie the other day. She is well cared for by Eli, but he is so cold and strict," Alice says, passing her mother another basket of wet shirts to wring out.

"Eli's religion is of the hellfire variety, rather than Christian love, Cissie's life is not what I'd have wanted for her. But Eli is determined that she won't go the way of her mother. Children belong to their father under the law, so we just have to accept his decision."

As Maggie puts the copper on again, to boil up the water to wash the soldiers' cotton long johns and underclothes, she is grateful that Eli allows Cissie to visit them regularly, so that she can at least keep an eye on her and give her a mother's care. She mops her brow with the hem of her apron, as she sorts through the pile of dirty washing, trying not to look at the soiling, ensuring that no stray-coloured items have got in amongst the whites.

"It's a shame everything happened when it did. Cissie was just beginning to come out of herself. She is progressing well at school with Miss

Briggs' extra classes. She has beautiful handwriting and is very good at arithmetic," Alice says.

It has made quite a difference that Cissie has clean clothes; once, when she was younger and had attended school regularly, the teachers had sent her home with a note saying that she was dirty and smelt unclean. But Ivy hadn't cared enough to see to the poor child, and had simply kept her home until Maggie had taken her in again, where she combed Cissie's hair for nits, and washed and patched her clothes. The other girls had called her names back then, but, as she got older, she had done her best to keep herself and Ernie washed.

"She will soon be starting her monthlies, and at least being with you and Dolly some of the time, she will soon get the hang of changing her sanitary rags," Maggie says.

"Talking of monthlies, I need to tell you that I'm late," Alice says in a rush, glad to find an opportunity to tell her mother, whilst she is too busy to whack her one.

Maggie gives her a hard stare, but doesn't break her stride in feeding the dirty washing into the bubbling copper. "You will have to wed Reggie, and any prospect of doing typewriting in the dockyard offices is over. Reggie is a nice lad, so it will probably be okay."

"Can you wait to tell Dad till I've told Reggie, please? I've got to find the right moment."

"Okay, I'll tell your Dad when he's in a good mood. I hope he won't lose his temper."

"Thanks, Mum," Alice says, and makes her escape, leaving Maggie to wonder; another one off my hands already. Where are the years going?

******

Miss Garrett doesn't know what to do with herself, now that summer is here. Every year, for as long as she has been a teacher, she has gone travelling during the harvest holidays. She and a select group of friends travel across Europe by train, to take the air in Switzerland, or explore the ruins in Rome. She hopes at some point to travel down to the south of France, to visit the towns favoured by the Impressionist artists, but the war has put a stop to all that.

It isn't even possible to do that much travelling at home, as some areas are designated as military zones, and there are restrictions on access. The whole of the Isle of Sheppey is designated as such, and you have to show the red identity *Defence of the Realm Permit Book,* if you go to the mainland, and again on your return. People have nicknamed it "Barbed Wire Island." Other seaside ports are also designated as military zones, such as Dover and Newhaven, which restricts the ability to travel abroad.

Even if you can visit other towns, rationing means that tea shops and restaurants are limited in what they can serve, and many hotels have been requisitioned for military use.

After the war, I will go travelling round Europe to see the impact of the fighting, and I will visit my friend Herr Klein in Germany, she promises herself, as she sits in the parlour and thumbs through the postcards she has collected on her travels over the years, along with other memorabilia.

Herr Klein was a local photographer of German Jewish origin. He had moved to Britain in the 1880s, when he was a young man. Before the war, Miss Garrett would often drop in on him to practice her German, although his accent was Bavarian, and not the *"Hochdeutsch"* – high

German, she had been taught. It is still good to speak with someone whose mother tongue it is.

Immediately after the outbreak of the war, the *Aliens Restriction Act* means that Germans can't move more than five miles, and have to register with the police. Herr Klein was over military age, and was deported, rather than interred like the younger men. She doesn't know where he is now, but she does have an address for his sister, who lives over the Austrian border, in Salzburg. She will start by writing to her, once the war is over.

But for this summer holiday, she will have to settle for a week visiting her married sister in Norfolk. The two of them can't stand one another, but blood is thicker than water, she thinks, as she reaches for her pen and some note paper, to send her sibling a letter, telling her when she will arrive.

******

The *Women's Day* soon comes round, much to everyone's excitement. John and Hattie are unable to find a men's team from the dockyard willing to play the *Naval Stores Ladies*, who have earned themselves a name for being skilful players. The possibility of losing to a bunch of women makes the prospect of playing them unacceptable to the men's teams. So, Hattie approaches Mr Pope and his VAD air raid wardens, to see if they will accept the challenge. Mr Pope's arrogance gets the better of him, and he ignores advice from his colleagues that they could possibly be humiliated, and accepts.

Kick-off is at one o'clock at the Wellmarsh recreation ground; it is timed to start early, as the *Women's Day* parade will start at five o'clock through the town, enabling people to be able to go to both events. A large crowd has gathered to watch this novelty football game of women versus men, and they pay sixpence each for the privilege. There are a good couple of hundred people there, and Hattie estimates they will raise at least five pounds towards the new recreation hut for the service women.

Alice, Tilly, and the other girls are feeling on top form; training sessions have recommenced, and they feel ready to test themselves against their male opponents, but, at the same time, they are daunted by the prospect, as men are generally stronger and faster than women. Hattie comes into the dressing room and calls the girls together for a team talk.

"Don't forget, girls, you won the *Dockyard Ladies Cup*! The VAD men don't play as a team, they don't know one another's strengths and weaknesses. Mr Pope has made himself captain and centre forward. He is fifty and overweight. Their goalie is Mr Palmer senior, the butcher. And he is no stranger to a roast dinner! Three of their team were rejected for military service because of poor eyesight, and a fourth was rejected because he has one leg shorter than the other. Only a couple are fit, but doing war work, or they would all be in the army. Otherwise, they are all old or unfit. You can beat them!"

The girls cheer Hattie's speech, as they prepare to run out onto the pitch in their familiar football kits.

Mr Pope is giving a similar pep talk in the men's dressing room.

"Well, we band of brothers," he starts, quoting Shakespeare with his whiney voice, "we ought to let the girls think they have the better of us, rather than run them into the ground too soon, or it will look unsporting. Hang back a bit for the first half, then we will show them how it's done in the second. By all means, let them score a goal, if any of them know how to kick properly. And be gallant if any of them look like they might swoon. Offer them your arm to help them across to the touch line for a sit down."

Mr Palmer interrupts him here. "Not bloody likely! If they want to play against men, then they should be bloody well prepared to be beaten!"

"Language, Mr Palmer! It is *Women's Day* after all! Now, let's get out there and show them what's what!"

The ill-matched assortment of men run out onto the pitch in an equal array of different kits. Mr Pope has new boots on, which he has never worn before, and his feet will soon be telling him that he should have used the old trick of urinating in them first.

By contrast, the *Naval Stores Ladies* look like a team in their red and white striped jerseys, and black socks and shorts. Their boots are polished and have seen active service recently. Each girl knows her place on the field and what her job is.

The day is hot, and the VAD men are flagging. Some are barely running, and for a little while it looks like Mr Bartlett, the greengrocer, is going to have a heart attack. Mr Palmer, their goalie, is worse than any of the others, as he is kept busy with all the goal mouth action being at his end. By the time the half time whistle goes, the *Naval Stores Ladies* are two – nil up, and it's a wonder to the watching crowd that it isn't more.

During the half time break, Miss Garrett comes to find Hattie in the dressing room. Everyone is amazed to see her there, but she walks in briskly, and announces, "Well done, girls, keep it up," before turning on her heels and walking out again, without waiting for a response. Hattie is least surprised, as she knows of the antipathy between Miss Garrett and Mr Pope, and guesses that is the reason for the headmistress' appearance at the game.

Alice disappears into the toilets, and she can be heard being sick.

"Are you okay, Alice?" Tilly calls out to her through the closed door, as Gladys comes and stands beside her to find out what is wrong.

Alice opens the door and confides. "I missed my monthly." Alice's face is as red as the stripes on her jersey. Gladys and Tilly exchange looks.

"You've no worries there," says Tilly, a little enviously, "Reggie will stand by you."

"Will you be okay to play the second half?" Hattie asks, with concern as she joins them in the washroom.

"I'll be fine," Alice responds to Hattie. "The nausea doesn't last long," she says, under her breath, so only Tilly and Gladys can hear her, and they all breathe a sigh of relief.

In the men's dressing room, Mr Palmer produces a bottle of whisky from nowhere, and passes it around for medicinal purposes. They are not looking forward to the second half, and most are smoking cigarettes like it will be their last. Mr Gooch, the undertaker, says he feels too unwell to play anymore. He changes back into his ordinary clothes leaving them one short. They hadn't expected to be losing so badly, and didn't want to be humiliated.

"We will just have to play them as though they are bloody well men, not bloody pussy foot around them with kid gloves," Palmer says, mixing his metaphors. "If they bloody well want to be treated like men, then I say we bloody well go for it."

There are nods of agreement, but some of the younger dockyard men are uncomfortable about this tactic, but are too shy to speak out against the majority of VADs.

When they run back onto the pitch, Mr Bartlett goes in goal, and Mr Palmer promotes himself to centre forward. The VADs play a lot more aggressively, and the referee is forever blowing his whistle to keep order. But the *Naval Stores Ladies* are still the better players, and their defending keeps Palmer and Pope away from the goal. As the time ticks on, Mr Palmer decides to take Alice out with a vicious tackle. She hits the ground with a thud and lays winded. Then, she feels a rushing of blood, and knows she has to get to the lavatory. The two teams are now both ten players a side, with only ten minutes to go. Palmer manages to score, just before the final whistle, pulling the score back to two – one in the ladies favour.

Tilly runs off the pitch to find Alice in the dressing room lavatories. "Are you okay?" she says through the closed door, for the second time that day.

Alice gives a little whimper. "My monthly has arrived. There's nothing to tell Reggie now."

"Oh, Alice," says Tilly, unable to decide if she should be pleased or sad for her friend.

Just then, Hattie comes in. "Are you all right, Alice? Do you need to go to the infirmary?"

"No, I'm fine, it's just my monthly and I wasn't prepared for it," she calls through the door.

They can hear rustling as Alice sorts herself out, then she unlocks the door and comes out looking very pale. The black of her shorts disguises the colour of the blood, but she has streaks down her legs.

"Get yourself cleaned up," says Hattie, full of concern, escorting Alice to the showers, and producing a large bath towel. "I have some Southall's sanitary towels you can use. Are you sure you are okay?"

Tilly pulls Hattie to one side and whispers, "She missed her last monthly. She thought she might be expecting."

"Oh dear, do we need to get a midwife to examine her?"

"I was just late," says Alice, with mixed feelings. She knows her Mum will be pleased, especially as she hasn't yet told Rab; now, she won't have to.

"I'd better check on the rest of the girls, but I have some leaflets from the *Malthusian League* on how to prevent pregnancy. I will lend them to you. I am also happy to go with you to buy a contraceptive diaphragm. Then, you shouldn't need to worry again," Hattie says quietly to Alice, as the rest of the team are in the changing room shouting and cheering that they've defeated the VAD men and helped raise money for a recreation hut for the service women. She leaves Tilly with Alice, and goes to congratulate the girls.

Alice is embarrassed by Hattie's frankness about preventing pregnancy, but decides that she wants to learn more.

"Did you know they are going to advertise some typewriting jobs in the dockyard at the end of the month?" Tilly asks Alice, as she comes out of the shower, "We can both apply!"

"That will be great. It's more pay, but not so much fun."

"But we will still have jobs after the war," Tilly says, with determination.

John Phillips knocks on the dressing room door, and asks, "Is everyone decent?" before opening the door, when they shout back, "Yes."

"Congratulations! You beat those pompous men!" he calls to the girls, before turning to Hattie and says, "Mrs West, Hattie, please allow me to escort you to the parade."

Hattie comes over all coy, before saying, "That will be lovely, John!" to a round of applause from the girls and calls of, "About time!" and, "What took you so long?!"

John offers Hattie his arm, and she takes it without a backward glance at the girls.

"I best tell my Mum that my monthly has arrived. Good thing I didn't tell Reggie! He's been talking about buying a motorbike after the war. A baby would have put paid to that. We can take things at our own pace now," Alice says, linking arms with Tilly. "But let's go and enjoy the parade first!"

******

Armistice Day

As autumn arrives in 1918, so does the Spanish flu. There are several cases in the barracks and amongst the ships anchored in the dockyard. But it doesn't confine itself to the servicemen. Miss Briggs has to leave school at nine o'clock on the morning of the twenty-fourth of October, as she is too ill with the influenza to carry on her duties. Lucy Hardcastle has to take over her classes, including cookery, which she knows little about, never having had to cook at home. Her mother always employed a cook, and now Mrs Bills cooks for her and Miss Garrett. Four girls can't attend the cookery class through sickness, and there is an anxious atmosphere throughout the school, as a result of so many absentees.

Miss Garrett is visibly ruffled as a total of forty-one children are away sick. The following day, the School Board are ordered by the medical authorities to close all the schools for a fortnight. Miss Garrett sends all the teachers and pupils home as directed and decides to visit Ena Briggs at home.

She goes via the florists to buy some chrysanthemums, both for their hardiness and because few other flowers are available late in the autumn. It is a shame they smell so earthy, but they do come in a variety of colours. Miss Garrett chooses some large purple ones, and having checked them personally for earwigs, she takes her purchase to Miss Briggs's home in Inkerman Street.

As she approaches her friend's house, the door opens, and Dr Pennyweight comes out. He tips his hat to Miss Garrett, and stops to speak to her. "I'm afraid Miss Briggs is not very well at all. The virus has hit her badly and has turned into pneumonia. Do you have any contacts for her family?"

"Sorry, she has been estranged from her family since she finished university, I believe," Miss Garrett replies, glancing up to Ena's bedroom window, where she can see the curtains are drawn.

"I don't think she will last the night," Dr Pennyweight says, matter of factly. "I will come back later, but there are several cases in town. There have already been a number of deaths. I suggest you refrain from any physical contact with her," he finishes, and gets into his Crossley motor car to visit his next patient.

Mrs Hancock, Miss Briggs' housekeeper, is waiting in the hallway and starts talking before Miss Garrett is through the door. "Oh, Miss Garrett, whatever should we do? Miss Briggs is shivering so hard that her teeth are chattering, and she complained of a tremendous headache before she took to her bed. She said her throat is sore and now she has a raging fever. What will become of us?" she asks, concerned about her own position, as well as the health of her mistress. Miss Garrett orders her to make tea and presents her with the flowers to find a vase for, then goes upstairs to see Ena for herself.

Hattie is sitting beside the bed and is reading aloud to Ena from *The Secret Garden* by Frances Hodgson Burnett. It doesn't look like Ena is able to take in the story, but Hattie can't think what else she can do, and she knows it is one of the stories that Miss Briggs likes to read to her pupils. Every so often, she will break off, and apply a cool cloth to her companion's head. Tibby the cat has curled up on the foot of the bed, and watches Ena with concerned eyes.

Miss Garrett says, "I saw the doctor," and exchanges a heartfelt look with Hattie, who stands up and offers the headmistress the chair.

The two women keep vigil over Ena's bed until around four o'clock in the afternoon, when their friend passes quietly away. Miss Garrett is overcome with grief and, quite unlike herself, gives into tears. The doctor returns shortly after, as promised, and signs the death certificate. "Dr Worth had three deaths today, and there will be more through the night, I expect. We are going to be busy," he imparts, before leaving.

****

Over the next few days, Miss Garrett and Hattie look through Miss Briggs's bureau and drawers to see if they can find any trace of a next of kin, but they draw a blank. Inwardly, Miss Garrett is annoyed at the disarray her friend's papers are in. She sorts them as they search, so that she will have all the documents ready to register the death and notify Ena's solicitor. There is a copy of the will, which Miss Garrett sneaks a look at, her curiosity as always getting the better of her. Ena has left money to herself, and the house and contents to Hattie. There are several bequests, especially of her jewellery, to friends and colleagues.

Ena's solicitor has already heard the news, and is ready to start the process of probate. He also puts a notice in *The London Gazette,* and in both local papers, so that any relatives can come forward, but nobody does. Miss Garrett and Hattie arrange the funeral at the Congregational Church, where Miss Briggs taught Sunday school. There are not as many people there as expected, as the Spanish flu is reaching epidemic proportions, and people are advised not to mix, if possible.

As Hattie is to inherit Miss Briggs' home, it is agreed that she will remain as a tenant until probate is confirmed, albeit on just a nominal rent. So, she assures Mrs Hancock that she can continue as housekeeper, and she will pay her wages. Mrs Hancock is so relieved, and keeps repeating, "Bless you, bless you!"

******

School reopens on the seventh of November, but only about half the girls return. Many have been dangerously ill, and whole families are hit with the flu. Five students have lost their mothers, and they have been buried the same week as Miss Briggs.

At about eleven thirty, there is a deafening crash as the pipe of the stove in the Bethel room, where Lucy Hardcastle is teaching, falls to the floor. Fortunately, there are no children sitting in the desk next to where it lands. All the girls jump up and shriek in surprise. The stove continues to belch out fumes, and smoke rapidly fills the room.

"Quickly girls, we need to get out," Lucy shouts, as she evacuates the girls out into the main part of the hall, and firmly shuts the door behind her. Those nearest are covered in soot, and they are all coughing, with some girls making the most of the drama.

"Is anyone hurt?" Miss Garrett asks, and is relieved that no one is, as there could easily have been a fatal accident.

"It's lucky so many children are still off with influenza, otherwise the nearest desk would have been occupied," Lucy says.

"Until the stove is mended, it won't be possible to heat the room sufficiently on cold days, so your class will have to squash into the main hall with the classes that are already billeted there. The sooner the war is over, and we get the Broadway school back, the better," says Miss Garrett, as she goes back to her office to write the incident up into her logbook, and to notify the Education Board.

******

The Allies and the German High Commands have been talking all through October. However, these negotiations have stalled, and it looks like Germany might decide to continue the war. But the

"Sailors Revolt" in the German military port of Wilhelmshaven has been spreading across the country and there are calls for the Kaiser to abdicate and a republic to be declared. Miss Garrett has been following the news in the papers avidly, and is hopeful that an armistice will be declared any day now.

Her wish, and that of many others, comes on November the eleventh. On November the tenth, the German High Command receives word that Kaiser Wilhelm II has abdicated, and they are given instructions by the new government that they should sign the armistice. At five o'clock the following morning, the armistice is agreed upon. Marshal Foch has sent word to the Allied commanders that *"Hostilities will be stopped on the entire front beginning at eleven o'clock, November eleventh."* The Allied troops will not go beyond the line reached at that hour, on that date, until further orders. The war on the Western Front has finally come to an end.

The announcement is made at twenty past ten. However, the officials in the Dockyard receive the news at quarter past nine. Although everyone is sworn to secrecy, the news is across the town before the official announcement is made. Nearly all the soldiers in the garrison are released from duty for the day and, together with their regimental bands, they march into town, where they are joined by hundreds of local residents.

Colonel Leahy of the Royal Garrison Artillery rides on horseback to the town clock in the Crescent to make the formal announcement. The gathered crowds are already there, waving flags and singing songs like *"When the Boys Come Home Again"* and *"It's a Long Way to Tipperary"*. Despite the torrential rain, a spontaneous procession, led by the various military bands, starts to wind to the far end of the Broadway, then back down through Coronation Road, then into the High Street. The girls from the WAAC link arms with the soldiers and sailors, and everyone makes merry.

******

When Maggie McDonald hears about the Armistice, she grabs little Rab's hand and they run all the way into the main town to get to the clock tower. She wants him to see the soldiers, whom she knows will be celebrating. She is so excited that she doesn't even bother to dodge the growing puddles. Nor do those neighbours hurrying with her, as they are so keen to be part of the momentous occasion. They are soaked through by the rain, but don't care.

"Your big brother Billie will come home soon!" she tells her youngest, overjoyed that her eldest has made it through, unlike so many. Little Rab can't remember Billie, as he had only been a baby when his brother had volunteered back in 1914, but his mother keeps a picture of Billie on the mantelpiece, so he knows who he is.

As they hurry towards the crowds, Maggie spots Mrs Symonds, Reggie's mother, standing at her door at the end of Kipling Road. The telegraph boy is cycling away back to the post office dodging the people gathering in the Crescent. Maggie knows instinctively what news has been delivered, as Mrs Symonds throws her apron up and buries her face, her shoulders heaving as she sobs.

Maggie goes to the other woman and puts her arm around her shoulder, "It's my Fred, he's been killed. How cruel is fate to deliver this news, today of all days?" Mrs Symonds cries.

Patch, the Manchester terrier, looks up at his mistress, full of concern, from his position of guarding the front door. He wonders if he should have chased the telegram boy down the road for making her cry.

Maggie doesn't know what to say in the face of this tragic news, but she feels guilty that she is so happy that Billie has made it through, and she hasn't received the much-dreaded telegram from his Regiment.

Mr Symonds comes through from the back room and leads Mrs Symonds inside, leaving Maggie and little Rab standing on the doorstep. "I'll ask next door if someone can pop down to the dockyard to tell our Reggie," he says, as he steers her to the back room, closing the door in Maggie's face without even seeing her. Little Rab pulls on her arm to re-join the crowd in the town centre, and she turns away.

******

Hattie, Lucy, and all the other teachers gathered the children together as they hear the procession approaching the temporary school accommodation, and lead the children out to join the parade. Despite the rain, the girls are happy to leave the dry of the classroom. For once, Miss Garrett doesn't complain, but instead dons her own hat and coat and joins them. Meanwhile, all the local church bells ring out and the dockyard siren that signalled when air raids are beginning or the "All Clear" at the end, sets to wailing and adding to the cacophony, much to everyone's delight, especially Polly the milkman's horse, who turns tail and sets off for his stable against the sea of people.

The crowd head for the Garrison Square, where everyone sings the National Anthem before giving three cheers of "*God Save the King!*" Miss Garrett and the other head teachers declare a half day's holiday, as the crowd disperses to return to the warmth of their own homes. The children are either collected by their parents, or walk back to the main town in groups of friends.

"I wish Ena had been here to see this," Miss Garrett confides to Hattie, as they walk back through the town.

"She will have been baking cakes and making flags in celebration," Hattie agrees.

Just then a voice calls out. "Mrs West!" and John Phillips runs to catch them up. "What wonderful news!" he exclaims, grabbing both her hands and swinging her around in an impromptu dance. He then catches her in his arms and kisses her soundly. "Will you marry me?" he asks, caught up in the moment.

"Yes!" declares Hattie, and kisses him soundly back.

"We will talk more tonight," John says, before returning to the dockyard as most of the servicemen are disappearing into the many pubs to celebrate the news.

Miss Garrett stands to one side sheltering under a shop awning, shaking hands with people in celebration, but keeping one ear out to hear what Hattie and John are saying. "Congratulations," she says, coming forward to walk with Hattie, once John has gone.

"Goodness, yes! I'd made up my mind to be single after I lost Bill."

"You never know what life has in store for you," Miss Garrett says. "Let's get in the dry and have some tea."

*****

Alice and Tilly join the parade, with the rest of the dockyard girls. The two friends have recently secured jobs in the office with their new typewriting skills, but Gladys and Gertie are beginning to wonder what will happen to their positions in the stores, once the men are demobbed and return to take back their jobs.

"It's all right for you two," says Gertie, with an edge to her voice, "You've got secure jobs now. But we will end up back in domestic service!"

"Yes, I'm not saying it's not right that the men will get their jobs back, but things shouldn't just go back as they are," Gladys responds.

"You can learn to typewrite and get a better job," Tilly says. "Miss Garrett says she will offer evening classes, once the school returns to its own building."

"How long will that take?" asks Gertie, pulling her shawl further over her head, in a vain attempt to keep the rain off. She'd laughed at Alice and Tilly when they gave up their free time to train in secretarial skills, but now she regrets not thinking about the future.

"I'm sure it won't be that long," Alice says. "Miss Garrett is always true to her word."

But as the girls head back to the office and the stores respectively, Gertie and Gladys experience some mixed feelings about the Armistice.

As they go back through the gate, Alice spots Reggie heading in the opposite direction, and waves to him. But as he gets closer, she can see something is terribly wrong.

"It's Fred," he says. "He hasn't made it. Mum got a telegram."

"I'm so sorry," Alice says. "Do you want me to come home with you?"

"No, I'll see you later," he responds, heading towards home, and leaving Alice feeling guilty that she had been so happy.

******

Gladys and Gertie are soon proved right. The War Office sets about the demobilisation of the troops in Europe in an orderly fashion. They want to avoid the chaos of everybody going home at once, as there are many things to consider, such as rationing and the possibility of unemployment. The Bolshevik Revolution makes the authorities acutely aware of what large numbers of unemployed men can lead to. So, there is a system of grading devised, in the form of groups. The priority groups are miners and agricultural workers, and those men who are essential for the satisfactory conduct of the economy. This means those dockyard workers who were conscripted last, will be amongst the first to return home. The Admiralty loses no time in releasing the women from their jobs.

Gladys and Gertie find themselves back at the Labour Exchange, looking for work. Tilly and Alice thank their lucky stars that they have learned to typewrite.

On the fourteenth of November, it is announced that Parliament, which has been sitting since 1910, and was extended by emergency wartime action, will dissolve on the twenty-fifth of November, with elections a month later, on the fourteenth of December.

Miss Garrett is looking forward to using her vote for the first time, although she is less than impressed with the choice of candidates. Hattie at first thinks she will be debarred, as she is a tenant until probate is granted. However, as she pays the rates on the house, she is the legal householder and old enough to vote, as she is now thirty-two.

"Ena had so been looking forward to voting!" Miss Garrett declares, on an almost daily basis, as she reads the hustings in the papers. Lloyd George's Coalition Party candidate is standing on a platform to protect women in the home against the revolution preached by the women leaders of the Labour Party; although, locally, the male Labour candidate is addressing himself to the soldiers, sailors, and working men, who are also all newly enfranchised, adding another couple of thousand to the electoral role. Typical men, she thinks, ignoring the thousands of women newly able to vote as they are householders.

The schools again shut again, because of the Spanish flu epidemic. Miss Parsons succumbs to the virus, leaving another vacancy on the school staff. Miss Garrett hopes that recruiting new staff will be easier, once the male teachers return. She is concerned that the influenza might take more pupils and teachers before it is done. They have lost a couple of girls, as well as Miss Briggs and Miss Parsons.

Then, the epidemic reaches into her own home. Mrs Bills, her housekeeper, takes to her bed and never gets up again. She has been with Miss Garrett since she purchased her home in Crimea Road, when she had first worked at the Broadway School. She doesn't know how she will replace her.

Then, most shocking of all, John Phillips is struck down. Hattie and he had begun to make wedding plans. They had decided on a civil ceremony, as they felt that after so many deaths during the war, and now with the epidemic taking the civilian population, that it would be wrong to be too showy, and neither of them were in the first flush of youth. But he left work early one day at the beginning of December, as he felt unwell, and was dead by the following day. His sister Biddy hadn't even had time to call out the doctor.

Hattie is devastated. She has lost her friend, Miss Briggs, then John, to the virus. She can't even throw herself into her work because of the school closures. Her friends Maisie and Rosie do their best to comfort her, but Hattie doesn't want to be around happily married women, and finds herself spending more time with Miss Garrett. I'm turning into an old spinster myself; Hattie thinks.

By the time the election comes round on December the fourteenth, everyone is looking forward to a new start. The war is over, and they need to rebuild the country. Hattie and Miss Garrett set off for the polling station together, with hope for the future.

"Let's hope that whoever wins the election will make a land fit for heroes," Miss Garrett says.

"And for heroines," adds Hattie, as they prepared to cast their votes for the first time.

******

Afterword

As part of the WWI commemorations, I was involved in a project funded by the Heritage Lottery to research the role of women on the Isle of Sheppey. I read every copy of our local newspaper, from 1 January 1914 to 31 July 1919, when Peace was officially declared, to see what work women were involved in.

I came across a story of how a female dockyard worker had unsuccessfully taken a male colleague to court for sexual assault. We think of sexual harassment in the workplace as being a modern issue, but over one hundred years ago, women were having to deal with the unwelcome attention of colleagues.

I also wanted to find out more about women's football, as a search of our local history Facebook page produced two photos of women in WWI football kits. I contacted the families, but neither knew who their grandmother had worked or played for during that first flowering of the beautiful game. My research in the local paper only produced one report of a women's game being played – that of the *Naval Stores Ladies* against the *St John Ambulance Brigade,* for a charity match. The women won, and a football playing colleague suggested the reason might be that the women were already in a team, and so had tactics and training which led them to beat the men. And, by coincidence, the Naval Stores is where the victim of the sexual assault case worked.

The King visited the dockyard 23 May 1918, and met workers as well as servicemen. He met women in the Colour Loft under Mrs Evans. The local paper report said most of the workers were widows of men who died at the front. He visited the Rigging Shop, meeting Mrs Dawson, Mrs Forrester, and Mrs Mayers, who were making stowing spars for lighters, and wire rope and wire hawsers. He met Miss Hoddinott in the foundry. The children from the local schools lined the streets and cheered the King when he passed by, and were given the rest of the day as a holiday. There are no photographs of his visit, but there are some of his visit to Chatham Dockyard the same day, and these show the women lining his route in the dockyard, wearing their heavy smocks and snoods. The scene would have been very much the same in Sheerness.

The character of Maggie is largely based on my own grandmother, and the tales my Dad used to tell of their lives in West Minster. As I was writing, her character got bigger, as I realised that she had her own story to tell.

The other historical source I used were the school logbooks. I had been sent selected transcripts from the Maidstone Archive. However, these only related to the war, and how it affected the children. I decided to visit the archive after lockdown ended, and read the logbooks for myself. There is a very sad entry on April 2nd, 1913, *"Bert Lucas was drowned during dinner hour by slipping into a pond at the cement works. Fruitless efforts to resuscitate took place for two hours."* There are other reports of drownings and children falling into unguarded fires. These days, such accidents would make the national news, but were far too commonplace then. Even the story of the boy taking a fog detonator to Sunday school is gleaned from the local paper, along with several stories of children losing an eye in an accident.

I hope you enjoyed meeting Miss Garrett and Hattie again. The names of the people they are based upon appear throughout the war years in the local papers; they all certainly stayed busy.

All names in the text have been changed, except where they are a matter of historical record.

Printed in Great Britain
by Amazon